PAINTER

The Stockholm Killings – Book 1

Venezia Miller

PAINTER

Copyright © 2025 by Venezia Miller.

All rights reserved. No part of this book may be used or reproduced in any manner whatsoever without written permission except in the case of brief quotations embodied in critical articles or reviews.

This book is a work of fiction.

Names, characters, businesses, organizations, places, events and incidents either are the product of the author's imagination or are used fictitiously. Any resemblance to actual persons, living or dead, events, or locales is entirely coincidental.

For information contact : venezia.miller@gmail.com

https://veneziamiller.wixsite.com/mysite

Book and cover design by V. Miller
ISBN: 9798280835467

First Edition: May 2025

CHAPTER ONE

STOCKHOLM, DECEMBER 2000. As Inspector Njord Dahlman approached the house, barely visible between the gnarled, twisted trees, a chill settled over him that no winter wind could explain. In over twenty years with the police force, few things could still unnerve him, but the recording of those desperate cries for help had done just that. The sound of a woman's screams—raw with terror, pain, and madness— had sent a cold spike down his spine. Even now, the memory of it clung to him, and it was impossible to shake. Whatever horror she had endured, Dahlman knew it was unlike anything he had ever faced before.

He recognized the house immediately. Over the years, he and his partner had been called here countless times for domestic violence involving Annika Svensson and her husband. The pattern was always the same: accusations of brutal beatings, a desperate call for help, and then silence when she inevitably went back to him.

But something felt different this time.

The house itself was a two-story structure nestled in the woods, which appeared to be in a state of neglect. The paint on the walls was faded and peeling in places, revealing the wood underneath. The windows were boarded up and cracked, and the roof sagged. The chimney was leaning to one side, and the garden was overgrown with weeds. The house had a sense of abandonment, as if it hadn't been lived in for some time.

He paused, his gaze sweeping over the crowd milling around the scene. Despite the number of people, an unnatural stillness clung to the air, as if the woods themselves were holding their breath, waiting for something to happen.

A sharp wind cut through the trees, stirring flurries of snow that danced around him and made him wish he'd worn something warmer. He pulled up the collar of his coat and continued along the snow-covered path, the crunch beneath his boots amplifying the uneasy silence.

As Dahlman approached one of his colleagues, he immediately noticed the young officer's distress. Leaning against a tree, the man was pale and visibly shaken, beads of sweat glistening on his forehead despite the biting cold. His hunched posture and trembling hands suggested he was barely holding himself together. When he finally looked up, his tear-streaked face and wide, terrified eyes told Dahlman everything: he'd seen something no one should ever see.

"What happened?" Dahlman asked.

The officer's gaze flickered to the house, then back to Dahlman. His lips parted, but no words came, only a broken stammer. "Sir, I... I can't. You have to see it for yourself." His breath hitched, and he turned away, gagging.

Dahlman hesitated. Whatever lay ahead, it was something no one was prepared for. Still, he forced himself forward, each step toward the house feeling heavier than the last, pulling him toward something vile.

Near the edge of the clearing, he spotted his partner, Adam Wallin, standing beneath a tall pine.

"Adam?" Dahlman called.

Adam flinched, as if snapped out of a trance. His wide-eyed expression quickly shifted to one of practiced composure. "Jeez, Dahlman," he muttered, running a hand through his hair.

"How bad is it?"

Adam put his hands in his pocket and said, "Bad."

"Is it her?"

"No, the children," Adam said.

The words stopped him in his tracks. "The children? How..."

"They're dead. He killed them."

"But... he never touched the children before. Never," Dahlman finally managed, turning toward the house. They were standing only a few meters away.

Men in coveralls came out of the house, carrying boxes.

"He wanted to get back at her," Adam said. "It's clear from the way the crime scene is set up, the way he orchestrated everything. He wanted to hurt her in the worst way possible, and he succeeded."

Dahlman sighed. He wasn't ready to go inside—he never was—but this time, the thought of crossing that threshold felt almost unbearable.

Death, raw and merciless, was waiting for him.

✳ ✳ ✳

The blood was still wet on the floor as Dahlman stepped inside, careful not to disturb anything that might serve as evidence. The sickly, metallic smell of death thickened the air with every step, clawing at his senses. His heart pounded, and cold sweat dampened his shirt as he followed the trail down the narrow hallway. He knew what he was walking into—he just didn't know how bad it would be.

He could still hear their laughter in his mind, faint echoes of innocence that clashed violently with the nightmare awaiting him. Seven children, ranging from fifteen to two years old. He'd seen them only days ago after he had passed by to check on their mother. And now their mother was being rushed to the hospital in an ambulance, alive but in shock and barely registering what had happened.

Dahlman reached the living room and froze. The scene before him was utterly still, a composed landscape of horror. The children's bodies were laid out in a line, side by side, their faces pale and frozen in expressions of terror. Their pajamas were soaked with blood, but their faces were eerily intact, as if death had paused just short of robbing them of their identities.

A wave of nausea rolled through him. He fought the urge to turn away, forcing himself to take in every detail. The juxtaposition of their innocence and the brutality inflicted upon them was almost too much to bear. He clenched his jaw, swallowing the bile rising in his throat.

This was worse than anything he had encountered in his twenty years on the force. He had seen death before—grisly, senseless deaths—but this felt different. The sheer magnitude of it, the betrayal of a father who should have protected these children, cut deeper than anything else.

Then a surge of anger flared in him, hot and all-consuming, before it was replaced by a crushing sadness. He had failed them. Not just as an officer but as a human being. The signs had been there—the escalating violence, the desperate cries for help—and yet, here they were.

Dahlman steadied himself, taking a shaky breath. There was no time for grief now. He began scanning the room methodically, cataloging every broken detail in his mind. The spilled toys in the corner. The faint smudge of a small handprint on the wall. The grotesque finality of the blood pooling beneath their fragile bodies.

He stood over them for a moment. They had been ripped from their sleep, their dreams shattered by violence. His hands balled into fists at his sides.

Dahlman just stood there, staring at the bodies, until he felt someone behind him. Turning, he saw Adam standing in the doorway. His partner's face was pale, his eyes wide and unblinking, a strange mix of horror and something darker flickering behind them. Dahlman felt a shiver run through him.

"What is it?" he asked.

Adam didn't respond at first, his gaze locked on the lifeless forms before them. Finally, he shook his head. "To think a father could do this to his own kids... It's sick. Unfathomable."

Dahlman sighed. "Yeah. It doesn't make sense."

Adam stepped closer, his voice dropping to a grim murmur. "Five of them were shot in their beds. The other two... somewhere else. Then he brought them all here and laid them out. Side by side, like... I don't know." He paused, rubbing the back of his neck. "It's almost like he was arranging something."

Dahlman's frown deepened. "Arranging what?"

Adam hesitated. "A message. Or... a display. The way he lined them up—it's almost like he was trying to create something. Like some twisted masterpiece. A painting."

Dahlman turned back to the scene, his stomach tightening. "You have a strange idea of art, Adam."

"I'm just saying," Adam continued. "The precision. The way they're positioned. It's not random. It's deliberate. He wanted us to see this and feel something—shock, revulsion, anger. He wanted us to remember."

Dahlman stared at the bodies. "If that's true, then he's even sicker than I thought."

He turned around and looked at the rest of the room. The house had been ransacked. Chairs were knocked over, pieces of glass on the floor.

A birthday cake sat on the dining table, half-crushed. Pink frosting smeared across the wood, mixed with something darker.

Maybe blood.

He couldn't think about this.

Dahlman's gaze shifted to Adam. "You said five were shot in the bedrooms upstairs. What about the other two?"

Adam's voice was subdued, almost hollow. "The youngest son, a six-year-old boy, and his nine-year-old sister were probably killed here in the living room."

Dahlman gestured toward the bodies. "The boy and the girl on the left?"

Adam didn't answer immediately. His eyes remained fixed on the scene, wide with a horrified intensity. Slowly, he walked closer to the row of bodies.

Their hands had been carefully arranged to look like they were holding each other. All of them lay on their backs—except for one. The blond-haired girl, the nine-year-old, was facedown, her pajama stained with a dark, spreading blotch on her back.

The rest had gaping wounds in their chests, the blood seeping through the fabric. Their faces were pale and lifeless, frozen in a haunting stillness.

Adam crouched, staring at them for a long moment. Then, his eyes locking onto the girl and her brother, he jerked back a step, his expression twisting. "That's... that's... It can't be."

CHAPTER TWO

STOCKHOLM, DECEMBER 2022. Stefan Eklund stood on the Västerbron bridge, the cold winter air biting at his cheeks as he took a drag from his cigarette. Snow fell gently, dusting the city in a blanket of white.

A few people trudged through the streets, heads bowed, their coats pulled tight against the wind. Their footsteps crunched in the snow, swallowed quickly by the stillness.

Christmas was coming.

A flicker of something stirred in his chest—anticipation, maybe. Or was it dread? He wasn't sure anymore.

He knew how it would go. His sister would call, ask him to come. He'd say no. She'd try again, a little more insistently this time. He'd still say no.

And then, like every year, he'd be alone.

Maybe that wasn't so bad.

He sighed.

Flicking his cigarette into the water below, Stefan pulled out his phone.

As the call rang, he stared out over the city. The skyline shimmered with scattered lights, their reflections breaking apart on the dark water like a fragmented mirror. A strange detachment settled over him, as if he were merely an observer, standing outside the world instead of in it.

"Hey, it's me," he said when the call connected. "Happy birthday, sis."

"Stefan! I thought you'd forgotten," Elena said.

"Of course not." He managed a small smile. "How could I forget your birthday?"

She laughed, but then her tone shifted. "Are you smoking?"

He frowned, glancing at his phone as if it might somehow betray him. "Uh... how do you know?"

"I know you," she said. "I know where you are. And you always smoke a cigarette there."

"Jeez, you know me too well."

"Maybe... but you're my little brother, and I don't want to lose you. So, stop smoking."

Stefan inhaled sharply, her words cutting through the cold more than the wind ever could. Frustration prickled at him—not because she was wrong, but because she was right. He let out a slow breath, watching it dissolve into the air.

"I know," he murmured. "Anyway, what are your plans for today?"

"Work. But... I'm having a birthday party this Saturday. You should come."

He hesitated. "Is Johan going to be there?"

"He's my husband. So, yeah."

Stefan was silent. He already knew the answer, but he'd asked anyway, as if hoping for a different one. His relationship with Johan was...

complicated. They never fought outright, but there was an unspoken tension between them, a constant undercurrent of irritation that neither could quite shake.

Johan thought Stefan was brooding and distant. Stefan thought Johan was arrogant and dismissive.

But at the heart of it, Stefan just didn't like the way Johan treated Elena sometimes. It was never anything obvious—nothing he could put his finger on—but he'd seen the way Johan's words cut, the way his presence could make her shrink just a little. And whenever Stefan tried to bring it up, she would brush it off, insisting everything was fine.

On Johan's side, Stefan's presence was a constant shadow in their marriage. Always there, always involved. Johan never said it outright, but Stefan knew—it made him feel like an outsider in his own home.

They had learned to stay out of each other's way.

To keep the peace.

For Elena.

"I don't know, Elena…"

"Please?" she said. "Just think about it?"

Stefan sighed, running a hand through his hair. "Who else is going to be there?"

"Friends, few colleagues."

"Elena... I don't know."

"Jeez, Stefan, how socially inadequate can you be?! Maybe you should get out there now and then... you know, be around real people. Not those obsessed macho colleagues of yours. And... find a good woman and marry her!"

"Do you know where I can find any?"

Elena laughed. "Well, you're in Stockholm, not some desolate wasteland. Just look around. Or better yet, I'll introduce you to some of my friends at the party. They're not all married, you know."

"Oh great, matchmaking. That's exactly what I need."

"Stefan, you're impossible. Just come to the party. It'll be fun, I promise. And who knows, maybe you'll actually enjoy yourself for once."

"Fine," he said after a pause. "But don't expect me to stay long."

"That's all I ask. See you Saturday."

"Yeah. See you," Stefan said, ending the call.

He pulled out his pack of cigarettes, taking one out and lighting it as he walked. He knew he should quit, not just for himself but for his sister too. She was the only person that mattered in his life.

As he walked, the streets were deserted, the snow falling softly around him. He felt that sense of isolation again. In fact, he had felt it his entire life.

He arrived at the police station and was immediately dropped into the familiar bustle of activity which did little to ease his frustration.

Inspector Stefan Eklund moved through the chaos with quiet efficiency, his sharp blue eyes scanning the room as if searching for a puzzle worth solving. In his late twenties, he had already built a reputation for untangling the most complex cases. But success hadn't brought him companionship—he was a loner by nature, preferring quiet moments to crowded social events. The few friendships he maintained were hard-earned and carefully guarded.

Physically, Stefan had an unpolished appeal. His lean, athletic frame reflected a life of restless energy, and his short blond hair was always slightly disheveled, as if he'd just stepped out into the wind. He wasn't conventionally handsome, but there was something magnetic about him—an intensity that unsettled some and intrigued others. Admirers came and went, but none had held on for long. He liked it that way. Commitment felt like a trap.

Well, maybe Katherine had come close.

Beneath his poised exterior, Stefan carried a weight he rarely acknowledged. Years of chasing shadows had left their mark, and lately, the fire that once drove him had dimmed. Even the chase, the thrill of the hunt, failed to stir him.

He made his way to his desk, eyeing the inevitable pile of paperwork before deciding coffee had a higher priority. But before he reached the break room, a voice stopped him.

"Eklund."

Superintendent Franck Juhlin stood in his path, arms crossed.

Franck Juhlin, once tipped for rapid advancement, had waited years for a promotion that materialized much later than expected. The job had certainly taken its toll, but no professional burden compared to the devastating loss of his wife when their daughter was still very young. He raised her single-handedly, constantly balancing fatherhood with his duties, and never remarried.

Time had eased the athleticism from his frame, and his face was etched with deep lines, each marking sleepless nights and battles waged away from public view. His graying hair, invariably neat, offered a small island of order in his otherwise unpredictable existence. Yet, his tired blue eyes held a sorrow that professionalism could not entirely mask.

Despite everything, there remained something steadfast about Franck Juhlin. A quiet resilience had carried him through grief, professional setbacks, and the long years of unfulfilled potential.

Stefan straightened, sensing that whatever came next would be important.

"Walk with me," Franck said.

Stefan raised an eyebrow. Superintendent Juhlin wasn't one for small talk, and the look on his face told Stefan this wasn't going to be good news.

"What is it, sir?" he asked, gauging the mood in the room.

Juhlin sighed. "Olavson is in deep shit. He's been suspended."

A knot formed in Stefan's stomach. His partnership with Inspector Olavson spanned two years, having started in the midst of a pandemic. Their connection was built on an almost unspoken understanding, a balance between Olavson's sharp instincts and reckless methods, and Stefan's own meticulous approach. Together, they had tackled—and solved—cases others wouldn't dare touch.

But Olavson had always been a storm waiting to break. Brilliant, unpredictable, and dangerously comfortable toeing the line. His methods often delivered results, but they left him one misstep away from disaster.

Stefan took a steadying breath. "What did he do?"

Juhlin shook his head. "The investigation is ongoing. I can't give you details, but his actions have compromised the department's integrity. We're taking it seriously."

Stefan clenched his jaw. "What now?"

"That's the other thing." Juhlin hesitated, then allowed a rare smirk. "Your new partner is Delara Holm. Transferred in from Nyköping. Highly recommended."

Stefan barely stopped himself from groaning.

Trust didn't come easy. Building a strong partnership took time—time he didn't have the patience for. He thought back to past partners, how many had come and gone, how often things had fallen apart. He had a reputation for being difficult. Olavson had been the exception. And now he had to start over. Again.

"Never heard of her."

"You will," Juhlin said. "Five years on the force, sharp instincts, relentless. I expect you two to work well together."

"When do I get to meet her?"

"She's waiting in conference room B." Juhlin's tone shifted. "And, Eklund—I expect great things from this partnership, because I'm giving you a new assignment."

Stefan narrowed his eyes. "Why do I get the feeling I won't like this?"

Juhlin folded his arms. "It's an idea I've been working on. The Police Commissioner finally gave his blessing. I want to create an elite unit—one that tackles the toughest, most complex cases."

Stefan exhaled sharply. "What kind of cases?"

"Serial killers, extreme violence, cold cases…"

Stefan snorted. "Sounds like you're trying to get rid of me."

Juhlin's expression darkened. "I'm giving you an opportunity. You're one of the best detectives I have, but you've been running on fumes. You need a change, a challenge, something to reignite that fire of yours. This isn't about getting rid of you—it's about pushing you to your full potential."

Stefan studied him, searching for the catch. "People don't like me. This will only make it worse."

Juhlin shrugged. "Since when you care what people think?"

"And how many of these cases do you think we'll actually have?" Stefan gestured around. "This city isn't exactly crawling with serial killers."

Juhlin's smirk returned. "There's a basement full of cold cases. And two months ago, we had a ritual killing in Gamla Stan. You think there's a shortage of work for a team like this?"

Stefan crossed his arms. "So, let me get this straight. You want me to lead a dream team of misfits, digging through the city's ugliest cases, with no guarantee of success? And if it falls apart, I'm the one taking the hit?"

Juhlin met his gaze, steady and unflinching. "It's a risk, yes. But it's also a chance to do something meaningful—to chase the cases others have given up on. I wouldn't offer you this if I didn't believe you could handle it."

Stefan sighed.

This was either a trap—or exactly what he'd been waiting for.

His hands rested on his hips as he stared at the floor. A part of him bristled at being thrust into this new role, but another part—one he wasn't ready to acknowledge—felt a flicker of intrigue.

"And Holm?" he asked, looking up. "Does she know?"

Juhlin nodded. "Yes. She's your partner in this—your equal. This isn't a solo gig, Eklund. You'll need to rely on her as much as she'll rely on you. From what I've heard, she's more than capable."

Stefan sighed, rubbing the back of his neck. "Fine. I'll meet her. But don't expect miracles."

"I don't," Juhlin said with a faint smile. "Just results."

With that, Stefan turned and walked toward the conference room. Through the glass door, he spotted a woman sitting at the table, reviewing a file with sharp focus.

Delara Holm.

Her dark hair was pulled back into a sleek ponytail, and her tailored blazer suggested a no-nonsense attitude. She glanced up as he opened the door, her dark eyes locking onto his.

"Inspector Eklund, I presume?" she said, standing and extending a hand.

"Delara Holm," he replied, shaking it. Her grip was firm, her demeanor professional and calm.

"I've heard a lot about you," she said, a faint smile tugging at the corners of her lips. "Looking forward to working together."

Stefan studied her, trying to gauge whether her words were genuine or just polite formalities. "Likewise. Looks like we're diving into the deep end together."

Holm raised an eyebrow, her smile widening. "Good. I prefer it that way."

Stefan sighed. He glanced at Delara, holding her gaze a beat longer than necessary.

"So, how do we start?" she asked.

He forced a small smile, a hint of dry humor creeping into his voice. "I guess I show you around this madhouse first. Welcome to Stockholm."

***

The warm light spilling from the windows filled him with an unexpected sense of longing. He lingered in the shadows, watching the two-story house as if it were a portrait of a life he had once known. The well-manicured lawn, the bright red door, the freshly painted shutters—every detail beckoned.

It wasn't his.

It never could be.

Laughter seeped through the closed window, muffled but unmistakable, blending with the faint clink of dishes and the low hum of a melody he couldn't place. Even through the glass, the warmth of their joy reached him, twisting something sharp inside. He shouldn't be here. He didn't belong.

Yet he couldn't leave.

His feet moved of their own accord, bringing him closer. The porch creaked faintly beneath his weight as he reached a trembling hand toward the red door. Just before his fingers touched the wood, his gaze shifted to the window.

For a moment, he simply stared.

He could almost see himself inside, sitting at the table, basking in their warmth. But that wasn't his place. His place was here, outside—cold, uninvited. The realization burned, igniting something darker within him.

How would they react if their perfect world shattered?

Would the father's confidence falter? Would the mother's hands tremble as she clutched her children close? Would the children scream, their laughter dissolving into cries when they saw his face?

The thought sent a surge of power through him—chilling and exhilarating. He stepped back, retreating into the shadows, his breath quickening with anticipation. The house still glowed, blissfully unaware of the storm lurking just beyond its walls.

It wouldn't stay that way for long.

* * *

Delara changed into her favorite sweatpants and an oversized T-shirt, the simple act shedding the weight of the day. She gathered her dark hair into a messy bun, curled up in her armchair with a glass of wine, and let out a slow exhale. Shadow, her sleek black cat, purred contentedly in her lap.

Her first day as chief inspector.

A quiet pride swelled in her chest. She had worked tirelessly for this moment, often questioning if the sacrifices were worth it. But now, in the stillness of her apartment, she felt a glimmer of validation.

Her thoughts drifted to Stefan. He was intense, almost disconcerting, with an energy she couldn't quite pin down.

Unpredictable.

She wasn't sure whether she found him intriguing or unsettling—or both. Either way, she would need to figure him out.

Shadow's purring stopped abruptly. His ears swiveled toward the front door.

Delara frowned. At first, she heard nothing. Then—a faint scratching sound.

Setting down her wine glass, she stood. Her stomach tightened at the thought of an uninvited visitor.

Peering through the peephole, she felt her breath catch.

Emil.

Her ex-boyfriend stood on the other side, his signature smirk in place, as if he knew exactly how disarming his presence could be. Emil had always been aware of his effect—his tousled blond hair, sharp blue eyes, easy charm. And he wielded it like a weapon.

Delara hesitated, her hand hovering over the lock. They hadn't spoken since their disastrous breakup, and she wasn't sure she wanted to break that silence now.

Emil knocked, leaning closer. His voice was smooth and casual. "Delara, I know you're in there."

Her grip on the doorknob tightened. Of course he would show up like this—uninvited, as if he still had any claim on her time or space.

Emil had always been that way: entitled, arrogant, convinced the world would bend to his will.

Shadow paced nervously at her feet. Delara's mind raced, torn between sending him away and confronting him.

Emil's voice took on a practiced vulnerability. "Look, I just want to talk. You owe me that much, don't you?"

The irony almost made her laugh. Owe him?

She thought of his betrayal—how he had taken her trust and crushed it under his selfish desires. How he had cheated with one of her closest friends and then blamed her for being 'too focused on work.'

Her hand fell away from the lock.

"Go home, Emil," she said.

Silence stretched between them. Then a chuckle. "Come on, Delara. Don't be like that. I made a mistake, sure. But you know I never stopped caring about you."

She clenched her jaw, anger bubbling beneath the surface. Emil only cared about one person—himself. His sudden reappearance wasn't about her. It was about his bruised ego, his inability to accept that she had moved on.

"Leave," she said.

The smirk in his tone faltered. "Fine. But don't act like you're better than me, Delara." He scoffed. "You're still the same workaholic who doesn't know how to let anyone in. Maybe that's why you'll always end up alone."

Her chest tightened, but she refused to let his words land. She waited until she heard his footsteps retreat before exhaling.

Shadow rubbed against her leg. She reached down, stroking his fur, her fingers trembling. Emil's parting words echoed in her mind, but she refused to let them take root.

Her world was no longer his playground.

And tonight, she had reminded him of that.

CHAPTER THREE

THE MAN'S EYES SNAPPED OPEN, his breath hitching as a wave of cold knifed through him. Snowflakes swirled above, blurring the dark sky. He blinked rapidly, trying to take in his surroundings, but his vision was hazy, and a sharp pain pulsed at his temple, forcing him to stop.

Instinctively, he reached up. His fingers came away wet and sticky.

Blood.

His stomach twisted at the sight, nausea clawing at his throat, but he shoved it down.

He needed clarity.

Answers.

He was on some sort of boat. The realization hit him like a slap. The small vessel rocked gently, the water lapping against its sides in a rhythm that did nothing to calm his rising panic.

He scanned the darkness, desperate for a landmark, a clue—*anything*. But there was nothing. Just the oppressive silence of isolation.

His clothes—a shirt, jacket, and jeans—clung to his skin like a second layer of ice. He shuddered, his body trembling violently.

How long have I been out here?

Move. Now.

Gritting his teeth, he dragged himself upright, fingers clawing at the boat's edge for balance. His muscles screamed—stiff from the cold, seizing with every movement. The shoreline loomed just ten meters away, but between him and safety stretched a fractured no-man's-land: half ice, half black water, the divide between them as jagged as a knife's edge.

He couldn't swim. Not now. Not with the cold ready to steal his breath and his strength in seconds.

Instead, he tested the ice near the bow, pressing down with agonizing slowness. It held. Arms outstretched like a tightrope walker, he shuffled forward, each step a battle against the groan of shifting ice.

Then—a snap.

His foot plunged through, the freezing water seizing his ankle like a vise. He gasped, yanking his leg back, pain shooting up his calf. But he couldn't stop. Not now.

Step by step, he forced himself toward the shore, his breath coming in ragged bursts. When his boots finally hit solid ground, he collapsed into the snow, his limbs leaden.

Where am I? How did I get here?

More importantly—who am I?

A sound cut through the silence. Footsteps. Crunching snow.

His pulse spiked as he turned, squinting into the darkness. A figure approached, flashlight beam slicing through the trees.

"Hey! Are you okay?"

The voice was distant, but the uniform was unmistakable—a park ranger.

Relief crashed over him, his knees buckling. The last thing he saw before the darkness took him was the ranger rushing forward.

***

"What happened to him?" Stefan said and took the notebook out of the pocket of his jacket. He quickly looked at the woman next to him. Delara had her hair in a bun and with her black blazer, black pants and white shirt she looked like a businesswoman about to close a deal rather than a police officer.

The ride to the hospital had been immersed in silence, both lost in their own thoughts. Those awkward silences, he knew, were so much worse when they settled in his chest like stones. He could sense the weight of them, growing heavier with each passing second.

He hated them.

It wasn't the silence itself that bothered him; it was what it represented—a failure to connect, to say the right thing, to bridge the gap between himself and someone else.

He had wanted to say something—anything—but the words wouldn't come. They never did, not in moments like these. The hesitation always clawed at him, gnawing at his resolve until the opportunity slipped away, leaving him stranded in the quiet.

Once he got past this stage, things would be different. They always were. He'd joke, he'd listen, he'd charm his way into their good graces, and they'd walk away thinking he was the most outgoing guy they'd ever met.

But the first step?

Breaking the ice?

It was like standing at the edge of a cliff, staring down at a churning sea, unable to make the leap.

He sighed, opened the notebook and clicked his pen, ready to take notes.

Back to business.

"We don't know yet," the doctor said. "But from the temperature of his body, we suspect he was outside in the cold for at least a few hours."

Stefan scribbled the information down, then looked back up at the doctor. "What about the blood?"

"It's human blood," the doctor said. "Not his. Different blood type, and he has no obvious injuries that could explain the amount of blood. But we won't know more until we run some tests."

Stefan nodded. "We need to find out who this man is and what happened to him. Can we talk to him?"

The doctor hesitated. "He's still unconscious at the moment, but we can try to wake him up and see if he's able to communicate. His injuries look bad but are, all in all, minor. Mostly frostbite, some cuts, and bruising. He's lucky—any longer out there, and the outcome might have been very different. When he was semi-lucid, he mumbled a few words, but nothing coherent. He's clearly confused, possibly due to the hypothermia or trauma."

Delara interrupted, "We can start by checking the missing persons reports."

Stefan agreed. "Let's start by canvassing the area around where he was found. Maybe someone saw something that could help us piece together what happened."

Stefan then turned to the doctor again. "Please do what you can. It's important that we find out what happened to him as soon as possible. Given the blood, someone else might be in danger."

The doctor nodded and led them to the room where the man was being treated. As they approached, Stefan noticed the man was in his mid-forties, with short, dark hair flecked with gray and a scruffy beard that hadn't seen a razor in days. His face was pale, almost grayish, the telltale signs of someone who'd been exposed to the cold for far too long. His hands, resting limply at his sides, were blotchy and swollen, the tips of his fingers an alarming shade of bluish-black.

Frostbite.

The man lay still, his breathing shallow but steady. His lips were cracked, and faint streaks of dried blood marked the edges of his mouth. An IV drip hung from a pole beside the bed, feeding him fluids. A heated pad was tucked around his feet, which were wrapped tightly in gauze.

"His condition?" Stefan asked, his eyes fixed on the man.

"Stable for now," the doctor replied. "The frostbite on his fingers and toes is severe, but it hasn't reached the point of needing amputation. We're monitoring him closely. He was hypothermic when they brought him in, but we've managed to get his core temperature back to normal. We've kept him sedated for now to help with recovery."

Stefan nodded, his jaw tightening as he took in the scene. "Maybe we shouldn't—"

"Wake him up, doctor," Delara interrupted. She didn't look at Stefan, whose frown deepened at her insistence.

The doctor hesitated, glancing between them, then checked the man's vitals before administering a mild stimulant.

After a few moments, the man stirred. His eyelids fluttered open, and he blinked, his gaze moving sluggishly around the room.

Stefan stepped forward. "Hello, sir. Can you hear me?"

The man's eyes landed on Stefan, unfocused and dazed. "Where... Where am I?"

"You're in the hospital," Stefan explained. "You were found outside in the cold. Do you remember anything about what happened?"

The man winced, his brow furrowing as he brought a hand to his temple. "No... I don't... I can't remember." His voice was tinged with frustration. "Why can't I remember? Why?"

Delara and Stefan exchanged a quick glance before Stefan said, "It's okay, sir. You've been through a lot. We're here to help you. Can you tell us your name? Anything at all?"

The man stared at Stefan, his expression shifting between panic and despair. "I... I don't know."

Stefan jotted down some notes in his notebook, then turned to Delara. "Let's start checking the surveillance cameras around the area where he was found. Maybe we can find something that could help us identify him or figure out what happened."

"The blood... there was blood everywhere," the man stammered.

Stefan turned to him. "Do you remember anything else? Anything at all that could help us?"

The man shook his head. "No, I'm sorry. It's all a blur. Except... I had the feeling someone was watching me."

"Who?"

Stefan leaned in, his eyes locked onto the man's. "Who was watching you? Can you describe them?"

The man furrowed his brow, clearly struggling to recall any details. "I don't know. It was dark, and I couldn't see anything. But I could feel it... someone was there."

"You told the doctors you were in a boat. Was it your boat? Did you recognize it?"

"No, I don't think I own a boat. I don't think I like the water."

"That's okay, sir. We'll keep looking into it. In the meantime, please try to rest and recover. We'll do everything we can to help you remember and find out what happened."

The man nodded.

"Sir, please try to recall if there is anything else," Delara insisted.

"Inspector Holm," Stefan said in a stern voice.

"Anyone you might have seen, anything else," Delara continued.

Stefan put a hand on Delara's shoulder. "Let him rest for now. We'll come back later and ask him more questions when he's feeling better."

Delara nodded, reluctantly. "Alright. But we need to find out what happened to him. It could be a matter of life and death."

Stefan gave her a reassuring smile. "Let's have a look at the area where the man was found. Maybe we'll find something that can give us some answers."

They left the hospital room and made their way to their car. Stefan started the engine. The tires crunched against the icy pavement as they pulled out of the hospital parking lot and headed toward the Nacka Nature Reserve, where the man had been found.

According to the police report, he had been drifting in a small, battered boat near a secluded cove by the eastern shore of Skrubbatjärn. The area was quiet, popular in the summer with joggers and kayakers, but deserted this time of year, with the icy grip of winter keeping most people away.

"What do you think? Could this be a case of assault or kidnapping?"

"He claims not knowing anything but maybe he's not a victim at all. The blood wasn't his. He had few injuries."

"Wow, nothing gets past you."

She looked at him with a stern glance. "I'm not here to make friends."

"I gather that. But you're right. We shouldn't assume anything."

As they drove southward, the city faded behind them, replaced by sprawling forests that seemed to stretch endlessly on both sides of the road. The snow-covered trees stood like silent sentinels, their branches heavy with the weight of the winter frost. The road narrowed, winding through the dense woods, and the occasional house or building was swallowed up by the trees.

After about half an hour, they reached the area where the man had been found. It was a small clearing in the woods, isolated and desolate, with only the wind rustling through bare branches above. Snow coated the ground, muffling every step, and the dirt road had all but vanished beneath the fresh layer of white.

As they approached, a strip of blue-and-white tape fluttered between two trees—*POLIS AVSPÄRRAT*. Beyond it, the ground bore clear signs of activity. The snow here had been trampled, shoveled, and smeared into slush. Tire marks cut deep through the mud, and colored flags stuck out of the ground where the forensic techs had marked points of interest.

"The boat was here," Stefan said, nodding toward a wide indentation in the ground near the water's edge. "You can still see the drag marks."

Delara crouched near one of the deeper impressions. "They really tore this place up."

"Had to," Stefan said. "The guy said he woke up inside the boat. They needed to preserve whatever trace evidence they could find."

The lake stretched beyond them, small and partly frozen, its murky water dark beneath a thin sheen of ice. Broken reeds lined the edge. There were no boats left behind—only scattered debris and churned earth.

Delara scanned the surroundings, her breath fogging in the cold air. "No hikers. No tire tracks but theirs. Why would someone come out here just to crawl into a boat and freeze?"

"Maybe he didn't come willingly," Stefan muttered.

Delara didn't answer. She turned away from the main area and began walking along the tree line, her boots crunching lightly in the snow. A few minutes later, she stopped abruptly, stared at the ground, then stepped between the trees. She vanished from view for a moment before reappearing, her expression more focused.

"Stefan. Over here."

He joined her, and she pointed to a spot near a pine tree, farther from the water—a place untouched by the earlier flurry of activity. Under a low-hanging branch, the snow had partially melted from body heat or pressure, revealing something underneath.

Delara knelt, brushing away the powdery snow to reveal a faint but definite footprint. Human. The edges had started to blur, but it was still discernible.

"There are a few more over there. This wasn't near the boat," she said. "Whoever left this wasn't involved in the rescue or the transport. Like someone standing here and watching."

Stefan crouched beside her, frowning. "Looks fresh. Could've been someone watching. Or leaving after dumping him."

"And look at this," she said, pointing to a tree near the edge of the clearing. "The bark's all scraped off, like something was trying to climb it."

Stefan stepped closer. The tree's bark was indeed marked in several places, with rough, jagged scrapes running vertically up the trunk. It looked as though someone—or something—had tried to climb it but had been unsuccessful. Lower down, near the base, there were scuff marks in the snow, as if someone had made a desperate attempt to push themselves up.

Delara crouched down, her gloved hand brushing against the snow, revealing small, broken twigs scattered around the base of the tree. Some of the branches higher up were bent or partially broken, their ends jagged, as if they had been used for support but couldn't bear the weight.

"Looks like a failed climb," Stefan murmured, inspecting the area more closely. "Someone was trying to get away from... something."

"Or maybe they were looking for something," Delara said quietly, her eyes scanning the clearing again.

Stefan nodded, still staring up at the tree. It seemed like a small detail and not really related to the case.

"Maybe an animal?" Stefan said.

Delara nodded. "Could be."

Stefan sighed, his gaze drifting across the clearing. "It snowed last night. Not sure if we'll find anything useful besides the footprints. Where do they lead?"

Delara straightened up, brushing snow from her gloves. "They head back into the woods. Sparse, but you can track the general direction."

She took a few careful steps, scanning ahead. The snow wasn't deep, but the footprints—when they appeared—were irregular, spaced like someone moving cautiously. Not running, but not just wandering either.

"They're leading away from the lake," she said. "Definitely not toward the road. So they didn't arrive the way we did. No vehicle tracks that way either. They came from the forest."

Stefan followed her, careful not to disturb the impressions. "So someone walked out here, stood near that tree, maybe tried to climb it, and then left again. All without going anywhere near the boat."

He took a pack of cigarettes from his pocket and lit one, exhaling a plume of smoke as he stared at the water, ignoring the frown on his partner's face. The nicotine barely took the edge off.

They walked in silence for a few more meters, the trees growing denser around them. The blue of the police tape was now barely visible through the trees behind them.

Then Delara crouched again. "Here."

Stefan joined her. The footprint here was clearer—sharper edges, maybe shielded from the wind by the slope of the ground. The heel was deeper, like the person had paused or turned sharply.

She looked up. The forest stretched out ahead, quiet and cold. "This wasn't just some bystander."

Stefan's jaw tightened. "Then we're missing a second person in this scene. Whoever they were, they didn't want to be seen."

Delara nodded slowly, her breath white in the air. "We should circle back. Get photos, cast this one before it fades." She paused, then added, "And we need to flag this with the Superintendent." She pulled out her phone and snapped a few quick photos. "Let's mark the coordinates and get a team out here to sweep further north. If we're lucky, they'll find more prints. Maybe a tire track. Something."

"Good idea."

"The boat was already here. Otherwise, we should have seen tire tracks... anything to suggest how it got moved." She scanned the shoreline, her eyes narrowing against the glare of snow. "Unless someone carried it in by hand. According to the picture, the boat wasn't that big. Which means—"

"—they're strong. Or had help," Stefan finished, following her gaze to the tree line where shadows stretched long across the snow.

A gust of wind sent powder swirling around their boots. Delara shivered, but it wasn't just from the cold. The stillness felt wrong.

"Back to the car?" Stefan asked.

She nodded.

They started heading back toward the clearing, retracing their own steps carefully.

Just before they reached the clearing again, Stefan said, "What if the guy in the boat was running from them?"

"Maybe... do you know what this reminds me of?"

"No, tell me," Stefan said as he quietly let the puffs of smoke disappear from his mouth.

"It reminds me of a case from a few years ago. A body was found in a pond not far from here, covered in blood. Turned out it was a drug deal gone sideways—one dealer teaching the other a brutal lesson."

Stefan raised an eyebrow. "Really? Do you think there's a connection?"

"No... I guess... just saying."

They moved in a slow, methodical circle around the lake.

Stefan's gaze lingered on the water, but his attention was split between the stillness of the scene and the nagging feeling that something was just out of reach. "Maybe you're right... maybe he's not a victim."

Delara glanced at him. "We really need to find out who he is."

"I agree. Missing person's reports first."

They both got back into the car, and Stefan started driving back to the station. The silence between them stretched for a moment before Delara suddenly spoke up, "You don't like me."

Stefan quickly glanced at her. "Why do you think that?"

Delara didn't look at him but kept her eyes on the road ahead. "The way you interrupted me in the hospital. And just now, out there—you didn't believe me."

Stefan sighed, his grip tightening on the steering wheel. "I just want you to be more aware of when to push and when to pull back. You interrogated that man like he was hiding something. What if he's just terrified? And why did you bring up the drug murder? It felt like you were already drawing conclusions about this man. I think you have a bias."

Delara was silent for a moment, processing his words. "I see. I do think I am allowed to express my opinion."

"Yes," Stefan said, his fingers tapping once on the wheel. "But opinions aren't facts. And that man in the hospital... right now, he's neither a suspect nor a witness. He's a victim of *something*—hypothermia at minimum, trauma at worst. Your job isn't to interrogate. It's to listen."

Delara's jaw tightened. "And your job isn't to patronize me."

A beat of silence. Stefan exhaled through his nose, then surprised her with a half-smile. "Fair."

There was another moment of silence before she said, "What happened to your previous partner? What was he like?"

"Yan Olavson," Stefan said and sighed. "He was... not easy to work with. We sometimes clashed, but that was okay. We respected each other... at least that's what I thought. But he... was a bit of a troubled man."

"Interesting," she said. "Many people think you are difficult to work with."

He frowned and quickly looked at her. "Really? Why?"

"You are eccentric, stubborn... you don't listen to authority..."

"But I heard you specifically asked to work with me," he said.

"Well, no one can deny it. Your closure rate is 20% above average. I didn't request you for your personality."

"You are ambitious." He turned the wheel.

"Is that a problem?"

"No, no, but remember we are here to help people in need, to make sure we find the culprits."

"Of course," Delara said surprised. "I want to make a difference."

"So, when we arrive at the police station, you can make a difference and start going through the missing person's reports."

Delara's grip tightened on the door handle, her knuckles whitening. The landscape blurred, but she didn't trust herself to speak.

Not when she felt so annoyed.

CHAPTER FOUR

THE POLICE OFFICERS STOOD OUTSIDE, pale and tense against the snowy backdrop. Their wide eyes and rigid stances betrayed their unease, as if any movement might disrupt the heavy silence around them.

Delara and Stefan got out of the car.

As they approached the officers standing near the house, Stefan could feel their fear and apprehension. He knew that whatever they had just seen must have been truly disturbing.

"What's going on?" Stefan asked.

One of the officers turned to face them, his eyes still wide with shock. "We found a body... bodies."

From the outside, the family home where the police officers were standing looked unassuming and quaint. It was a small house with a sloping roof, nestled in the midst of a quiet suburban neighborhood. The brick exterior was painted a muted shade of beige, and a small porch with a wooden railing led up to the front door. The windows were all shuttered, as if the occupants were trying to keep the world out. Despite its unremarkable appearance, there was something eerie and unsettling about the house.

"What happened?"

"The neighbor called it in," the officer said. "Said the door was wide open, and there was blood on the doorstep. When we got here, it was just as he described—door ajar, blood pooled just inside, and footprints tracked through it. Be careful when you go in." He held out a box of shoe covers. "You'll need these."

"You went inside?" Stefan asked, taking a pair of blue shoe covers from the box and handing it to Delara.

"Yeah... it's... not a pretty sight," the police officer stammered.

Stefan sighed, then strode toward the door but stopped just short of crossing the threshold. He turned to Delara.

"Are you going to be okay in there?" he asked, studying the young woman beside him.

"Yeah... sure," she said, though the hesitation in her voice betrayed her uncertainty.

Stefan frowned. "Look, I don't want to deal with you throwing or freezing up. Keep your eyes open and your antennas sharp. Every detail matters."

Delara's jaw tightened, his comment clearly hitting a nerve. "Inspector Eklund, I've seen my fair share of disturbing scenes. I may be young, but I know how to do my job. You don't need to babysit me."

"Perfect. Then we shouldn't have a problem," Stefan said and stepped inside.

Delara followed, her expression set with determination, though her knuckles tightened around the edge of her coat as she crossed the threshold behind him.

As they stepped into the dark hallway, a chill ran down her spine. With each step, the unease grew.

The hallway stretched ahead, its once-white walls streaked with crimson. Delara's eyes caught the blood smeared along the staircase banister. A jolt of unease flickered through her, but she forced it down.

Then they moved toward the living room. Broken glass littered the floor—clear evidence of a struggle. A small cupboard in the hallway was overturned, belongings scattered, as if violence had ripped through it.

As she stepped inside, Delara's eyes immediately locked onto the blood smeared across the wallpaper. The silence was suffocating, broken only by their steady breaths.

Stefan's words echoed in her mind, but she pushed aside any lingering apprehension. Now wasn't the time for hesitation. Her training took over, sharpening her focus as she scanned the room.

She drew a deep breath, ready to move forward—but before she could take another step, hurried footsteps pounded behind her. She spun around, her pulse quickening.

For a moment, she couldn't process what she was seeing. It wasn't just what stood before her—it was who.

"Torre?"

Standing in the doorway of the living room was Torre—a young man with a quiet, almost otherworldly presence. He was handsome in a way that was uniquely his own, with finely chiseled features, his dark hair tousled in a careless manner, and eyes that seemed to hold a mixture of something vulnerable and unreadable at the same time.

Delara's heart skipped, but she quickly masked it. She had always found Torre more intriguing than his older brother Emil—softer, more approachable, but also hiding something beneath the surface. It was hard to pinpoint, but there was a pull she couldn't ignore.

Torre shifted nervously, his eyes flickering between Delara and Stefan. His posture was awkward, like he didn't quite know where he fit.

"Torre, what are you doing here?"

"Didn't Emil tell you?" he stammered.

She frowned, confusion knitting her brows. "Tell me what?"

"I'm with the police force now... I started a month ago." He seemed unsure of himself, his gaze drifting briefly to the floor before snapping back to her.

Delara's lips parted in surprise. "Emil and I broke up. He didn't tell me anything."

Torre's expression faltered, a brief flicker of something unreadable crossing his face. "You... did? I didn't know. Well... anyway, I'm the new forensic psychologist. I specialize in behavioral analysis."

Delara remembered hearing Emil mention something like this, but it hadn't registered at the time. Torre had always been the quieter one, the one who often stayed in the background, and it had been easy to overlook him. But now, standing in front of her, there was something different about him—something that made her feel uneasy in a way she couldn't explain.

"Oh, okay... so they put you on this case... as a profiler or something?"

"Yes... you could say that," Torre nodded, his voice a little more steady, though there was still an undercurrent of nervousness.

Delara's gaze lingered on him just a moment longer than necessary before she tore her attention back to the room. But something about his presence stayed with her—unsettling, yet strangely magnetic.

"Inspector Holm," Stefan said in a stern voice, his eyes flicking between Delara and Torre as he observed their exchange. "Do you two know each other?"

"Yeah," Delara answered quickly, her voice steady but her gaze flickering briefly to Torre.

"Is this going to be a problem?" Stefan pressed.

"No, no," Delara said, her eyes meeting Torre's for a moment, and then turning back to Stefan. "No, not at all."

"Good," Stefan nodded and turned to Torre. "Inspector...?"

"Dr. Torre Nylander," Torre replied.

"Okay then... let's get to work," Stefan said, stepping further into the living room.

Stefan's breath fogged in the air as he stepped forward—then froze. At first, his brain refused to process it. The wall wasn't a wall anymore. It was a canvas. The woman's outstretched arms formed a grotesque 'V', each wrist pinned with industrial staples that gleamed like chrome teeth. Blood had dripped downward, creating macabre 'strings' that connected to her children's smaller bodies below. A toddler and a boy of seven, eight years old. The toddler's left foot twitched slightly—just a nerve spasm, but Stefan's stomach lurched.

Then the smell hit him: copper, bile, and beneath it all, the sour tang of urine. Someone had pissed themselves. Maybe all of them.

"Oh, my God," Delara whispered.

Stefan stood frozen and hadn't taken his eyes off the wall.

Torre was standing a bit further away as the room was now filling with men and women in coveralls.

The forensic team had arrived.

"This is a massacre," Delara let out.

"He made them watch," Torre said suddenly.

"What?" Stefan turned around. He looked pale and confused, like he had witnessed the entire scene play out himself.

"The chairs," Torre said and pointed at the four wooden chairs placed in the middle of the room facing the wall. Three of them were drenched in blood. Tape was hanging from the armrests, and bloody footprints on the floor were surrounding them.

"Uh... you think he made the others watch as he butchered them one by one," Stefan said.

"The children were likely murdered first," Torre said. "To torture the parents. The youngest, then the oldest. Then the mother. I wouldn't be surprised if the blood on the mother's hands belonged to her sons. She either had to make the drawings or help him kill them."

"Why four chairs?" Delara said and quickly looked at her partner who hadn't said much since they had entered the room.

"Where is the father?" Torre said.

Delara looked around. "Somewhere else."

"We need to find him."

Delara walked over to one of the police officers standing at the door.

"Are you okay?" Torre said.

Stefan turned to him. "No. This brings back memories."

"Of what?"

"Nothing I want to share today. I'll be fine. What did you say? He wanted them to watch."

"No, even worse. He wanted them to be part of it."

Their conversation was interrupted by a tall man who had just entered the room. "What the fuck are *you* doing here?"

Quinten Arning. Not exactly Stefan's best friend at the police station.

Stefan barely had time to register the familiar voice before Quinten stormed toward them, his glare sharp enough to cut through glass.

"I asked you a question," Quinten snapped. "What the fuck are you doing here?" His tone dripped with hostility, his posture stiff with barely contained irritation.

Delara exchanged a glance with Stefan, already bracing for the inevitable clash.

"We're investigating," Stefan said calmly.

Quinten let out a sharp, humorless laugh. "Investigating? Right. The so-called 'elite' squad, swooping in like you own the place." His gaze flicked to Delara. "Didn't realize we needed a babysitting service now."

Delara's jaw tightened, but she stayed silent.

"Last I checked," Stefan said, "this case falls under our jurisdiction."

Quinten scoffed. "Your jurisdiction? Funny, because last I checked, I was the first one called here." He stepped closer, eyes narrowing. "This is my crime scene. You two can fuck off back to your little ghost-chasing squad."

Stefan took a slow breath, keeping his temper in check. "We're not here to argue, Arning. We're here to do our jobs."

Quinten smirked. "Yeah? Then stay out of my way."

He turned and strode toward the evidence markers, barking orders at the officers nearby. Stefan watched him go, jaw tightening.

"Charming," Delara muttered under her breath.

Stefan exhaled through his nose. "Let's just focus on the case." But he knew Quinten wasn't going to make that easy.

Pushing aside his irritation, Stefan turned his attention back to the room. He started toward the blood-smeared wall, scanning the scene for details—but before he could get any closer, a tall woman in a coverall stepped into his path.

"Stefan, what are you doing?" she said in a stern voice.

"How did they die?"

"You know I can only make an official statement after I examined them in the lab."

"But you can have a guess," he tried.

A faint smile appeared on her face and then became serious again when she turned to the victims. "He cut the children's throats. There is a massive amount of blood on the floor near the chairs and where they are hanging. The blood drenched their pajamas. Then he stabled them to the wall. That's hard to do alone. He must have gotten help. The mother... I don't know. Beside the pins in her hands and arms there are no obvious wounds."

She sighed and looked at the woman. "Her trousers and knickers are missing. Maybe sexual assault."

"And the father?"

"He's not here. He's missing."

"Okay, I'll leave you to it."

Torre's gaze fixed on the scene, his eyes tracing every detail with unsettling intensity.

"Dr. Nylander?"

Then Torre looked at him, as if he was still in a trance. "It's like a painting."

"What did you say?"

"A painting. A piece of art he wants everyone to see."

Stefan held his breath. "Do you think he did this before?"

"Maybe... no, he did. This must have taken hours. He had to plan this very carefully. It's not the first time he did this. But you know..."

"What?"

"I think I've seen this before."

Stefan held his breath. "Where?"

"I mean the painting exists. I know I've seen it before. I can't remember who the painter is."

"In a book? A museum?"

"It's not in a book or a museum," Torre murmured. "I feel like I've encountered this painting before, but I can't quite place it. It's as if the image has been imprinted in my mind, waiting to be discovered."

"Is there anything specific about the painting that stands out? Any distinctive elements?"

Torre closed his eyes. After a brief moment of reflection, his eyes snapped open.

"I remember now," Torre exclaimed. "The painting... it's called 'The Puppeteer's Symphony.' I don't recall the artist's name, but the title... I do remember. It depicts a similar scene of marionettes manipulated by invisible strings. It's... scary."

Stefan put his hand on his shoulder. "I'm sorry that you need to go through this..."

"It's my job," Torre said. "This is what I'm good at."

Delara walked up to them. "The father..." And she took her

notebook. "Gustav Gyllenstierna... he's not here. Likely he was taken by the killer."

Stefan kept staring at the wall, until she noticed that it wasn't the wall he was looking at, but the pictures on the cupboard.

"Maybe we do know where mister Gyllenstierna is," he said and pointed at a picture of the family.

She froze. "It's the man in the hospital."

"And maybe you were right. Maybe he isn't that innocent after all."

※ ※ ※

The tension was mounting as Stefan and Quinten stood in Superintendent Franck Juhlin's cramped office, their postures stiff, their expressions equally determined. Delara had opted to stay outside, knowing this was about to turn into a battle of egos.

Quinten leaned forward, hands braced on the edge of Franck's desk. "With all due respect, sir, I was the first one at the scene. I'm the senior officer here. This was my scene. My evidence. My victim statements."

Franck rubbed his temple. "And yet here we are," he muttered, glancing at Stefan, who stood with arms crossed on the other side of the room.

"This isn't just another homicide," Stefan said. "The circumstances are unusual—bizarre even. That's exactly the kind of case our unit is meant to handle."

Quinten scoffed. "Unusual? Bizarre? Come on. Just because there's some blood on the walls doesn't mean it's one of your spooky cases."

Stefan didn't rise to the bait. "The preliminary report suggests no signs of forced entry, no clear explanation for this kind of brutality. That fits our mandate."

Quinten scoffed. "Fits a lot of things, including a standard homicide investigation. The husband's the obvious suspect, but instead of following real leads, you want to chase shadows. I'm more than capable of handling this case."

Franck leaned back in his chair, steepling his fingers as he regarded them both. "I understand both of your positions. Quinten, you're right—you have seniority, and you've been with this department longer. But Stefan is also right. This case does have elements that suggest it falls under the elite unit's jurisdiction."

Quinten straightened. "Sir, you can't seriously be telling me you're giving it to them."

Franck sighed. "What I'm telling you is that this case has too many unknowns to be treated as routine. The elite unit was created for a reason. If we keep treating these cases like ordinary crimes, we'll keep hitting dead ends."

Quinten's expression darkened. "So that's it? You're siding with them?"

Franck met his gaze. "I'm making the decision that's best for the case. Stefan's team will take the lead, but you'll be kept in the loop."

Quinten's hands curled into fists at his sides. "You're making a mistake."

Franck's voice hardened. "That's my call to make."

For a moment, it looked like Quinten might argue further, but then he let out a sharp breath, shaking his head in frustration. Without another word, he turned on his heel and stormed out.

Stefan remained still, watching the door swing shut behind him.

"You'd better solve this fast," Franck said. "The last thing I need is him breathing down my neck about it."

Stefan gave a small nod. "We'll do our job."

"Good." Franck leaned forward. "And Stefan—watch your back. He's not going to take this lightly. Quinten's got friends everywhere."

Stefan didn't need the warning.

He already knew.

***

Gustav Gyllenstierna sat with his hands tangled in his hair, his body trembling uncontrollably. He had vomited the moment the police confronted him with the bodies of his wife and sons.

"What happened?"

"I... I... don't know," he cried out.

"Mr. Gyllenstierna, calm down. We need to know what happened. You want to find whoever did this to your family, no?"

Stefan was looking from behind the one-way glass and sighed seeing the arrogance and incompetence of his colleagues. His gut tightened. Quinten had gone behind his back. He was already questioning Gustav—despite the fact that he had been clearly told to let Stefan's team handle this. It wasn't a surprise, but it didn't make it any easier to swallow. Stefan could have made a scene, stormed in and put Quinten in his place, but he didn't. It wasn't worth it, not yet.

Instead, he looked at it with growing amazement and frustration at the same time. They had been questioning the man for two hours now. They had gone in with almost blunt force, so sure they would crack him in half an hour. But Gustav had given them nothing.

"I don't even remember who I am," the man cried out.

Stefan's frustration grew with each passing minute. He had hoped for a breakthrough in the interrogation, a crack in the façade of the man they believed to be the killer. But instead, what he witnessed was a scene of despair and confusion.

Quinten and the other detective in the room seemed equally puzzled by Gustav's response. Their initial confidence had given way to a sense of unease and bewilderment. It was evident that their aggressive tactics had not yielded the expected results. Stefan knew that this approach would only push Gustav further into himself, making it even harder to extract the truth.

"Psychogenic amnesia," a voice said.

Stefan turned around and saw Torre standing behind him.

"He knows what happened to his family. His brain just can't handle it, and to protect itself from the deep emotional pain, it has blocked out those memories completely. It is a defense mechanism triggered by severe psychological trauma," Torre explained.

"Or he's faking it?"

Torre gave a small, knowing shrug. "I'm not excluding that he can be lying. It's a possibility. We're dealing with extreme trauma here. It could be a way for him to protect himself, especially if he's guilty. Some people shut down completely when confronted with guilt. Others, well, they go into denial."

Stefan nodded and then fixed his gaze again on the man being questioned in the interrogation room. "So, he may genuinely have no recollection of what he did or what happened to his family?"

"Indeed," Torre replied. "The mind can be a fragile thing, capable of extraordinary measures to shield itself from unbearable memories." Torre pressed a hand to the glass. "The human brain can erase years in milliseconds. Soldiers can, for example, forget entire deployments." His finger traced Gustav's trembling form. "But the body remembers. His pupils dilated when they mentioned the children's pajamas. His left thumb has been rubbing his wedding band nonstop. Some parts of his body already remember."

Stefan's eyes narrowed as he observed the detectives in the room, still pressuring the amnesiac man for answers he might not be able to provide. "They're not going to get anywhere with him like this. He needs specialized care, not a hostile interrogation."

Torre nodded in agreement. "I'll speak with them, try to explain the situation, and suggest a different approach."

A sarcastic grin played on his lips and then Stefan said, "I know you mean well, but my colleagues unfortunately... they don't seem to grasp the importance of handling this case with sensitivity and understanding. Gustav is not going to talk."

"Not like that." Torre sighed. "We could try hypnosis to retrieve the lost memories."

"Hypnosis? No, they will never go for that."

"I understand their skepticism... and yours for that matter," Torre started. "Hypnosis can be a controversial technique, and it's not widely accepted within the field. But in some cases, it has shown promising results in accessing repressed memories."

"The blood on his body was his wife's and his children's. He either witnessed it or he did it."

Torre calmly turned to Stefan. "And if you want to know what happened, this is the solution I offer you. It might also help *you*."

Stefan frowned. "What do you mean?"

"You froze out there. That is more than a cop's instinct. It's personal for you. Your past experiences are affecting your ability to handle this case objectively. Hypnosis might provide you with some closure and healing."

"I know perfectly what happened to me. I don't need hypnosis for that."

"So, something did happen," Torre said quickly.

"I'm only going to say this once... I don't want to talk about it."

Stefan looked at the man in the interview room again, frustration simmering beneath his calm exterior. His colleagues were still pressing Gustav, but the man remained a broken shell, trapped in his own mind. The aggressive tactics only seemed to drive him further into himself.

Idiots.

"Let him be," Stefan muttered.

Torre stood silently beside him for a moment, then spoke, his voice quieter now. "You can't save him like this."

Stefan didn't respond, but his jaw tightened. His instincts told him

Gustav was hiding the truth, but his own experience with trauma made him pause. The guilt, the raw emotion that had crippled him in the past... Stefan knew too well the deep scars that left one paralyzed.

As Gustav continued to cry in the interview room, Stefan finally turned away, the sound of his sobs still echoing in his ears. "Get him help. And tell them to lay off. You're right. We need to approach this differently."

CHAPTER FIVE

HE WAS HAPPY.

For once, everything had gone exactly as planned. The timing, the execution. Perfect. No mistakes, no unexpected variables. He closed his eyes and drew in the icy air, feeling it burn his lungs. The water lapped gently at the frozen shore, black and still. It had to be near freezing.

That's how he liked it.

The moon cast its pale glow over the landscape, turning the world into something ghostly, untouched. Headlights flickered in the distance—a police cruiser crawling along the lakeside road. He didn't flinch.

Let them look.

The silence stretched around him, broken only by the occasional snap of shifting ice. He let the sound settle inside him, let it quiet the lingering hum of adrenaline.

Planning had never been the problem. He was good at it. He knew how to wait, how to anticipate. He had studied every angle, imagined every possible failure until there was no room left for it. And yesterday, finally, it had all come together.

Satisfaction curled through him like warmth against the cold.

He opened his eyes, exhaling slowly. The water fascinated him—how it preserved what it took. Last winter, he'd watched a deer carcass float beneath the ice for months, flesh peeling back in slow, graceful ribbons.

Like a gallery exhibit.

A small smile tugged at his lips. This was just the beginning.

This was so liberating.

But it wouldn't last. It never did. The rush would fade, the satisfaction would dull, and then—his tongue found the groove of his back molar, where he'd cracked a tooth biting down last time. The phantom ache pulsed.

He clenched his jaw, already feeling the first stirrings of restlessness beneath his skin. The high never lasted long enough.

But he had to be patient. It was all about control. Timing. Precision.

The water remained still, indifferent to what had been given to it.

He envied that.

* * *

The doctor pulled back the sheet.

Stefan's breath caught. The toddler's small, lifeless body lay pale and still, too fragile for this world. Wide, vacant eyes. Slightly parted lips. He had seen death before, but this... this was different.

The boy's pajamas—blue with rocket ships—were stiff with dried blood. It looked so much like... He wrenched his gaze away before the memory could fully form.

Delara glanced at him, noting his clenched jaw, but said nothing. The silence in the room pressed in, heavier than ever. Stefan gave her a stare as she took out her notebook.

"The children died of massive blood loss after their throats were slit," the doctor said. A slow inhale. A measured exhale. Then, "There were no defensive wounds."

"They trusted whoever did this," Delara murmured, jotting it down.

"Or they were tied up," Stefan added. "There was tape on the armrests of the chair."

The doctor continued, "We found DNA from the mother and father on their bodies. Nothing else."

"And the mother?" Stefan asked.

"That's a different story." The doctor covered the boy's body and moved to the next table.

Delara's hand trembled as she continued to write, while Stefan kept his eyes on the doctor.

"The mother's cause of death is more complex," she said. "She also died of blood loss, but her torture lasted for hours. Her hands and arms were nailed to the wall with a nail gun. Her body was covered in bruises and lacerations."

"Sexual assault?" Delara asked.

"No. She had no underwear, but there were no signs of sexual violence. The killer wanted her to suffer, wanted her to be humiliated. My guess? She had to watch her boys die first. Psychological torment, followed by unimaginable pain. He broke her arms and legs, nailed her to the wall in an unnatural position. The agony must have been beyond words."

"What about the blood in the room? The chairs?" Stefan asked.

"All the blood came from the mother and her children. Nothing from the father or anyone else. His DNA was found on the chairs, but that's expected. The chairs were part of the living room."

Stefan's gaze drifted to the mother's body. Pale, empty, stripped of everything she once was. She must have been beautiful once. Now, her face only held the echoes of suffering. His stomach tightened.

He forced himself to look away. "Anything else?"

The doctor hesitated, then nodded. "It might be nothing, but their marriage was in trouble."

"How do you know?"

"My colleague, Dr. Quarnström, treated them for a while. Not recently though. He's a marriage counselor. I don't know the details, and maybe he shouldn't have told me, but..."

"That's interesting," Delara said. "So, they were having problems."

"Let's confirm that first," Stefan said.

"Is the father saying anything?" the doctor asked.

"No... he's in some kind of denial. Dr. Torre Nylander suggested hypnosis."

The doctor smirked. "Torre Nylander?"

"You know him?"

"I do. He took some of my classes. He's good—more than good. Brilliant even. His papers—written during his PhD—on trauma and memory are some of the most highly cited in forensic science."

"Torre?" Delara said. "Really? I know he has a PhD, but he seems to have left quite an impression."

"You know him well?" the doctor asked.

"I know his brother. Emil."

"Ah, Emil. He got the looks, not the brains."

Stefan couldn't hide his smile.

"But... Torre can be intense," the doctor continued.

"How?"

"He's obsessed with his work. I've seen it during his PhD. Some people find it... unsettling."

"But he's good," Stefan said.

The doctor nodded. "I'd trust him."

A phone rang, breaking the silence. Stefan pulled his out, glancing at the caller ID. He frowned and then said, "I need to take this."

He stepped outside. "Hey, sis. What's so urgent? I saw you've been calling all day."

"And you've been ignoring me," she said.

He couldn't see her face, but he knew her forehead would be creased, that deep line forming between her brows.

"I've been busy."

"That's exactly why I'm calling."

"Why?"

"Stef, a family was murdered. I saw it on the news."

"Yes, I know. We don't know if the father did it," he said, sighing.

"Don't do that."

"Do what?"

"Pretend this doesn't affect you."

"I'm a professional."

"But I know you," she said softly.

His sister wasn't wrong. This case—it was too close. Too familiar. Memories lurked beneath the surface, waiting for any excuse to break free. And maybe he could push them down, ignore them, but she couldn't.

"We'll talk on Saturday, okay?" she said.

He frowned. "Saturday?"

"Stef... my birthday."

Right. He had been hoping to quietly ignore it.

"Okay."

He just wanted the call to end.

"Stef—"

"I'll see you Saturday."

He shoved his phone into his pocket and stared at the wall.

"You good?"

He jumped at the voice. Delara stood there, watching him.

"Yeah... yeah." Then he said, "I have a question for you."

Delara raised an eyebrow. "Okay?"

"What do I buy a thirty-one-year-old woman who already has everything?"

Delara blinked. "We're not talking about the case anymore, are we?"

"Nope."

"And you're asking me because...?"

"Because I need advice."

She smirked. "What does she like?"

"How am I supposed to know? She's my sister."

Delara folded her arms. "Uh... that's exactly why you *should* know."

He sighed. "Never mind. Do you have all the information you need from the doctor?"

She nodded.

"Okay, let's go and talk to Mr. Gyllenstierna again."

*** * * ***

"Torre, are you coming downstairs?"

Her youngest son was sitting cross-legged on the floor of the study, surrounded by a chaotic sprawl of books and papers. The room, lined with towering shelves packed tightly with books, carried the unmistakable scent of aged paper and ink. Sunlight filtered softly through the half-drawn curtains, casting warm, golden streaks across the worn carpet.

"Torre?" she called again when he didn't respond.

He turned to her, his gaze distant, as if emerging from a dream.

She stepped inside and sat on the sofa against the wall, watching him. "What are you doing?"

"Uh... my first case," he said, sitting up straighter and looking up at her.

Her knee was brushing a stack of files. One slid open—a photograph of a stapled wrist. A grimace flickered across her face—such unpleasantness—before she snapped it shut. "I see. What's it about?"

"I... can't tell you," he murmured, glancing back at his scattered notes.

A faint smile touched her lips as her eyes fell on a book about paintings lying beside him. "I love you so much, Torre."

"I love you too, Mom. But... that's not why you're here, is it?"

They never needed many words. Though sometimes she wished he were more forthcoming.

She took his hand. His fingers were ink-stained, the nails bitten raw. A familiar, slightly unkempt sight she wished he'd grow out of.

"Torre," she began, "you know I wasn't in favor of you joining the police."

His thumb tapped against her palm—one, two, three, pause. The rhythm he'd learned in the psychiatric ward. A "safeguard." Her chest tightened—a pang of that old embarrassment mixed with worry.

"I know."

"And I still worry. A lot."

"About what?"

She hesitated. She knew the dangers all too well. Her own father, a police officer, forced into early retirement. She had wanted something safer, less disruptive, for Torre. His relentless mind, while impressive in its way, caused so much turmoil.

"I worry about your safety, Torre," she said. "This line of work... it's dangerous."

"I know, Mom," he replied. "But it's what I love."

"It's not just your physical safety," she pressed. "It's your mind. You get so... intense, so consumed. It's unsettling for everyone around you, Torre. It scares me."

Torre moved to sit beside her, taking her hand. "I know."

"It's not the first time it's made you—" Her voice faltered as she looked into his eyes. Her youngest son, so brilliant—a reflection of the sharp minds in the family—yet so frustratingly fragile.

Their family of three boys couldn't have been more different. Torre was the intellectual, his brilliance undeniable, if only he could channel it into something less... volatile. Emil, the middle child, was all charm and trouble, coasting through life. And Sam, the eldest, had chosen stability, becoming a successful lawyer—a comfort, really—with a growing family of his own.

But Torre's brilliance came with a cost. She still remembered, with a knot in her stomach, how his obsession had spiraled. It was during his PhD—he'd become consumed by a patient's case, crossing lines with a lack of judgment that had landed him—and by extension, the entire family—in an embarrassing situation requiring psychiatric intervention.

His fixation had been all-consuming... notes, photographs, diagrams plastered across the walls. Day and night... Meals went uneaten, disrupting household routines, time slipped away... Friends drifted away, and his family watched, frustrated, as his obsession consumed him. Admitting Torre had been unavoidable, one of the hardest burdens she'd had to manage. She had done it out of love, yes, but also fear—and a desperate need to restore some semblance of normalcy. Slowly, he had clawed his way back, thankfully.

Even now, the memory of those days haunted her.

"You know what I mean," she said softly.

"Crazy," Torre replied with a sad smile. "You can say it. I can be crazy sometimes."

Her throat tightened. Such difficult phases they'd weathered.

"I know what you're thinking," Torre said quietly. "But don't worry. I can see the signs now. I track my sleep. My meals. The intrusive thoughts. It's okay."

She nodded, though the practicalities didn't entirely soothe the underlying anxiety about potential future episodes and their fallout. "Just promise me you'll take care of yourself."

"I will," he said. Then, after a pause, "Delara is there."

"Delara?" she asked, her voice sharp with surprise. "Here? What's she doing in Stockholm?"

"She joined the Stockholm police force," Torre said, his tone casual, but the revelation left her stunned. Delara, inserting herself here.

"Emil didn't mention a word. I thought she was going to quit the police force and study law. Why wasn't I told...?"

"She told me she was thinking of it, but finally didn't," Torre said.

His mother sighed, shaking her head. "I don't know what that girl is thinking. She's so... I don't know. I never felt she was right for Emil."

Torre looked at her. "Mom, I know you have your reservations about Delara, but she's not a bad person. Emil treated her horribly. You should talk to him."

"And I will," she replied quickly. "But he's my son, and a mother protects her own. That girl was always trouble for him. I need to protect you too."

"Mom, you're wrong about Delara."

"I just don't think she was right for Emil. She's too... strong. Too ambitious, perhaps. He needs someone... gentler."

"More obedient? Someone who worships him?" Torre cut in. "Mom, it's the twenty-first century. You can be a little... old-fashioned sometimes."

She bristled slightly, pulling her hand back almost imperceptibly. As a psychiatrist, she was used to dissecting behavior, analyzing relationships—but when it came to her own family, such labels felt reductive and unfair. His father, her husband, had often reminded her to separate her clinical instincts from her role as a mother. But it wasn't easy, especially when her concerns were clearly valid.

"Maybe," she conceded coolly, taking his hand again as if nothing had happened. "I just want you all to be safe and settled. This world can be dark, Torre. Just promise me you'll look after yourself and not let... unsuitable influences... take advantage of your good nature."

Torre nodded. "I promise."

"Good," she said, patting his hand, the capable professional momentarily surfacing. "Now, a break is clearly indicated. Come downstairs with me? I've got some chocolate cake waiting—your favorite."

He smiled, rising to his feet. "You know I can't say no to that."

With that, he followed her down the stairs, reassured by her concern, if only for a moment, while the shadows of their conversation lingered beneath the surface.

CHAPTER SIX

STEFAN LOOKED AT THE WOMAN next to him. "Since when?"

Her long black hair shielded her eyes. When she finally looked at him, he saw the tears welling up, threatening to spill over.

"Two months," she said quietly. "I'm sorry."

Stefan turned to stare through the windshield. They had been sitting in his car for nearly an hour. He had picked her up from her house, but before he could even start the engine, she had dropped the bombshell.

"Two months," he repeated, trying to wrap his head around it. "Why didn't you tell me earlier? We knew this wouldn't last, and... it was only sex. I care about you, but I never wanted to be in a relationship with someone else's fiancée. Why keep this from me?"

Her voice cracked as she answered, "I didn't know how. I guess... I wanted everything. You and Xander."

The words struck him like a blow. His chest tightened, and he could feel the sting of betrayal—why did it hurt this much if it was only supposed to be casual? He had tried not to get too close, but somehow, against his better judgment, he had fallen for her.

He reached for her hand, his voice softer now. "I just... I thought what we had meant something more. You should've been honest with me from the start. If nothing else, I deserved that."

Katherine's tears slipped down her cheeks, and she shook her head. "I never meant to hurt you, Stefan. I didn't think it would get this far. But now..." She faltered, looking down at her lap.

"What?" he asked.

"I'm pregnant," she whispered.

For a moment, the air seemed to leave the car. Stefan felt his pulse roar in his ears as the word sank in.

Pregnant.

"Is it mine?" The question came out harsher than he intended.

"I don't know," she admitted, her hands trembling in her lap. "It could be yours. Or it could be Xander's."

"How long?"

"I... I just found out. Eight weeks."

Stefan let out a bitter laugh, his hand running through his hair. "Shit. I don't know what to say." He looked at her, his voice dropping. "What are you going to do?"

She took a deep breath, wiping her face. "I don't know. I need time to figure it out. I'm not asking anything of you. This is my responsibility, and I'll handle it."

"Katherine, wait—" He reached for her again, but she pushed his hand away and opened the car door.

Before stepping out, she turned back to him. Her voice was steady now, though her eyes still glistened with tears. "I hope you find what you're looking for. It wasn't just sex for me. I loved you. I truly did."

"Katherine," he stammered, but the door slammed shut before he could say another word.

In the rear-view mirror, he watched her walk away, disappearing into the distance. He sat motionless, the silence in the car suffocating. She was gone—the only woman who had come close to breaking through the walls he had built—and he had let her go.

※ ※ ※

"Mr. Gyllenstierna," Dr. Gersson said.

In the observation room, Stefan, Delara, and Torre sat in silence, their eyes fixed on the one-way glass. Beyond it, Dr. Gersson faced Gustav Gyllenstierna, his voice calm, steady. The soft glow of the office lamp and the faint hum of instrumental music set a carefully curated atmosphere of reassurance.

Torre leaned forward, anticipation tightening his posture. He trusted Gersson—an expert in his field, a friend—but hypnosis was unpredictable.

Gustav sat motionless in the chair, his expression unreadable. He said nothing—just watched.

Dr. Gersson continued, "I understand this process may feel unfamiliar, even uncomfortable. But I am here to help you uncover the memories you've buried. Together, we can bring clarity to what happened. You are safe here. Trust the process."

Gustav's lips parted. "I... I don't think..."

"It's alright," Dr. Gersson said. "Remember, you're in control. If at any point you feel uneasy or wish to stop, let me know. Your well-being is my priority."

Gustav shifted uncomfortably but eventually nodded.

"Good. Let's begin. Close your eyes and take a deep breath. As you exhale, release any tension in your body. Picture yourself in a peaceful setting—somewhere calm and secure."

After a moment of hesitation, Gustav complied. His shoulders began to relax, and his breathing slowed.

Then Dr. Gersson guided him deeper into relaxation. His words took on a soft, rhythmic cadence.

"Now," Dr. Gersson continued, "I want you to go back to the night of the incident. Imagine yourself observing it from a distance, like watching a scene unfold on a screen. Let the memories come to you, piece by piece."

In the observation room, Stefan, Delara, and Torre watched intently.

"I... I was in the study," Gustav whispered. "Upstairs. I remember hearing footsteps... they were getting closer."

"What happened next?"

"Before that... there was the sound of the doorbell... and stumbling. I thought the boys were running around again."

"Focus, Gustav. Go back to the moment you heard the footsteps. What do you see?"

Gustav's body stiffened. His fingers twitched and a sheen of sweat formed on his brow. "No... no, please!"

"You're safe," Dr. Gersson reassured him. "These memories cannot harm you. You're just an observer now."

Gustav's breathing quickened, but after a moment, he nodded. "Okay."

"Good. Let's take it step by step. What happened when the door opened?"

"It was... him," Gustav said. "He had a gun. He was pointing it at me."

"Can you describe him?"

"He... he wore a black coverall. Completely covered. His face was hidden, but his eyes... they were glowing. Red glowing eyes. And that terrifying smile. Like... like pure evil."

In the observation room, Delara's brow furrowed. "I don't believe him. He's faking it."

Stefan glanced at her. "Why not?"

"Glowing eyes? Really? Rather theatrical don't you think. It sounds like he's describing a movie monster, not a real person."

Torre interjected, "His reactions seem genuine. The panic, the distress—it's hard to fake that."

"People fake things all the time," Delara snapped.

"You're making claims without proof," Torre replied.

Delara narrowed her eyes. "I've dealt with enough liars to recognize a fabrication. And you're not a detective."

"No, but I have a degree in psychology. I can assess credibility," Torre said.

"Alright, enough," Stefan cut in. "This argument isn't helping. It's possible he's faking, but I don't think so. He stopped because he's scared, not because he's lying."

Delara crossed her arms. "That doesn't mean he didn't do it."

"True," Stefan admitted. "But if he's hiding something, it's not because he's making it up entirely."

At that moment, the office door opened, and Dr. Gersson stepped into the observation room.

"We'll need to stop for today," he said. "Gustav can't handle more right now."

"What's your take, Doctor?" Stefan asked.

Dr. Gersson hesitated. "He genuinely believes there was someone else in the house. But dissociative projection is a possibility—he could be projecting his guilt onto an imagined figure as a defense mechanism."

"So, he might still have killed his family," Delara said.

"It's possible," Gersson admitted. "But it's too early to draw conclusions."

Stefan sighed. "We need to check the house and the lake where he was found. If there's evidence of someone else, it might still be there. Though... the forensics team didn't find anything."

Gersson nodded. "I'll arrange a follow-up session when Gustav is ready."

After the doctor left, Stefan turned to Delara, stopping her before she could follow Torre who was leaving. "I thought you said you were fine working with him."

"I am," she replied, confused.

"Then what was that?" Stefan asked, hands on his hips. "You were picking a fight. Don't project your issues with his brother onto Torre."

"I'm not!"

"It sure looked like it." His gaze was sharp. "Now, come on. We're going to look for a mask."

"A mask?"

"Glowing eyes. That's what Gustav said. The man was wearing a mask."

Delara frowned but followed him, muttering under her breath. "Fine."

✳ ✳ ✳

Five toy shops and a few florists later, Delara's irritation was growing with each passing minute. Stefan seemed oblivious to her annoyance as he insisted on visiting another store. It wasn't just about finding the mask with the glowing eyes anymore; he had made an additional detour to buy a gift for his sister. Delara felt her patience wearing thin.

She had reluctantly agreed to accompany Stefan, hoping their focus would remain solely on the investigation. But now, their outing had turned into a meandering expedition, wasting valuable time she believed could be better spent at the crime scene or pursuing other leads.

"Stefan, seriously? We've been to five toy shops already, and now you want to stop at yet another florist?" Delara couldn't hide her annoyance any longer.

He turned to her with an apologetic smile. "I know it's taking longer than expected, but I promised my sister I'd bring her something. It won't take much longer, I promise."

Delara crossed her arms. "And what about our investigation?"

Stefan's smile faded. "Let's make this quick, and then we can get back to the case."

They entered the florist, where Stefan quickly selected a bouquet. Delara's irritation simmered as she let out, "Roses? Really? Next time, don't ask for my opinion if you're not going to consider it."

"Sorry," he said. "Now, one last stop. There's a shop with knick-knacks further down the main road. I remember they had great costumes for Halloween. Last stop, I promise."

She shot him a skeptical look, but something about his insistence made her relent. "Fine. Let's just get this over with."

They continued down the main road until they reached the shop. The storefront displayed an array of colorful costumes, masks, and various trinkets. Stefan's eyes lit up as he stepped inside, followed by Delara, who tried to suppress her lingering irritation.

The shop was filled with toys, Christmas gifts, and a small assortment of leftover Halloween decorations. Delara's mood began to shift as the whimsical atmosphere momentarily distracted her. Stefan eagerly scanned the shelves, searching for the mask Gustav had described. Delara watched him, her curiosity piqued despite herself.

After a few minutes, Stefan finally spotted it—a Halloween mask with neon glowing eyes. He picked it up, examining it closely. "This is it. This could be the mask Gustav was talking about. Red glowing eyes. I remember it was quite popular this Halloween."

Delara leaned in. The dark mask was crafted with unsettling precision, its black surface contrasting sharply with the neon-red glow of its eyes, which pulsed with an eerie, otherworldly light. A ghastly white smile stretched across the face, jagged teeth painted in stark detail. The mask's grin seemed to widen as she stared—a trick of the light, maybe. Delara's fingers itched to smash it.

Then she said, "Looks like Gustav's description wasn't too far off.

It's... unsettling."

Stefan held up the mask, its red eyes pulsing faintly in the dim shop light. Delara's fingers twitched—something about it felt wrong, like holding a piece of someone's nightmare. Then a voice cut through the silence.

"Interesting mask, no?" the voice said, startling them both. They turned to see a tall, slim young man with freckles and messy brown hair standing nearby.

"Yeah," Stefan replied. "You sell many of these?"

"They were very popular. End of October, they sold out in just a few days. We even had trouble restocking. And not just for Halloween—a few weeks ago, there was a small incident with a father who absolutely wanted one, but we didn't have any left."

"That's interesting," Stefan said. "Who was this man?"

"Just some random bloke... middle-aged, slightly balding. He had two boys with him. They looked scared. To be honest, we were scared too. He was yelling."

Stefan pulled out his phone and showed the young man a picture of Gustav Gyllenstierna. "Was it him?"

The young man nodded. "Yes, that's him."

"Why was he so angry?" Delara asked.

The young man shrugged. "I'm not entirely sure. He seemed agitated, demanding that specific mask. When we told him we were sold out and that we might have a few coming in later—it was already November—he got more and more frustrated. He kept saying it was important, like—life or death, or something. Honestly, it was creepy."

Delara exchanged a glance with Stefan. "Did he mention why he needed it? Anything specific?"

"No, he didn't explain. He was just fixated on getting that mask. Eventually, he stormed out with his boys, still fuming."

"Did he return?" Stefan pressed.

"I don't know. Maybe my colleagues know. He could have found it elsewhere."

Stefan gave him a faint smile and nodded. "Thanks."

"If I can help with anything else...," the young man offered.

"We're fine. Thanks," Stefan replied curtly.

"Oh, okay..." The young man hesitated before walking away.

As soon as he was gone, Delara's voice was sharp. "Gyllenstierna bought the mask. Whatever story he's spinning, it is bullshit."

Stefan sighed. "We still don't know if he actually bought it. Or if there was even an intruder wearing a mask."

"So, now what?" Delara asked.

"The crime scene. Then the lake," Stefan said decisively. "And I'd like to take Torre with us."

Delara's face tightened in annoyance. "Do we have to?"

"You really should give him a chance," Stefan said with a sigh.

Delara's expression tightened, though her irritation wasn't entirely directed at Torre. There was something about him—too quiet, too sharp. Like he saw things others didn't. And she hated how aware she was.

She let out an exasperated breath. "Fine."

CHAPTER SEVEN

"YOU DIDN'T SAY WE WERE GOING to your sister," Delara let out, folding her arms.

"Five minutes," Stefan replied, scanning the rows of snow-covered suburban houses.

Delara sighed, her irritation fading a bit as she took in the quiet charm of the neighborhood. Snowmen stood in the front yards, some proudly upright, others wearing mismatched scarves and hats. Frosted trees glittered in the weak sunlight, and the crunch of their footsteps mixed with the distant laughter of children playing.

They stopped in front of a house draped in festive decorations. A wreath hung on the door, twinkling lights traced the eaves, their glow softened by the snow. Stefan rang the doorbell.

"She's not home," Delara said after a moment.

"Be patient... she's there," Stefan muttered, his eyes fixed on the door.

"Well, she's taking her time."

Stefan shot her a look but didn't respond.

Finally, the door opened, revealing a blonde woman with striking blue eyes and an angelic face. But Delara's gaze immediately dropped to the wheelchair.

Stefan's sister greeted them with a bright smile. "Hello, I'm Elena," she said, extending her hand.

Delara hesitated.

"Go ahead, I won't break," Elena teased.

Delara flushed but then shook her hand. "Delara. Nice to meet you."

"Come in," Elena said, ushering them inside. The foyer was warm and inviting, filled with the scent of freshly baked cookies. Holiday decorations lined the walls, and the soft glow of candlelight added to the cozy atmosphere.

Stefan knelt beside his sister. "How are you feeling?"

"I'm a year older, not dying." She wheeled toward the kitchen as the rich scent of cookies grew stronger.

"Happy birthday," Stefan said, pulling a bouquet from behind his back.

Elena's sarcastic grin faded into something softer as she took the flowers. She filled a vase with water and arranged them with practiced ease. "So, I assume you're not coming tomorrow."

He sighed. "I've got a lot going on. The new case, other stuff. I wouldn't be great company. Besides… I barely know anyone there. And you have Johan."

Elena's eyes narrowed. "Wouldn't you want to save me from him, then? Since you don't like my husband?"

"He's fine," Stefan muttered.

Elena turned to Delara. "Sorry you have to witness the sibling drama."

Delara gave her a small smile. "I don't mind."

Then Elena shot Stefan a pointed look. "I need a word with my brother. The living room is on your right."

Delara nodded, glancing at Stefan before stepping away.

As soon as she was gone, Elena folded her arms. "What's wrong?"

"What do you mean?"

"I know you. You're hiding something. And bringing that girl as a buffer won't distract me."

"That's not—"

"Cut the crap," Elena interrupted as the oven timer beeped. She slid out a tray of golden cookies, setting them on a cooling rack.

Stefan raised an eyebrow. "Since when do you bake?"

"Since Johan's kids are coming over," she said. "Besides... it distracts me."

"Elena, I know you love them, but you're thirty-one, taking care of three kids that aren't yours. Are you sure this is what you want?"

Elena's expression hardened. "Yes, it is. I love Johan, and the kids come with the package. This is as close as I'll get to being a mother."

Stefan sighed. "I'm sorry. Are you still trying IVF?"

"Yes, but let's not get into that now." Her voice softened briefly before sharpening again. "You're deflecting. What's really going on? Is it... you know... the anniversary? I've been to the cemetery..."

He hesitated, then blurted out, "Katherine's pregnant."

Elena's eyes widened. "Yours?"

"She doesn't know," he admitted. "And... there's a fiancé."

"Jesus, Stefan." She let out a slow breath. "And what are you going to do?"

"Nothing. Not yet." He turned to the window, watching the fresh snowflakes drift down.

Elena wheeled closer, resting a hand on his arm. "You'll figure it out."

"I don't know if I can handle this," he muttered before sinking to his knees, resting his head in her lap. "Not now. It's... that time of the year."

Elena ran her fingers through his hair. "I get it... probably better than anyone."

He looked up. "Why did you go see him?"

"Dad?"

"Yeah."

"You should talk to him." Elena's voice dropped. "I think... I remember a woman's voice. *Her* voice. She was there that night."

"Elena, memories can play tricks, especially after so many years. Don't let this pull you under."

She held his gaze for a moment, then nodded. "Just let me know if I can help. With Katherine. With anything."

"Thanks," Stefan said quietly.

Five minutes later, he and Delara were back in the car.

"Sorry for leaving you stranded in the living room," Stefan said.

Delara shrugged. "It's fine." She hesitated before adding, "I didn't know your sister was... in a wheelchair."

Stefan gave a faint smile as he started the car. "She's tougher than most people I know."

Delara nodded, watching the snowy streets as they pulled away. She leaned her head against the window. There was so much she didn't know about Stefan.

And now... she wasn't sure she wanted to.

※ ※ ※

Daylight now poured through the windows, softening the blood smears on the walls—almost making them look like ordinary red paint. But Delara couldn't forget how oppressive it had felt that morning when she'd stood in this room for the first time, staring at the bodies of the boys and their mother nailed to the wall.

"Now what?" she muttered.

Her gaze swept the room. She'd seen her fair share of gruesome crime scenes, but this one lingered, refusing to fade. The violence of it gnawed at her, but she pushed it aside—there was work to be done.

Torre stood next to her, his eyes closed and his breathing slow.

"What are you doing?" she snapped.

He made her nervous.

"Quiet," Torre said and raised a hand. He took a slow breath, as if tuning in to something just beyond their reach.

Delara's patience snapped. She shot him an angry glare and turned to Stefan. "I don't think we'll find anything new. Forensics already combed through this place."

"Maybe," Stefan replied, and his gaze briefly flicked to Torre before returning to her, "but they look at things differently than we do."

He crossed the room to a cupboard lined with family photographs. He picked one up with gloved hands and studied it.

"A happy family," he murmured.

Before Delara could respond, Torre suddenly bolted from the room, disappearing into the hallway.

"What the hell is wrong with him?" Delara hissed.

Stefan shrugged. "He's... different."

"Yeah, but what does that even mean?"

"It just means he's not like the rest of us."

Delara rolled her eyes and turned her attention back to the room.

They moved carefully through the living room, eyes scanning for anything they might've missed. A few minutes later, Torre returned, his expression sharp with focus.

"It's evening," he began. "The doorbell rings. Why would Mrs. Gyllenstierna open the door to a stranger?"

"Maybe he wasn't a stranger," Stefan said.

Torre shook his head. "It's confusing. Why the mask? And why would she let someone in wearing a coverall?"

Delara frowned. "Maybe he put the coverall on later—before starting the killings."

"That doesn't make any sense," Torre countered. "He didn't want to leave any traces behind."

Delara sighed, crossing her arms. "Or maybe we're looking at this all wrong. Suppose there was no intruder. No man with a mask or coverall."

"You're saying that he's lying," Stefan said slowly.

Delara nodded.

But Torre interjected, "Or... his memories are distorted. Trauma can twist what people think they saw or heard."

"So, he's making things up?" Delara pressed.

Torre's jaw tightened. "Not intentionally. Trauma affects everyone differently. If he didn't do this, he's experienced an unimaginable horror. His mind might be shielding him from the truth—or filling in blanks with things that never happened."

"That sounds like nonsense," Delara muttered, shaking her head.

Torre sighed. She was clearly getting on his nerves. "Delara, trauma doesn't follow logic. It can create false memories, confuse timelines, or blur reality. Mr. Gyllenstierna might truly believe what he's saying, even if it conflicts with the evidence."

"But the facts don't lie," Delara said. "There were no other fingerprints. No DNA. No sign of anyone else being here."

"And I think you could be right," Stefan interjected.

Both Delara and Torre turned to him, startled. Stefan stood by the scattered toys in the corner, holding something up.

A mask.

Rigid, dark, with intricate carvings.

"This is the mask he described," he said quietly. "The one we saw at the toy shop."

Delara approached. "So... forensics missed it?"

"They weren't looking for it," Stefan replied. "But we are."

Torre stepped closer, his eyes fixed on the mask. "We need to analyze it. There could be trace evidence—DNA, fibers, something."

Delara's lips curled into a slight smirk. "If he wore it, we'll know."

Stefan frowned at her reaction.

He wanted Torre to be right.

Needed him to be—because the alternative was worse than he could admit.

A man killing his entire family.

***

Gustav flinched as the mask hit the table, sealed in a plastic evidence bag, its blank stare catching the light. Delara's gaze was locked on him. Beside her, Stefan was sitting, calm, composed, his eyes shifting between them.

"Mr. Gyllenstierna," Delara said. "We found this mask among your son's toys. Care to explain?"

Gustav's hands gripped the table. "It was just for Halloween. For school."

"We know you made a scene at the shop weeks before the murders. Why was it so important to get that mask?"

"I promised my son," Gustav stammered.

"This was after Halloween," Delara pointed out.

Silence.

"We found your DNA on it," Stefan said. "Not your son's."

Gustav's breath hitched. "I don't know why. I swear."

Delara leaned in. "You said the intruder wore a mask. Was it this one?"

"A mask?"

"Glowing eyes," Delara said. "So... is this the mask?"

Gustav hesitated, eyes darting between her and the evidence bag. "It... it could be."

"There's no evidence anyone else wore it but you," she pressed.

Gustav squeezed his eyes shut, his fingers digging into his temples. "I can't explain it, but I had nothing to do with this. There must be a mistake."

Delara's voice cut sharper than before. "Isn't it true there was no intruder? That you killed your wife and children? That this mask was part of it?"

"No!" Gustav's voice cracked. "He came in with a gun. He threatened me. I had no choice."

Delara tilted her head. "What exactly did he *make* you do, Gustav?"

Gustav's words tumbled out in a frantic rush. "He made me wear it. Tied me up. I had to watch."

"Watch what?"

His body shook, sobs choking his words. "Watch as he... killed them... I was helpless," he sobbed, slumping forward until his forehead hit the table.

Delara studied him, something unreadable flickering across her face. Stefan reached for the recorder. "We'll pause here."

She and Stefan stood and left the room. Outside, Torre stood by the one-way glass, arms crossed. "He believes what he's saying."

Delara scoffed. "The blood was his wife's and children's. No other prints, no other DNA. The mask has his DNA. We have enough to arrest him."

"And the motive?" Torre asked.

"His wife wanted to leave. He refused counseling after a while. Friends said he had 'better ways to make her listen.'"

Torre frowned. "Why did they stop counseling?"

"The doctor wouldn't say. Confidentiality."

Stefan let out a deep breath, fingers grazing his jawline. "The evidence is there, but something feels off."

"He's hiding something," Torre murmured. "Maybe he blocked details. Maybe he's protecting someone. Either way, arresting him might maybe be the only way to break through."

Delara's expression hardened. "We can't ignore the facts. He's our suspect."

Stefan studied Gustav through the glass—head down, shoulders trembling. "Alright. We make the arrest. But we're not closing the case. We need to visit the site where he was found. There's a reason the killer chose that place."

As they left, Stefan's thoughts drifted to Katherine.

To the child she carried.

Maybe his.

And how, in a world like this, he was supposed to be a father.

✳ ✳ ✳

The lake was still, but the silence didn't feel the same. Something had shifted. Foot traffic had thinned the snow in places, revealing patches of slick mud and half-frozen leaves along the shoreline. Stefan and Delara moved carefully, their boots sinking into the softened ground.

Behind them, Torre lingered, hands in his pockets, eyes fixed on the water.

Stefan glanced back.

"Should we wait for Torre?" he asked. "He seems... distant."

Delara barely looked over her shoulder. "He's a grown man. We're not his babysitters."

Her tone was sharp, the tension between them still simmering. Stefan had sensed it from the start. Before he could say anything, Delara pointed to the ground. "Look at the fresh tracks."

Stefan crouched, examining the partially obscured footprints in the mud. "Yeah... someone was here recently."

"Likely hikers," Delara said.

"Maybe," Stefan said. He scanned the trees. "But why was Gustav here? Five kilometers from the house, covered in blood. Did he walk here himself? How did no one see him?"

"He could've taken the forest road," Delara suggested.

Stefan frowned. "But why come here at all?"

Before she could answer, Delara let out a sharp breath. "What the hell is he doing?"

Without a word, Torre approached the nearest tree and started climbing, his movements deliberate, as if following an invisible trail. Higher and higher, until he perched above them, staring at the lake.

"I... don't know," Stefan had to admit. "Your guess is as good as mine."

Torre's voice carried down. "He was here."

Delara rolled her eyes. "We already know that."

"I'm not talking about Gustav." Torre looked down at them. "The killer. He climbed this tree. He watched everything from here. The boat. Gustav."

"What do you mean?" Delara asked.

"He put Gustav in the boat, climbed the tree and watched."

Stefan studied the bark—deep scratches marked the trunk. "You might be right."

"But why?" Delara countered.

Torre climbed down, landing on the moss and leaf-covered ground. "Darkness and light."

Delara frowned. "What?"

Torre pulled a folded piece of paper from his coat. "It's from a series by Benjamin Hartmann." He handed it to Stefan, who unfolded it carefully.

A winter scene—familiar. Snow-laden trees, a frozen lake beneath a pale sky. At the center, a wooden boat drifted across the ice. A man lay inside—still, peaceful at first glance. But then the bruises. The dried blood. The cracked skin.

"Solitude in Frost," Torre said. "From Benjamin Hartmann's *Darkness and Light* series."

Stefan couldn't look away. There was something intimate in the violence, like the killer had staged a confession only the right eyes could read.

Delara stared at it. "This is disturbing."

"Is the killer obsessed with Hartmann?" Stefan asked. "This isn't a coincidence."

"Gyllenstierna's library was full of art books," Delara noted. "Especially paintings and sculptures."

"Maybe we should talk to Hartmann," Torre suggested.

Delara raised an eyebrow. "Why? What could he tell us?"

"Maybe he can explain the themes behind his paintings," Torre said. "It might help us understand what the killer is trying to say."

Delara shook her head. "You're grasping at straws."

Stefan stepped in. "Delara, I get it. But we're running out of leads. If these paintings are connected, Hartmann might help us make sense of them. It's worth a shot."

Delara sighed. "Fine. Let's go see Mr. Hartmann then."

CHAPTER EIGHT

BENJAMIN HARTMANN WASN'T WHAT Delara expected. No eccentricity, no theatrics. He was controlled, deliberate. A tailored suit, measured movements, but eyes that held more sadness than warmth. He was handsome in a certain way—refined, polished, with an intensity that made it hard to look away.

His studio reflected the same precision. Canvases arranged neatly, brushes aligned, every surface free of clutter. The scent of oil paint and turpentine hung in the air, grounding the space in something tangible, something real.

When he greeted them, his voice was calm, but his expression unreadable. "Three of you. That seems excessive."

Before they could respond, he continued, "I assume this is about my son."

"What about your son?" Stefan asked and dropped into one of the chairs the man had offered them.

"Uh... let's say, he's not unknown to the police."

"Why?" Delara asked.

Benjamin's somber mood deepened as he hesitated before responding to Delara's question. He seemed to choose his words carefully. "He has a history of troubles," Benjamin finally said, his gaze momentarily drifting to the paintings on the walls before returning to meet Delara's eyes. "Substance abuse, theft, fraud, you name it. I blame his mother."

"That's easy," Delara let out.

He fixed his gaze on her, his eyes narrowing with deliberate intensity. The shift was subtle but powerful, a cold tension curling through her. Benjamin Hartmann wasn't one for confrontation, but his silence spoke volumes. She realized, too late, that she had struck a nerve.

"You're quick to judge," Benjamin said, lowering himself into the armchair opposite Stefan, Delara, and Torre.

"In my experience both parents carry a certain level of responsibility," Delara said and looked him in the eye. He was undeniably handsome, with an air of danger that made him even more intriguing. Middle-aged, he was old enough to be her father—but then again, she'd always had a weakness for older men.

"Maybe you should explain to my son why, at three years old, his mother locked him in his room and left. When I came home that evening, I found him lying in his own filth, having cried himself to sleep. There was a typed note on the kitchen table. She said she regretted only two things in her life: marrying me and giving birth to him. From that day, she was no mother to him. I've endured his nightmares, his fears, his anger..." He paused, his breath catching. "I've done all of that," Benjamin said, while his voice started trembling. "All these years, I've tried to shield him from the pain, to give him the love and care he deserved. But I couldn't erase the scars his mother left behind when she walked away. So yes... if that's what you mean by responsibility."

"I didn't mean to...," Delara stammered, her voice trailing off.

"We're not here about your son," Stefan cut in.

Benjamin exhaled deeply, steadying himself. His eyes settled back on Stefan. "That's... good to hear."

Stefan reached into his jacket pocket and produced a photo of Gustav Gyllenstierna, sliding it across the table. "Do you know this man?"

Benjamin's gaze dropped to the image. He studied the photo carefully, his brow furrowing before he shook his head. "No," he said, leaning back in his chair with deliberate ease. "I don't recognize him. Who is he?"

"Are you sure? Maybe his name rings a bell. Gustav Gyllenstierna?"

A second time Benjamin Hartmann shook his head. "What is this about?"

Stefan hesitated for a moment. "Mr. Gyllenstierna is a person of interest in an ongoing investigation. There have been some... disturbing incidents related to your paintings, and we're trying to piece together any potential connections."

"Disturbing incidents? What disturbing incidents?" Benjamin's eyes widened with concern.

"Let's not beat around the bush... murder," Torre said suddenly. He had kept quiet until then. When Stefan gave him an angry look, he ignored it and continued, "Someone murdered Mr. Gyllenstierna's wife and children... someone with an obsession for your art."

Delara stiffened. Torre's tone left no room for argument—sharp, authoritative. Since when did he drop the polite shrink act and start giving orders?

"How?" Benjamin asked, narrowing his eyes. He didn't appear upset by the revelation; instead, a flicker of curiosity crossed his face, his interest piqued in a way that felt almost unsettling.

"He set up the scene like one of your paintings," Torre said.

"Dr. Nylander," Stefan began, but Torre ignored him, causing another flash of irritation in Stefan's eyes.

"Which one?"

"The Puppeteer's Symphony," Torre answered.

"And Solitude in Frost," Benjamin added. Then, something shifted—his expression hardened, only to betray a flicker of fear.

Torre narrowed his eyes. "Why would you say that? There are plenty of paintings in the 'Darkness and Light' series. Are they connected? Why did you choose that one just now?"

"Because...," Benjamin said and got up. He walked to a cupboard against the wall, hesitating for a moment before unlocking it and retrieving a stack of old letters tied with a faded ribbon. He brought the bundle back to the table and placed it before them.

"These are letters I've been receiving for years," Benjamin said. "At first, they were innocent expressions of admiration for my art. People would write to tell me how my paintings touched them, how they felt a connection to the emotions depicted on the canvas."

Delara took the bundle of letters and started leafing through them.

"The letters started to change over time," Benjamin continued. "They became more personal, intrusive, and fixated on the emotions portrayed in my paintings. At first, I didn't think much of it, but as the years passed, they began to disturb me."

Torre leaned forward. "Did any of the letters mention 'The Puppeteer's Symphony' or 'Solitude in Frost' specifically?"

"Yes," Benjamin replied, his eyes still fixed on the stack of letters. "Several letters mentioned those two paintings specifically. One particular writer seemed drawn to the dark emotions depicted in 'The Puppeteer's Symphony' and the sense of isolation in 'Solitude in Frost' and the paintings of 'Darkness and Light' in general.'"

"Do you know who sent them?" Delara asked.

"No," Benjamin said. "The letters were unsigned, and there was no return address. I never knew who was behind them, and they stopped coming until recently."

"What happened?"

Benjamin took a deep breath before continuing, "A few weeks ago, I received a new letter. It was different from the previous ones. This time, it wasn't just admiration for my art or fixation on the emotions portrayed. It was... threatening."

Delara's eyes widened, and she leaned in closer. "Threatening? What did the letter say?"

"Maybe that's a wrong word. It was disturbing. The writer suggested a new painting."

"What?" Torre asked.

"An addition to 'Darkness and Light.' You can read it yourself. It's the last letter in the bundle."

Delara took the last letter, her fingers tightening around the paper as she unfolded it. The handwriting was erratic—sharp slashes of ink that dug deep into the paper, as if the writer's hand had trembled with intensity.

The letter didn't just describe a painting. It conjured something grotesque, something that felt more like a premonition than a concept. The writer envisioned a dark room, its cracked walls smeared with something too viscous to be paint. A woman sat slumped in a high-backed chair, her head tilted at an unnatural angle, eyes hollowed out into empty sockets. Blood streaked down her face in thin, deliberate lines, pooling at the hollow of her throat. The writer had been meticulous in detailing the wounds—how the flesh would split, how the bruises would bloom like ink stains beneath pale skin.

And then, the children.

Two of them, barefoot and silent, their mouths sewn shut with coarse black thread. Their hands, small and trembling, held paintbrushes dipped in something far thicker than oil paint. The writer insisted that their expressions remain frozen, their glassy eyes reflecting nothing but endless suffering. They would be positioned as if painting their own mother's corpse, their tiny fingers dragging brushstrokes of crimson across her lifeless skin.

Delara swallowed hard, her throat dry. The final lines of the letter were scrawled more feverishly than the rest, the ink almost gouging through the paper:

"I see it so clearly. The agony, the beauty, the silence. But I lack the hands to bring it to life. You must paint it for me. You must make it real."

The words weren't just admiration—they were a demand. A plea from someone who had stared too long into the abyss and now wanted Benjamin Hartmann to pull that darkness into the waking world.

"This is... disturbing," Delara said. "The writer seems to be fixated on the darkest aspects of your art, as if they want to bring the emotions... the paintings to life in the most horrifying way."

Torre took the letter from her hands, scanned through it, and then looked Benjamin straight in the eye. "Extreme violence toward women and children. Whoever wrote this, is writing off his frustrations and trauma. Anger that has been boiling for years. But it's not clear if he just wants attention or really wants to act on those ideas."

Torre gave the paper back to Delara and she carefully put the letter back in the bundle. "It's possible that the admirer of your art became obsessed to the point of replicating the emotions and scenes from your paintings in real life," she suggested. "But Dr. Nylander is right, it's not sure if he's going one step further. Why didn't you go to the police?"

"I never imagined my art could have such a dark influence on someone," he said. "I still thought it was a prank."

"It's indeed too early to say... these letters might have nothing to do with what happened," Stefan said in a serious voice. "Do you mind if we take them with us? There might be some clues in there."

"Of course," Benjamin said. "Go ahead." He looked at them for a few seconds and then continued, "Anything else?"

"Where were you last Monday evening, the day of the murders?" Delara asked.

"I was at home," Benjamin replied with a sigh. "Alone, as usual. I spend most of my evenings in my studio or reading. I'm not much of a social person."

"Do you have anyone who can vouch for your whereabouts?" Stefan inquired.

"I'm afraid not," Benjamin said. Delara glanced at her notes. "You mentioned earlier that your son has had troubles in the past. Could he have any connection to Gustav Gyllenstierna?"

Benjamin's eyes darkened. "I highly doubt it. My son has been trying to turn his life around. He's been attending therapy and trying to overcome his past. He wouldn't involve himself in something like this."

"We'll need to talk to him," Torre said firmly. "It's essential to rule out any potential connections."

"Of course."

* * *

Benjamin's hand rested on the door handle, his fingers tightening until his knuckles turned white. He sighed, staring at the metal as though it might provide some answers. The police officers were gone now.

There was confusion. But above all, there was anger. Raging, unrelenting anger.

He squeezed the handle harder. Anger at whoever had defiled the sanctity of his art, twisting it into something grotesque. Anger at the letters that had seeped into his life like poison, corrupting everything they touched. But most of all, anger at himself—at his own blindness, his own stupidity.

He knew what he had to do. And it wouldn't be pretty.

The fire in his chest fueled him as he turned abruptly. He climbed the stairs two at a time, his focus narrowing to a single destination. One of the bedrooms. The one he had locked away from the world—and himself.

At the door, he stopped, the torrent of emotions swirling within him. His hand trembled as he reached into his pocket and pulled out the key.

With a deep breath, he steadied himself. The key slid into the lock, and the click rang out, sharp and final. The door creaked open, and Benjamin stepped inside.

The room was dark, and for a moment, Benjamin stood on the doorstep, listening to the soft noise coming from the back of the room. He hesitated before switching on the light. As he stepped inside, the sound became clearer—soft, muffled sobs echoing in the room.

The room inside appeared ordinary at first glance—a neatly made bed, a small desk with books, and a window adorned with green curtains. But Benjamin knew better.

As he moved farther in, he noticed a figure huddled on the floor near the window, naked, trembling, consumed by his demons. The scars of his addiction were written all over him—needle marks, greasy hair, unshaven face.

For a fleeting moment, Benjamin felt a pang of compassion. Then came the anger again. He had seen this act too many times before—the pleading, the lies, the pathetic display of vulnerability. It was a familiar script, one he no longer had patience for.

"Get up," he barked.

The young man rocked back and forth, lost in the throes of the withdrawal.

"I said, get up!"

No response.

"You asked for it," Benjamin muttered while pulling the belt from his trousers.

As he raised it, his son flinched, fear flashing in his sunken eyes. "No, please."

"What did you do?" Benjamin demanded, stepping closer.

"What do you mean?" his son stammered, crawling into the corner, hands shielding his face.

Benjamin knelt, placing the belt on the floor beside him. His voice softened, but the edge remained. "I won't hurt you if you tell me the truth. Where were you last Monday? What did you do?"

"I don't know," the young man mumbled, strands of hair hanging over his eyes. "I just..."

Benjamin's hand reached out, running gently over his son's head, as if to comfort him.

Then the belt struck.

The scream tore through the room, raw and desperate. The hits came fast and relentless, each one fueled by years of frustration, disappointment, and self-loathing. Benjamin didn't stop until the sobbing turned to silence.

He stood over the crumpled figure, streams of blood and tears marking his son's battered body. How could this be his child? He saw his ex-wife in him—weak, plain, a failure in every way.

"You don't fool me," Benjamin spat. "This act won't work on me."

"Dad... please," his son whimpered.

"You're not my son," Benjamin said coldly. "If I could do it over, I'd have left you in that room and thrown away the key."

The young man's head lifted, his voice trembling. "Then why did you take me in? Why didn't you leave me to die?"

Benjamin stared at him. "A mistake. You're a monster. Just like me. And I need to protect the world from someone like you."

He turned, ignoring the desperate pleas and sobbing that followed. At the door, he switched off the light and locked the door behind him.

"No! Don't leave me!" his son screamed. The sound was punctuated by soft thuds against the wall.

By the time Benjamin descended the stairs, the screams had faded to muffled sobs. He would return when the boy was ready to talk. He always did. It was a game of power and Benjamin Hartmann was always the winner.

CHAPTER NINE

TORRE COULDN'T STOP LOOKING at the pictures of paintings on the screen of his computer. Benjamin Hartmann's 'Darkness and Light' collection. Thirteen paintings. An odd number. The final masterpiece of the collection was terrifying. A real descent to hell. Like Dante's inferno. Darkness had won in the end. There was no redemption, no salvation to be found in those brushstrokes.

Torre's eyes scanned the intricate details of the painting, each stroke of the artist's hand seemingly etching a deeper sense of despair onto the canvas. The colors were vivid, yet they seemed to bleed into one another, creating a disorienting effect that mirrored the chaos in the scene.

The figures in the painting were twisted, contorted, and tormented, as if trapped in a never-ending cycle of suffering. The title of the painting, 'Eternal Desolation,' seemed to encapsulate the overwhelming sense of hopelessness that emanated from the artwork.

He wondered about the mind that had conceived such a masterpiece, and the darkness that must have resided in the artist's own soul. It was as if Hartmann had captured a fragment of his own torment and transferred it onto the canvas, inviting anyone who gazed upon it to share in his anguish.

He closed his eyes for a moment, the afterimage of the painting still burned into his mind. When he reopened them, he found himself staring at the other paintings in the collection, each with its own unique portrayal of the interplay between light and darkness. It was a journey through emotions, through human experience, and through the unknown recesses of the human psyche.

He understood why people were drawn to these paintings. They were unsettling, yet he couldn't look away.

Had it been the same for Gustav Gyllenstierna?

Torre's fingers hovered over the keyboard. The next moment he jumped up as he felt a hand on his shoulder.

"Are you still looking at those?" Stefan's voice sounded.

Torre looked up and then said, "There is something about these paintings. Hartmann started painting them after his wife left. There is so much anger and hate in them. Even the works that supposed to represent 'light' are tinged with darkness. It's as if he channeled all his negative emotions onto the canvas."

Stefan nodded slowly, his gaze shifting from the screen to Torre's face. "Gyllenstierna confessed. The case is closed."

"What? No. This isn't right. Why? Why did he do it?"

"His wife was going to leave him. They had been going through marriage counseling for years. A few weeks ago, she pulled the plug on their marriage. He was angry. He wanted to punish her."

"What about the children?"

Stefan's expression darkened. "According to his confession, he believed that by taking away the children, he would make her suffer even more. He said he wanted to break her, to destroy her."

Torre's frustration grew. "But what about the letters, the paintings? There's more to this, I'm sure of it. It can't just be about a failing marriage."

Stefan sighed. "I agree that there might be more layers to this, but sometimes, people do terrible things for deeply personal reasons. It might not always make logical sense to us."

Torre shook his head. "I need to talk to Gyllenstierna. I need to understand what drove him to this point. There's something about those paintings that has a hold on him, something that pushed him over the edge."

Stefan placed a reassuring hand on Torre's shoulder. "You can try, but keep in mind that he's already confessed. He might not be very cooperative now that the case is closed. Just... let it go."

Torre took a deep breath. "I still think we're wrong."

"Noted," Stefan said. "But I do need your help in finalizing the report. Delara is already busy with it."

"Delara? Oh, okay. Sure."

Stefan narrowed his eyes and then said, "What's going on between the two of you? If this is going to interfere with our work, I'd rather..."

"No, it's okay. We're fine. It's just... she had a relationship with my brother, and they broke up. Personally, I have nothing against her, but she obviously has some reservations about me... because of him. That's all."

"Then see that it doesn't become anything more," Stefan said. He quickly checked his phone that was buzzing and left, walking in the direction of the exit.

As Torre settled into his chair and resumed typing, his mind drifted. Investigations were never as simple as they seemed—human emotion ensured that. The case of Gustav Gyllenstierna had been proof of that, a brutal reminder of how personal demons could drive a man to unspeakable acts.

He had seen it before. Over and over. The razor-thin line between love and hate, passion and fury. The way desire curdled into something violent, something monstrous.

His thoughts drifted to Delara, and he realized that even within their team, those same tangled complexities existed. The tension between him and Delara wasn't just about their past. It ran deeper, threading through their every interaction, an unspoken thing neither of them had dared to name. He told himself to keep his personal life separate from his work. But that was easier said than done.

And then there was home. Lately, something had shifted. Conversations with his family carried an unfamiliar weight, an edge he couldn't explain. He didn't know when it had started, only that it was there—a silent pressure, like a storm waiting to break. Maybe it was the past, finally demanding to be acknowledged. Maybe it was something else entirely.

Torre sighed, shaking the thoughts from his head.

Focus.

He glanced at the painting on his screen one last time.

A line of bodies.

Children.

Dead children.

And Death watching over them.

* * *

Stefan took a drag from his cigarette, the cold air biting at his fingers as he held the phone to his ear.

"Katherine?"

"Can we meet?" Her voice was tight, restrained.

He exhaled slowly, watching the smoke curl into the night. "I think everything has been said. You made your decision without involving me. Or him."

"I lied."

His grip on the phone tightened. The cigarette burned forgotten between his fingers, ash crumbling onto his coat.

A pause.

"About what?" he asked.

"I know you're hurting, Stefan. But there are things you deserve to know." A breath, then, softer— "I love you. I want you. I left him."

The city noise dulled. The cold faded. For a moment, all he heard was the echo of her words. Love. Left. Truth unraveling at the seams.

Across the street, a woman and child crossed through the snow, their footprints disappearing almost as quickly as they formed.

A perfect, fleeting moment.

Stefan swallowed. "I don't know what to say." He leaned back against the brick wall, grounding himself. He couldn't afford this—this spiral, this sudden pull of hope. Their affair had been about sex. Or at least, that's what he told himself. But then the sleepless nights came. The quiet realizations. The weight of wanting something he knew he couldn't have.

"I understand if you need time," she said. "But I needed you to know the truth. I care for you, and…"

A child's laughter rang out from the corner. Innocent. Uncomplicated.

Katherine's next words cut through him like ice.

"It's yours," she whispered. "The baby is yours."

Stefan's breath caught. The streetlights blurred, his pulse a hammer against his ribs.

"How do you suddenly know?" His voice was sharper than he had anticipated. "You told me you didn't know."

Silence.

"Did you really think I wouldn't know?" Her voice cracked. "I just... couldn't face it."

A bitter laugh escaped him. "Another lie. And if you had stayed with him? What then? Would you have told him it was his?"

"I don't know."

At least she was honest about that.

He ran a hand down his face, his mind racing. "Did he find out?"

"Stefan... I love you. I don't want to lose you. I want to be with you. Can't you give us a chance?"

He closed his eyes.

"Katherine, I need time. I just—"

His voice died in his throat as he pulled the phone away from his ear, thumb hovering over the *END CALL* screen. The conversation was over—cut short with a tap—but the storm inside him raged on, untethered.

Snow, lights, laughter. Life went on.

But not his.

Everything had changed.

* * *

He had never seen anything like it before. It was more beautiful than he had imagined.

A slow breath escaped him, forming misty clouds in the cold air. The world stretched before him, silent and untouched, blanketed in white.

Perfect.

But beneath that quiet surface lay something else. Something only he could see.

The memories played in his mind, a slow, deliberate symphony of violence. The way their eyes lost their light. The way the blood spread, carving patterns across the floor like brushstrokes on a canvas.

A masterpiece. His masterpiece.

He closed his eyes. The faces flickered behind his lids, merging with the stillness of the snow-covered landscape. Chaos and calm. Life and death. Beauty in its purest, rawest form.

And the hunger. Always the hunger.

It was never enough. The rush faded too quickly, leaving behind an emptiness, a craving that only grew stronger. It pulled at him, whispered to him, demanded more. More fear. More pain. More perfection.

A shiver ran through him—not from the cold, but from the high. The power. The way he had shaped something so final, so absolute.

He was in control. He decided when it ended.

But the hunger never let him stop for long.

And standing there, surrounded by the quiet of the night, he knew one thing with certainty.

This was only the beginning.

CHAPTER TEN

THE HOUSE WAS NEARLY IDENTICAL to the Gyllenstierna residence. Torre stood in the hallway, his breath shallow. Memories of that horrific scene surged back.

The déjà vu was suffocating.

As Torre moved through the house, the paintings and photographs on the walls seemed to watch him, their gazes unsettling, their silent scrutiny amplifying the tension.

His pulse hammered as he stepped into the room. The signs of violence were undeniable—a grotesque tapestry of blood and terror. The metallic tang of it clung to the air, sharp and suffocating. Torre closed his eyes, bracing against the wave of nausea and dread clawing at his gut.

When he reopened them, he let his gaze sweep the scene with cold precision. The arrangement was chillingly familiar—bodies placed with eerie deliberation, their final moments twisted into something almost ritualistic.

This was no outburst of rage. It was the work of a mind as calculated as it was depraved.

Harvest of Sorrow.

The image of the painting was burned into his mind. A family, seated around a dining table, posed in a grotesque parody of domestic bliss. Their faces were frozen in terror. At the head of the table sat Death itself, a figure cloaked in shadow.

Now he saw a live version of it.

There, in front of him.

Near the window sat a girl, nine maybe ten years old, her hair neatly braided, her features delicate, innocent. The pale light filtering through the glass bathed her lifeless face in an eerie glow. No visible wounds, but a dark stain of dried blood on the carpet told the entire story of her suffering. But when he looked at bit closer, he saw that her mouth had been sewn shut. Her eyes were gone. Just hollow sockets remained.

Across from her, her younger brother—still a toddler. The same horror.

Up close, the horror was unmistakable, but from afar peaceful. Stitched mouths, vacant stares, the quiet violence in every carefully arranged detail.

Torre's breath hitched.

"Are you okay?" Stefan's voice shattered the silence.

Torre took a deep breath. "We were wrong. He did this. The killer. It wasn't Gustav Gyllenstierna."

Stefan nodded. "Yes. I know." Then he looked at the children. "Why sew their mouths shut?"

Torre's jaw tightened. "Silence. Or maybe… someone who grew up being told to shut up." He looked around and then asked, "Where are the parents?"

"The father was found outside in the garden," Stefan said. "Lying in the snow, covered in blood—just like Gyllenstierna. He's still alive. They took him to the hospital."

"And the mother?"

"Upstairs," Stefan replied, pointing to the ceiling.

The two men ascended the staircase, the creaking wood beneath their feet adding an ominous rhythm to their climb. The walls were lined with family photos, moments of joy and love frozen in time. Now, they felt like cruel mockeries of the horror that had consumed this house.

As they reached the upper floor, Torre's eyes swept over the hallway. The doors to the bedrooms were closed. Stefan led the way, his hand resting on the doorknob of the first room.

With a slight hesitation, he entered.

Twisted bed sheets and a woman's lifeless figure were sprawled across the bed. Torre's breath caught as he saw the body. Stefan's face was composed, but his eyes said something entirely different. Fear. Anger.

Just like the children, her eyes were gone and her mouth was sewn shut.

"So much blood," Torre whispered.

"He stabbed her in the neck."

"Why is she here? Why not downstairs with the children?"

"He took his time with her," Stefan said. "Look at the bruises, cuts. This was before her death. He tortured her."

"Sexual assault?"

"We need to wait for the examiner's report, but there are no obvious signs."

"This is different from Mrs. Gyllenstierna," Torre said and sighed.

"Is it? Mrs. Gyllenstierna was forced to watch her children die. Torture. Mental torture first, then physical torture."

"I bet Mrs. Castner here was also made to witness the death of her kids, but why didn't he kill her downstairs?"

"Is this another Hartmann painting?" Stefan asked.

Torre nodded. "But the mother is in the painting."

"How?"

"The father and kids are sitting at the table. Death at the head. The mother is sitting on the floor. She's tied up like a dog and naked, almost begging."

"That's... interesting," Stefan said.

"All Hartmann's paintings are like that... since the departure of his wife."

"Maybe we should have another chat with him."

Torre shook his head. "It's not him, but it's somehow connected to him."

"Hey," a voice sounded from behind them.

They turned and saw Delara standing in front of them.

"This puts our theory on shaky ground," she said. "We need to rethink the Gyllenstierna case." And gave them a faint smile.

"And where were you?" Stefan said in a stern voice.

"Uh... meeting a friend," she said quickly.

"Now?"

Delara's response was quick. "It was important. I only saw your message half an hour ago. I tried to be here as soon as I could."

Stefan sighed and then turned back to the body on the bed. "Well, this brings us back to square one."

Torre shook his head. "This brings us back to Gustav Gyllenstierna. Mr. Castner is in a coma. He won't say anything for now. Only Gustav Gyllenstierna can tell us more about what happened. He hasn't said much so far. He's keeping things from us, and I need to know why. Why is he taking the blame?"

"Good point," Stefan said and threw Delara, who was staring at her phone, another glance. He took a deep breath and then said, "I agree, we should press Gyllenstierna for more information."

"We need to be fast," Torre said. "I think the killer has done this before, and he won't stop until *we* stop him."

"You think so?"

"This takes a lot of planning. Keeping a family under control. He has practiced this before. Maybe on a smaller scale, maybe he failed. We need to look at old cases."

"How far do we need to go back?" Delara asked.

"No idea," Torre said. "But the paintings can lead us."

Stefan's brow furrowed as he considered Torre's words. "You might be right. This level of orchestration and brutality suggests experience. We should definitely dig into older cases, even if they weren't as extreme."

The team fell into a contemplative silence as the forensics team came in and the pathologist meticulously started examining the scene.

After a while, she spoke up, her voice measured and focused. "There are signs of a struggle, defensive wounds on the mother's hands. It seems like she fought back against her attacker."

"How did she die?" Stefan asked as he stood next to her.

"She was stabbed multiple times in the neck and back with a sharp blade. I would estimate approximately three centimeters wide. The carotid artery was likely severed. I'll need to examine her more closely in the morgue."

"And the murder weapon?" Delara asked.

"We found a knife, a kitchen knife with blood on it in the husband's hand. He's severely hypothermic and unresponsive. They brought him to the Karolinska hospital."

"Thanks, Dr. Thulin," Torre said.

She gave him a radiant smile and then turned her attention to the victim. For a moment, he didn't know how to behave. He was always pretty awkward about the little attention he got from women. He wasn't exactly Don Juan and didn't enjoy being the center of attention.

He shifted his feet and cleared his throat.

Stefan motioned for Torre to step aside, his expression hinting at a smirk. "Smooth, Torre."

Torre shot him a half-amused, half-annoyed look.

"But what connects the Castners and the Gyllenstiernas?" Delara said, unaware of the subtle exchange between Torre and Stefan.

Stefan's eyebrows furrowed in contemplation. "That's the question, isn't it? The similarities are uncanny, but why these families?"

"A bad marriage," Torre said.

Delara frowned. "Why?"

"The Castners weren't sleeping together anymore. Look at the nightstands. A book, tissues, alarm clock on one nightstand... likely hers. Nothing on the other. It's clean. Mr. Castner was sleeping somewhere else."

"That doesn't mean a thing," Delara said. "My father and mother have different rooms because my dad snores."

"This is a young couple," Torre said. "They should be sharing a bed, not just a house."

Stefan nodded. "Could be, but we need something more than just speculation. Let's talk to the rest of the family, neighbors, friends."

"Suppose Torre is right...," Delara started.

Torre threw her an annoyed look.

"... how does the killer know both marriages were going through a rough time?"

"Good point," Stefan said. "I don't know, but it means the killer has somehow access to privileged information. It could be a friend or family... someone close to the families."

"He punishes the mother," Torre whispered. "But why the children?"

Delara shook her head. "I can't even begin to understand the mind of someone capable of this."

"I think we're done here," Stefan said. "Let's leave it to forensics to sweep the house. But we need to talk to Gyllenstierna."

"And Mr. Castner," Torre added.

"If he ever regains consciousness."

For a moment Torre stared at Delara without actually seeing her.

"What is it?" Delara said.

"Benjamin Hartmann. We need to speak with him again—and his son. The killer seems fascinated by his work and understands the meaning behind the paintings. We should also investigate how much Hartmann has made public about his marital problems."

"You think he might be part of his inner circle?" Stefan asked.

"Maybe... I just wonder... why is the killer escalating? Why now? Why so fast?"

"Something put him over the edge," Delara said.

"Do you want me to talk to Dr. Gersson again?" Stefan said and looked at the phone in his hand. The buzzing had stopped, but the messages hadn't disappeared. Katherine had been trying to contact him since yesterday... in fact after their last call. He looked at the messages with mixed feelings. He didn't know what to do.

He sighed, his gaze still fixed on the phone. He put it back in his pocket and then looked at Torre and Delara.

"It couldn't hurt," Torre said and walked to the door. "Meanwhile I'll dive into Hartmann again. There is something off about that guy. And I can be at the autopsy of Mrs. Castner and her children."

Dr. Thulin quickly turned around and gave him a smile.

"Sure," Stefan said with a smirk. "We need to keep close contact with our forensic colleagues."

* * *

Stefan stood frozen, his gaze locked on the horrifying tableau before him—*The Children*, a masterpiece by Benjamin Hartmann. Seven lifeless bodies—two boys and five girls—lay in a grotesque circle, their small hands intertwined in a macabre unity. The artist had captured their despair with haunting precision.

The room seemed to close in around Stefan as he absorbed the brutal details. Torre's voice, explaining the link between Hartmann's paintings and the escalating crimes, suddenly became a distant echo.

This felt different.

This was personal.

"What's wrong?" Torre asked.

"I... I forgot something," Stefan stammered.

He couldn't breathe. The sudden panic clawed at him, a rising tide of dread he couldn't suppress. He stumbled out of the office, each step a struggle against the weight crushing his chest.

The corridor's flickering lights toyed with his frayed nerves, casting shifting shadows that amplified his unease. When he finally reached the exit, he fumbled with the doorknob. It took him a while before he could get it open.

The cool air outside hit him like a lifeline, but the suffocating pressure in him refused to relent.

It was dark. So very dark.

This doesn't make sense. How can this be?

The city sounds surrounded him, but they felt distant.

It was already late.

Stefan's world tilted with each step. The pitying stares of midnight survivors blurred at the edges, swallowed by Stockholm's indifferent glow.

How can this be?

There was no oxygen.

No air.

His breaths came in rapid gasps, chest tightening, as if the very air conspired against him. Few people moved past, offering fleeting glances of concern, but Stefan felt detached, lost in a surreal dreamscape where the boundaries between art and life dissolved.

His hands trembled as he took out his cell phone and dialed the number. As he waited for the call to connect, he felt the strain in his body tighten.

"Do you know what time it is?" the voice said through the speaker.

"Elena..."

"Stefan, I do need my sleep. You might..."

"Elena, open your computer," he interrupted.

"What for?"

"Just do it... please," Stefan pleaded, his breaths still uneven as he navigated the tumult of emotions.

Elena sighed audibly. "Okay, okay, give me a moment."

He drew deep breaths as he awaited Elena's response. In the background, he heard Johan's voice mumbling, "What the hell... it's 1 a.m. Can't this wait?"

A door slammed, followed by Elena's hissed "Johan, not now—" before the line crackled with staticky tension.

Then he heard her say, "Tell me... what is it?"

He couldn't push out the words.

"Stefan... what is it?" Elena's voice cut through the silence. He heard the concern in her voice.

"The Children."

"What?"

"Open your browser and search for 'The Children' by Benjamin Hartmann."

He listened to the faint sound of her typing on the keyboard. And then it was as if her breathing suddenly increased. Fast, unsteady puffs echoed through the phone, creating a disconcerting rhythm reminiscent of someone running a marathon.

Stefan could almost feel the panic seeping through the connection.

"Elena," he called out.

The silence stretched, broken only by the rapid cadence of Elena's breathing. It felt like an eternity.

Finally, Elena's voice, strained and breathless, cut through the phone.

"Stefan, this... this is... I can't..." Her words faltered.

Stefan listened, a knot tightening in his chest as he sensed his sister navigating the images that likely unfolded on her screen.

"I know," he said.

"This can't be. How? What does it mean? Is this Benjamin a killer?"

"I don't know," he whispered. He suddenly felt an eerie calm come over him. "Maybe you were right. Maybe Dad is innocent. After all those years..."

"Stef, the painting dates back from 2001."

"2001? Then... I don't understand. It doesn't make sense."

He heard her sigh.

"Stefan, he heard about the case in the news, and he made a painting about it. It's disgusting and immoral, but that's all. Don't go all..."

"The details," he interrupted. "The hands, the circle of bodies. These details were never revealed. How does he know?"

"Ask him."

"Sis... this... I thought I had this under control and..."

"I know," she said with the softest voice he had ever heard. "Our balance is always fragile. It's the same with me. We will never be able to leave it behind us. This will always be there, lingering in the background."

"I just want him to tell me why. After more than twenty years, we still don't know. He keeps silent, and Mom... she can't tell us anything anymore."

There was a strange tension at the other end of the line.

"Elena?"

"There's going to be a hearing," she said.

"Uh... about his case?"

"About his parole... next week."

He felt his mood sink. "He can't be released. It's... I'm just not ready."

"Five minutes ago, you were over the moon because there was a small chance he could have been innocent, that someone else was responsible for murdering five innocent children, and now you're prepared to throw him under the bus again. I don't understand you, Stef."

"It's not easy."

"Yeah... I know. I was there." Her voice was harsh, edged with the bitterness of shared trauma. "Look, Stefan, talk to him. For years, I'm trying to tell you to listen to his story. You'll see there is something not right about it. He might be innocent, or maybe not. I haven't made up my mind." She tried to suppress a yawn. "It's late... I need to get up really early and... I want to sleep. And so should you."

"Elena..."

"Just talk to him."

The line fell silent.

CHAPTER ELEVEN

BENJAMIN HARTMANN AVOIDED looking at the pictures in front of him.

Another one.

He didn't understand.

Harvest of sorrow.

A painting that nearly wouldn't have existed if his girlfriend at that time hadn't insisted. He had found it too dark, too humiliating, too uncomfortable. He had painted and repainted it so many times. It had never clicked. It had never felt right. He often wanted to forget about it, together with the feeling of love and hate that accompanied it.

Now the painting, in all its ugliness, was staring him in the face.

Harvest of Sorrow, not only on the canvas, but in real life.

Benjamin's gaze lingered on the frozen figures. If he didn't know better, he would have thought it were the results of his brushstrokes. But these were real people.

Children.

His stomach turned and he took a quick sip of the water to quench the nausea.

"A third painting," Stefan said. "Where were you last night?"

"You seriously don't think I could do something like this. Why would I use my own paintings?"

"Your paintings depict scenes eerily similar to the crime scenes we've been investigating," Stefan pressed. "How do you explain that?"

Benjamin's eyes darted around the room, avoiding Stefan's stare. He ran a shaky hand through his disheveled hair and then said, "I create art. I don't orchestrate tragedies."

Stefan leaned in. "Where is your son, Mr. Hartmann?"

"I don't know. And why would he have anything to do with this atrocity?"

Stefan put pictures of other paintings on the table. "Interesting scenes. Each one of them depicts women being tormented, humiliated, murdered, tortured. I wonder what was going through your mind when you made them?"

"I think you already know," Benjamin said and crossed his arms. "A man and his son left by a wife... that should make for a lot of trauma. But my art is an expression of my own struggles, not a blueprint for violence. I can't help it if lunatics want to use this to get their own revenge."

"So, you think it's about revenge?"

"That's what I felt when painting them," he said with an indifferent tone in his voice.

Stefan placed a final picture on the table—The Children. Shock and confusion flickered across Benjamin's face as his eyes locked onto the image.

The Children, with its seven lifeless figures.

"Why do you put this in front of me? This piece is not part of the collection 'Darkness and Light.' This one is special."

"Why?"

"I... because it's not mine."

Stefan looked at Torre sitting next to him. He hadn't said a word yet.

"Your name is there," Torre pointed out.

"In 2001, I was in an all-time low. He already wrote to me then. It wasn't the first time he proposed a scene for a painting."

"The killer described this painting?" Stefan asked.

"I'm not sure if it's the same man," Benjamin stammered. "He sent me a letter in the summer of 2001, describing his dream."

"A dream?" Stefan frowned.

Benjamin hesitated. "Yes, a dream. Or at least, that's what I thought. A disturbing vision of seven children, lifeless and bound together. I thought it was just a twisted idea, something born out of his troubled mind. I never thought it was a gruesome reality."

Stefan's expression darkened. "You received this letter in 2001, and you painted The Children based on that description?"

"I didn't know it was an actual crime until recently. I thought it was a sick fantasy, not a premonition," Benjamin explained.

Stefan's mind raced. "Recently? So you do know?"

Benjamin sighed, went into the pocket of his jacket and threw the letter in front of them. "He sent me these clippings."

Stefan's hand trembled as he examined the yellowing clippings. The articles were dated back to 2000, detailing a gruesome crime with the title "Father kills his five children, injures two." A cold shiver ran down Stefan's spine. He knew this all too well. "Did you know the details in this article when you created the painting?"

Benjamin's face paled, and he ran a hand through his hair, visibly distressed. "I... I can't be sure. I remembered the case, but... at that time, I didn't realize it was about this case. I had a lot on my mind. But the details in the letter were a lot more disturbing."

"What details?"

"The details of the scene, where each of the bodies was. The injuries of the children. Everything."

"He was there," Stefan whispered.

Torre's eyes settled on Stefan. It was like his colleague had seen a ghost.

"He knows me," Benjamin said.

"Why do you think that?"

"At least now, he knows me... maybe not then. His letters have become more personal over the years."

"How?"

"He started mentioning things only someone close would know. My struggles, my personal life, my emotions. It became clear that he had some insight into my world. He's been watching me."

"Or someone close to you," Torre added.

"Your son," Stefan said. "He's a liability, isn't it?"

Benjamin frowned. "What would you know about my son?"

"He is too much like his mother," Torre said and fixed his eyes on the man. "Weak. No spine. A nuisance. A drug addict."

"He could never have written these letters or have anything to do with these killings," Benjamin let out. He was nervous. Fidgeting with the strap of his watch. The strong man of before was breaking down under the weight of accusations. "You're wrong. He's not capable of this. He's broken, yes, but he's not a monster."

Stefan studied Benjamin's reaction. The mention of his son had struck a nerve.

"Maybe we are not dealing with the same person," Torre remarked. "You told us the tone of the letters has changed over the years."

"Not so much the tone," Benjamin said. "But the level of information."

"Did you ever tell your son about the letters?"

Benjamin's eyes flickered with a mix of anger and annoyance. "Of course not."

"Where is your son?" Stefan tried again.

Benjamin sighed. "I don't know. He's a junkie. Try his so-called friends on the street, his supplier or... in his better days his psychiatrist."

"Psychiatrist? Who?"

"Dr. Elsa Larsson. She's been treating him for a while. I thought she could help him, but..." Benjamin's voice trailed off. Then he threw his head backwards, looked at the ceiling for a moment and said, "... not really. Wasted money and time."

"You think so?" Torre asked.

"Yes," Benjamin replied with a bitter chuckle. "He's beyond help. I don't even know why I bother. Maybe it's the guilt. Maybe it's because I'm his father, and I feel I should do something."

"I gather he is no longer a patient of Dr. Larsson?"

Benjamin shook his head. "He stopped seeing her a while ago. Stubborn as he is, he thinks he can handle everything on his own."

Torre exchanged a glance with Stefan. "We might need to talk to Dr. Larsson."

"Good luck with that," Benjamin muttered. "She won't say anything, but feel free to try. And I think you're wrong. My son couldn't have done this. He was just a baby when I got those letters."

"Who says the person who sent you the letters and the killer are one and the same person?" Torre suddenly said.

✳ ✳ ✳

"What's going on?" Torre asked.

Stefan sighed, his eyes fixed on the collection of papers scattered across his desk. "We're still no step closer to finding the killer. We need to talk to Gustav Gyllenstierna again."

"That's not what I was talking about."

Stefan looked up and met Torre's inquisitive gaze. "The Children. Why is this important to you?"

"It's not," Stefan said surprised.

"I don't believe you."

Stefan raised an eyebrow, studying Torre's expression. "What are you getting at?"

Torre leaned against the desk. "That painting has stirred something in you, something beyond the case. What is it?"

Stefan hesitated, but then said, "It's personal. The details in that painting, the scene it depicts... it hits too close to home."

"Why?"

"I can't tell you," Stefan said and looked down while his thumb grazed the edge of the crime-scene photo.

Torre's voice softened, but his gaze didn't waver. "I need to know if this will blind you. The killer won't hesitate to exploit weakness. If this case is affecting you to this extent, maybe you should consider stepping back, at least from the more emotionally charged aspects."

Torre's eyes dropped to Stefan's hand—the photo edge was crumpled where he'd gripped it too tight. "You're not okay."

Stefan's laugh was brittle. "I don't have the luxury of not being okay."

* * *

Dr. Gersson had reluctantly agreed to continue the hypnosis session. Gustav was sitting in the chair again, eyes closed. He looked a lot older than the last time Stefan and Torre had seen him. Unshaven, with dark circles under his eyes.

Dr. Gersson began with his usual calm and reassuring tone. "Mr. Gyllenstierna, I want you to take a deep breath and let yourself relax. You are in a safe place, surrounded by people who want to help you." Gustav's shoulders sagged as he followed the instructions, his breathing gradually slowing.

Stefan and Torre watched from the observation room again. The previous session had yielded some fragments, but they needed more concrete details to move forward in the investigation.

"Gustav," Dr. Gersson continued, "we are going to revisit the night of the incident. Remember, you are just an observer, and nothing can harm you. Let your mind drift back to that night. Where are you?"

Gustav's voice was barely a whisper, "I'm in the study... upstairs."

"Good," Dr. Gersson said gently. "You mentioned hearing footsteps. Can you focus on that moment again? Tell me what happens next."

"There were footsteps... coming closer. The door... it opened."

Gustav's face tightened, reflecting the stress of reliving the memory.

But Dr. Gersson's voice remained soothing. "You're doing well. Stay with the memory. Can you see who opened the door?"

"It's him," Gustav's voice quivered. "The man in the black coverall. He has a gun..."

Stefan leaned forward, his attention fully on Gustav's words.

"Focus on his appearance," Dr. Gersson guided. "Can you see any distinguishing features? Anything that stands out?"

"The eyes... they're glowing. He's pointing the gun at me. I... I can't move."

"Remember, Gustav, you are safe. This is just a memory. What happens next?"

Gustav's breathing quickened. "He wants me to go downstairs. I don't want to."

"What then?"

"He's angry and tells me they will die if I don't do what he says. I get up and go downstairs. I... no, I don't want to..."

"Remember, you are just an observer. You are not really there. What happens next?"

"I go into the living room. He's behind me... with the gun. I can almost feel it pressing against my back."

"Where are your wife and kids?"

"They... are in the living room... Oh, God... I don't want to..."

Gustav's breathing became labored.

"You're doing great, Gustav. Remember, you're just an observer. You're safe. What do you see in the living room?"

"They're tied up... sitting on different chairs. My wife, my children... they're so scared. I can see the fear in their eyes."

"Stay with it, Gustav," Dr. Gersson encouraged. "You're doing very well. What does the man in the black coverall do next?"

"He forces me to sit down on the chair in front of them. The next moment I feel the rope around my hands. He ties them... just like my wife and the children. It's strange. He... knows their names."

"What does he say?"

"I don't understand. How can he know?"

"What?"

Gustav shook his head. Dr. Gersson leaned forward, maintaining his calm, guiding voice. "Try to stay with the memory. What does the man in the black coverall say?"

Gustav's breathing steadied slightly as he focused. "He says... 'Who do you want to die first?' He aimed the gun at my wife and then the boys. He knows I..."

"What does he know?"

"He knows I have doubts about my family. I..." Tears started to run down his cheeks. "He knows I didn't want them. Please, let me go!"

"What do you mean you didn't want them?" Dr. Gersson asked and a deep frown appeared on his forehead.

"Please...," Gustav whispered, tears running down his cheeks.

Dr. Gersson looked at the one-way glass. The session was clearly taking a toll on Gustav.

"What doubts did you have?" he then asked and turned to Gustav.

Gustav's breathing was ragged, and his voice trembled as he spoke. "I... I never wanted to be a father or a husband. I told my wife... I wished we'd never met. I thought... The responsibility... it was overwhelming. He knew my fears, my insecurities. He taunted me with them."

Stefan braced one palm against the cool glass, his reflection ghosting over Gustav's tormented face. The other hand kept unconsciously drifting toward his sidearm.

Dr. Gersson continued, "Stay with the memory. What happens next? What does the man do?"

Gustav's body tensed, and his voice dropped to a whisper. "He... he says if I don't choose, he'll kill them all. He points the gun at my wife again, then at my children. I... I couldn't..."

"What did you do, Gustav? It's important for us to know."

Gustav's face contorted with agony as he relived the moment. "I couldn't choose. I begged him to let them go, to take me instead. But he just laughed. He said I had to choose, or he would make the choice for me."

"And then?"

"They are crying, pleading to spare them."

"And..."

Gustav shook his head again, his distress growing. "I don't want to. I need to go."

"You're doing great, Gustav. Remember, you're just an observer. What does he do next?"

"He... he moves to the other side, facing me. He puts the gun against my wife's head."

Stefan and Torre leaned in closer, their faces tense with anticipation.

Dr. Gersson's voice remained calm and steady. "You're safe, Gustav. What does he say to you?"

"He crouches beside Lisa's chair, tilting his head. He... he says it's my fault. That it's their fault. He says... 'If they'd been worth keeping, you wouldn't have hated them so much.' Then he... he pulls out a knife."

"A knife?"

"Yes," Gustav whispered, his voice quivering. "He holds it to her throat and says... he says he's going to make me watch."

"What happens next, Gustav?"

Gustav's face contorted with pain. "He... he suddenly moves to the children. Then he..." Gustav's voice broke, and tears streamed down his face. "Oh God, he cuts Willie's throat... Lisa and Joshua are screaming..."

Dr. Gersson nodded, but for a fleeting moment, the horror of the memory cracked through his professional composure before he steadied himself.

"He... he's laughing. It's like he enjoys it. He says... he says it's my fault they're going to die. He makes me watch as he... moves to Joshua and kills him. The blood is so massive... and there's nothing I can do. Make it stop! Make it stop!"

Gustav couldn't continue, and Dr. Gersson gently brought him out of the hypnotic state. "That's enough for now, Gustav. You've been incredibly brave. We'll stop here."

Dr. Gersson stepped back, his hand resting on Gustav's shoulder as the man broke down in silent sobs. Behind the glass, Stefan and Torre exchanged a grim look, knowing the horrors they'd just heard were only part of the truth they still needed to uncover.

CHAPTER TWELVE

THE PERSON AT THE FRONT DOOR WAS persistent. The doorbell's shrill cry sliced through the house like a scalpel through scar tissue.

It rang again. And again.

Elena tightened her grip on the wheels of her wheelchair, her left leg spasming—the old wound sending phantom pains up her thigh. The wheelchair's armrest groaned under her white-knuckled grip as she navigated the narrow hallway with deliberate effort.

She reached the door and hesitated. Her pulse drummed in her ears.

Then, with a steadying breath, she unlocked the latch.

"Who is it?" Elena called out.

"It's Delara," came the reply. "I hope you remember me. I'm Stefan's partner."

Elena frowned. What could she possibly want at this hour?

The chain lock rattled as Elena opened the door slightly, peering through the gap.

Why was she here?

Delara stood on the doorstep, her expression serious. "Can I come in?"

Elena hesitated, then opened the door wider. "What's this about?"

Delara stepped inside. "I need to talk to you about Stefan."

Elena's grip on her wheelchair tightened. "Why?"

Delara took a deep breath, steadying herself. "He might have already told you, but there's a case we're working on. A killer is murdering entire families and displaying them as paintings by Benjamin Hartmann. And there is one particular painting I want to talk to you about: 'The Children.' Seven dead children on the floor, holding hands."

Elena's face hardened. "I don't know anything about that. You're wasting your time."

"I don't think so," Delara said.

Elena's eyes narrowed, and she wheeled herself back. "What do you mean?"

Delara stepped closer. "Stefan has been acting strangely. He's obsessed with that painting. It's like it's consuming him, and I believe it has something to do with your past."

Elena shook her head, her jaw set in defiance. "Our past is none of your business. That's between him and me."

"Families are being murdered, Elena," Delara said. "Displayed in horrific ways, just like in Hartmann's paintings. If there's something—anything—you know that can help us to stop this, you have to tell me."

Elena's anger flared, but she took a deep breath, trying to maintain control. "You think you can just waltz in here and demand answers? Our past isn't something you can just pry into."

"I'm not here to pry. I'm here to help. But I can't do that without your help. Please, Elena. Stefan is on edge. He needs you. We all do. I need to know if he's okay."

Silence.

"I tried checking the database," Delara admitted. "But you're not there. You changed your last name."

Elena's expression wavered, the tension in her shoulders easing slightly. She glanced away, memories flooding back despite her attempts to suppress them. "That painting... it's not just art. It's a nightmare."

Delara's eyes widened. "A nightmare?"

Elena nodded slowly. "The Children... that's us. The Svensson family."

Delara frowned and stammered, "What do you mean? I don't understand."

"We were seven siblings. Stefan was six at the time. I was nine. I don't think he remembers much, but I do."

She sighed and put her hands in her lap.

"What happened?"

"Our dad... there had been struggles for years between Mom and Dad. Fights... every night. She wanted to leave him and one evening... he decided he would never allow her to leave with the children... us. He decided to..."

Elena's voice broke, and she paused to collect herself. Delara watched. The woman in the wheelchair suddenly seemed so frail, so broken.

"He decided to kill us all," Elena continued. "He took his rifle, went to the bedrooms and shot his children. Stefan and I shared a room. He had woken up in the night... thirsty... and he was whining so much, I took him downstairs. It's where we were when we heard the shots. Before we knew what was going on, he shot us too. Then Dad carried the bodies to the living room and put us on the floor, hand in hand, and waited until the police arrived. Stefan and I were the only ones who survived. I barely made it... now I'm here in a wheelchair for the rest of my life."

Delara's face paled. "I had no idea."

Elena's eyes filled with tears, but she quickly blinked them away. Her voice sounded harsh when she said, "Indeed, you have no idea. You have no idea what I felt when I was lying there, barely alive, my hand touching Stefan's and the other hand touching my brother Lukas. I felt the life drain out of him... it became cold, and I so much wanted... So, forgive us if we don't want to talk about it. Mom went crazy. Lucky for us, our grandparents took us in and gave us the best childhood they could give us. They had to deal with the knowledge that their son was a murderer, that he had killed almost his entire family. It's like they had to make up for where our dad had gone so horribly wrong."

"Where is your dad now?"

"In prison."

"I'm sorry I didn't mean to upset you."

"But you did, and I am not sure what you exactly achieved by forcing me to reveal this."

"Obviously, Stefan talked to you about Benjamin Hartmann. What do you think happened? Did you father know him? Admire him?"

"Not sure Dad was an art lover. Though... my mother was. Also... Hartmann painted this in 2001. The... incident happened in 2000."

Delara frowned. "So, the painting came after the incident. In principle, Hartmann could have used the reporting on your case as inspiration, but he said that he received a letter describing the scene. He later decided to use it."

"I saw the painting," Elena said. "Some of the details were never revealed in the press, like the fact the bodies were staged like that."

"Then the letter was written by someone who was there. Maybe your father..."

She looked at Elena who immediately gave her an angry look. "Don't go there! I have been thinking about that, and to be honest the last years I have made myself crazy with the hope that maybe he did not do it."

"Do you think that someone else could have done it?"

Elena turned her wheelchair and gestured for Delara to follow. She led her into the living room, navigating smoothly toward a small, cluttered desk in the corner. With practiced ease, she pulled open a drawer, her fingers brushing past scattered papers before retrieving a worn, leather-bound journal, which she handed to Delara.

"Read this," Elena said. "It's my father's journal. My grandmother told me he always wanted to be a journalist, but... anyway, I found it hidden away in our old house a few years ago. My mother never sold the house... I don't know why. I've read it a hundred times, trying to make sense of it all."

"Where is your mom?"

"She's in a nursing home. After the incident, she has been in and out of psychiatric hospitals... so many times. She's a broken woman. She tried to take her own life twice, but..."

"But?"

"I don't know if it was sincere," Elena said and narrowed her eyes.

"What are you saying?"

She shook her head. "Probably nothing."

Delara took the journal, flipping through the pages filled with cramped, erratic handwriting. She paused on a page dated a few days before the tragic night, her eyes scanning the fevered entries. "This entry... the day before. He writes about taking you all to the zoo. There's nothing about—"

"Exactly." Elena's wheelchair creaked as she leaned forward. "The man who documented every grocery receipt and dry cleaner visit didn't mention planning a massacre? Either he's the most disciplined liar in history..." She met Delara's gaze. "Or someone else is responsible for this."

"Maybe he didn't want to implicate himself."

Elena shook her head. "He confessed almost immediately. I don't think he wrote that letter. I doubt he knows Hartmann. But if my dad didn't write to Hartmann, then who did?"

Delara's brow furrowed. "The letter had to come from someone with intimate knowledge of the crime scene. Someone who was there or who had access to the police files."

Elena's eyes darkened with a glimmer of suspicion. "The police?"

"Jeez, I don't want to go there," Delara sighed.

"Why not?"

Delara looked away, her shoulders tense. "Because if it's the police, it means we're up against more than just a killer. It means the very people we should be able to trust are part of the coverup."

Elena crossed her arms. "We can't afford not to go there, Delara. If we're right, then they have the power to bury the truth and silence anyone who gets too close."

"Who was the lead investigator on the case?"

Elena shook her head, while putting the journal on the table in front of her. "I don't know, but you should be able to find out. 6 December 2000, Rinkeby."

"Rinkeby?" Delara echoed with a hint of surprise in her voice.

Elena looked her straight in the eye. "Yes, Rinkeby."

"So, you've come a long way. It's not easy to grow up in Rinkeby."

Elena's expression softened. "No, it's not. It was tough, although the mix of cultures and social dynamics taught me resilience and adaptability. I learned to see the beauty in diversity and the strength in community, even when things were hard. But... to be honest, I don't remember much. My grandparents, on the other hand, lived in Östermalm. That's where I really grew up."

"Okay, I'll check in the files."

"One thing... and it's not negotiable," Elena said. "I have to tell Stefan. He's my brother, and I don't want to blindsight him. Besides, he might have some insights or remember details that I don't... although I doubt that. He was very young."

"Okay. I'll start digging through the files, and you talk to Stefan. Maybe we can finally get somewhere."

※ ※ ※

Dr. Elsa Larsson sat behind her polished mahogany desk, the afternoon light catching the gold frames of her glasses. At fifty, she carried herself with the effortless grace of someone used to being the smartest person in the room. Her crimson nails tapped once against her appointment book as she regarded the two detectives. "Gentlemen, I assume this isn't a social call."

Torre stepped forward, his notebook already open. "We need information about two of your patients—Gustav Gyllenstierna and Sebastian Hartmann."

Elsa's eyebrow arched. "You know I can't discuss patients without—"

"Entire families are being butchered," Stefan interrupted, slapping a crime scene photo on her desk. The image showed a woman posed grotesquely, her limbs arranged in deliberate angles. "Like this."

Elsa's gaze shifted to the photo, then moved away. There was a barely perceptible tightening around her eyes. "Even if I wanted to help, patient confidentiality—"

Torre clenched his jaw. "At least can you tell us if Seb Hartmann knew Gustav Gyllenstierna? Could they have met each other?"

"I..."

"Look, I can do this the official way," Stefan said, his hands firmly planted on Elsa's desk. He lowered his face to her level, locking eyes with her.

Stefan's intensity was met with Elsa's calm resolve.

It was a silent standoff.

Torre glanced between them. He knew Stefan's desperate approach could yield results, but it also risked escalating the situation.

"Dr. Larsson, please," Torre urged. "We just need to know if there's any connection between Seb and Gustav."

"As far as I know, they didn't know each other, but I cannot be sure that they didn't meet at a given time in the waiting room."

"Can you check when the appointments took place?" Stefan asked.

"But..."

"Please," Torre added. "This could be the key to preventing more deaths."

After a long pause, Elsa finally nodded. "I'll check my records. But I'm doing this unofficially, and you must promise to keep my involvement confidential."

"Of course," Stefan said.

She opened her laptop and started typing, her fingers moving swiftly over the keys. The screen's glow carved shadows across her face, softening nothing—her cheekbones still sharp, her gaze still cutting. Even now, she seemed more like a judge than a doctor.

Torre and Stefan watched in silence. Elsa's brows furrowed as she scanned through the records, her eyes darting back and forth across the screen.

"Gyllenstierna and Hartmann were in the same building the same day. An hour apart." A pause. "Close enough to share a waiting room."

"Do the records show wait times?"

Elsa gave a dry smile. "No. But if one arrived early—or the other ran late—they might have crossed paths."

"What about Marnix Castner?" Torre asked.

Elsa suddenly looked up. "Marnix? Why do you bring him up?"

"So, he was a patient of yours?"

"Was?" Elsa asked.

"Mr. Castner died yesterday in the hospital. His family died a few days ago," Stefan said. "Murdered in the same brutal way as Gustav's family, enacting a painting of Benjamin Hartmann."

"Dr. Larsson, everything leads to you," Torre said.

"No," she said in a stern voice. "It leads to Seb Hartmann."

"How?"

Elsa took a deep breath, her eyes narrowing as she collected her thoughts. "Seb and Castner had an altercation a few months ago. Seb was in the waiting room when Castner came in. You have to understand, I wasn't seeing Seb anymore as patient."

Torre leaned in closer. "Why?"

"I... I can't say," she stammered.

"Dr. Larsson, this is about protecting innocent people," Torre pressed.

Elsa hesitated, the conflict evident in her eyes. Finally, she sighed and spoke. "Seb's behavior became increasingly erratic and aggressive. He refused to take his medication, missed appointments, and began displaying signs of severe paranoia. I had to refer him to another specialist because I was no longer able to manage his case effectively."

"So, it wasn't him who stopped coming to you?" Stefan interjected.

"Indeed," she said. "Did he claim otherwise?"

"No, not exactly." Then Stefan frowned. "Why didn't you tell us this earlier?"

Elsa looked down. "Because I don't believe he is capable of something like this."

"So, what happened with Castner?" Torre asked.

Elsa took a deep breath. "Seb desperately wanted to see me. He had a fight with his dad that day and was visibly upset, but Castner wouldn't let him. It was his slot."

"And how did Seb react to that?" Stefan asked.

Elsa sighed. "Seb was furious. He accused Castner of being selfish and insensitive. The argument escalated quickly. Castner remained firm, saying Seb had to wait his turn, but Seb stormed out, shouting that he would make everyone pay for dismissing him."

"Did it get physical?"

"No."

Torre exchanged a glance with Stefan. "This makes Seb's motive even clearer—he felt not just betrayed by Castner but dismissed by everyone who refused to take him seriously."

Stefan nodded. "We need to find Seb Hartmann. He's the key to unraveling this whole mess."

"Be careful," she said. "Seb is unstable and unpredictable. If he's truly behind these murders, he won't hesitate to protect his twisted sense of justice."

"Why is he doing this?" Stefan asked.

"These families represent everything he didn't have. A loving father and mother. A real family."

Torre shook his head. "It's a plausible theory, but it feels too convenient. We need more concrete evidence before we can be sure Seb is our guy. Seb is erratic, chaotic. He's a drug addict. The killings were meticulously planned. He doesn't fit the profile."

Then he turned to Elsa. "Why was Castner a patient of yours?"

"You know I can't tell you," Elsa spit out.

Torre remained calm, his eyes steady on hers. "We're not asking for specific details about his treatment, Dr. Larsson. But any context you can provide might help us understand why he was targeted."

Elsa hesitated, clearly torn between her professional ethics and the urgency of the situation. Finally, she sighed and said, "Castner was dealing with severe anxiety and depression. He was under a lot of pressure at work and at home, and he had trouble coping."

"At home? Why?"

Elsa looked down at her hands for a moment before meeting Torre's gaze again. "His marriage was strained. She had an affair and wanted to leave him. He felt humiliated and betrayed. He talked about his fears that his wife was setting up the kids against him. He had lost any connection with his family."

"So, he could have been under so much stress that he was vulnerable to manipulation," Torre finished. "A perfect target for someone looking to exploit his emotional turmoil. The killer doesn't just strike. He weaponizes the men—turns their rage and pain against their own families. Seb Hartmann might be involved, but he's not the one orchestrating these murders. There's a level of sophistication and precision that he simply doesn't possess."

"Speculation... but everything points to him and his father," Stefan said. "What if Benjamin is involved?"

Torre frowned. "Benjamin Hartmann. It's possible. He's manipulative and strategic. If anyone could devise a plan like this, it would be him."

Elsa interjected. "Benjamin Hartmann is a powerful man. Why would he even do this?"

"His wife left him," Stefan said. "The women were punished more than the children or the men. It's a pattern—revenge against those he believes wronged him."

Torre glanced at Elsa. "Dr. Larsson, have you ever had any dealings with Benjamin Hartmann?"

Elsa shook her head, then looked at the laptop on her desk. "No, not really."

"Not really?" Torre pressed.

"I mean... he's Seb's dad. Benjamin was the one who forced him to go into therapy. He paid for everything, but he never interacted with me directly about Seb's treatment."

Torre shook his head. "Benjamin fits the profile, but why would he put the spotlight on him. It doesn't make sense."

"This entire case doesn't make sense," Stefan said and then looked at Dr. Larsson. "You have been most helpful, doctor, but we'll need your notes on Seb Hartmann."

"A warrant, gentlemen," she said with a straight face. "Only then, I can share my notes."

Stefan sighed.

He knew it wouldn't be that easy.

CHAPTER THIRTEEN

SEB HARTMANN STUMBLED THROUGH the dark streets of Stockholm, his body wracked with pain and tremors. Each step sent sharp jolts of agony through his limbs, and his muscles twitched uncontrollably. His skin was slick with cold sweat, his clothes clinging to him as he shivered violently despite the mild night air. The craving for a fix was an insatiable beast inside him, clawing at his sanity and driving him to desperation.

His vision blurred, and he clutched at his sides, feeling like his organs were being twisted and torn apart. Every nerve in his body screamed for relief, for the sweet oblivion that only a hit could provide. But his pockets were empty, and the streets offered no solace. He had sold everything of value, every possession, and pawned every item he could think of. Now, there was nothing left but the cold, harsh reality of his addiction.

Seb's breath came in ragged gasps as he staggered into a desolate alley, the faint light of a flickering streetlamp casting eerie shadows on the walls. He leaned against the cold, rough brick, sliding down until he was sitting on the grimy ground, his head cradled in his hands. The tremors wracked his body, each wave of withdrawal more intense than the last. He clenched his teeth, trying to stifle the whimpers of pain that escaped his lips.

As he sat there, lost in his agony, a group of young men emerged from the shadows. Their eyes glinted with malice as they approached. Seb looked up, his bloodshot eyes filled with desperation and fear.

"Hey, you got any money?" one of them sneered.

Seb shook his head. "No... nothing."

He slowly got up.

The gang leader's face twisted in anger. "Then what the hell are you doing here, junkie?" He turned to the other men. "Fuck... he said he would have money."

One of them muttered, "He's lying."

Before Seb could say anything, a fist connected with his jaw, sending him sprawling to the ground. Pain exploded in his head. The gang descended upon him like a pack of wolves, kicking and punching him relentlessly. Each blow was a fresh wave of agony, adding to the torment already coursing through his body.

"Got nothing, huh? Useless piece of trash!" one of them spat, delivering a particularly vicious kick to Seb's ribs.

Seb curled into a ball, trying to protect himself from the onslaught. His cries of pain echoed in the alley, but no help came. The beating seemed to go on forever, each moment stretching into an eternity of suffering. When the gang finally tired of their sport, they left him there, broken and bleeding on the cold, hard ground.

He gasped for breath, his body a mass of bruises and lacerations. His ribs screamed where they'd been kicked, but the ache in his veins—the absence of the drug—hurt worse. He needed a fix.

And he would do anything, anything, to make the pain stop.

※ ※ ※

Sex with Katherine had always been all-consuming, confusing and exhilarating at the same time. Passionate, like he had to possess her, all of her.

He had found her in her car in front of his house after a frustratingly long day, where they hadn't gotten any closer to finding the killer of the Gyllenstiernas and the Castners. Exhaustion clung to him like a second skin. Now, sweat slicked both their bodies, tangled in the sheets.

Even as his fingers traced the curve of her neck, the heaviness returned. "You shouldn't be here."

Katherine sighed and then said, "Maybe."

He kissed the naked skin of her back and then let his fingers trace the slight indentation at the base of her spine. A stab of something unwelcome, a tenderness he couldn't afford, twisted in his gut.

"Are you going back to him?" he finally asked.

Katherine turned to face him and tilted her head back, the moonlight catching the glint of a tear in her eye.

A tear from Katherine Bergenstråhle? It was a sight that defied logic. He had never seen her so vulnerable.

"Xander is... was... safety," she whispered. "He loves me but this..." She gestured vaguely at her stomach, "this changes everything."

He had warned her from the start. But the flicker of pain in her eyes still cut deeper than he'd expected.

He wasn't marriage material, he wasn't parent material. Still, deep down, the thought of losing her gnawed at him in ways he couldn't fully comprehend.

Her eyes were searching his with a mixture of sadness and longing. "And what about you? What do you really want?"

He looked away, unable to meet her gaze. "I want you to be happy. I want you to be safe. And if that means being with Xander, then that's what you should do... go back to him."

Katherine's hand reached out, brushing his cheek. "But what if I want *you*?"

His heart ached at her words. "You deserve more than I can give. You deserve stability, someone who can be there for you and the baby."

"It's hard to let go... hard to let *you* go."

He pulled her into a tight embrace. "I know, Kat. I know."

For a moment, they just held each other.

Katherine pulled back and whispered, "I need to go."

She dressed quietly, and he watched her go, feeling a sense of loss that he couldn't quite put into words. As the door closed behind her, he lay back on the bed, staring at the ceiling. The case, the murders, and the tangled web of his personal life all swirled in his mind.

He *had* to find the killer—not just for the victims, but to restore some order to his own chaos. But tonight, as the weight of exhaustion and heartbreak pressed down on him, all he could do was lie there and hope that, somehow, everything would eventually make sense.

But the clarity never came. The reality was that Katherine had blindsided him. She had never told him she had a boyfriend, and when she first revealed her pregnancy, she had claimed she didn't know who the father was.

He replayed the conversation in his mind, the shock and betrayal still fresh.

He had wanted to be angry, to lash out, but all he felt was a deep, hollow ache. The trauma of his childhood, the memory of his father's brutality, loomed over him like a dark cloud. He had sworn never to repeat his father's mistakes, never to bring a child into a world where he might cause them the same pain.

And yet, here he was, tangled in a web of love, duty, and fear.

The thought of becoming a father terrified him, haunted him. He couldn't risk turning into the monster his father had been. He couldn't bear the thought of hurting the people he loved.

Stefan closed his eyes, the image of Katherine's tear-streaked face imprinted on his mind. He had to let her go, giving her the safety he could never offer. But was it really the right thing—or just the easier way out?

* * *

Seb lay in the desolate alley, his body battered and aching from the beating he had just endured. Pain radiated through his limbs, mingling with the relentless tremors of withdrawal. His vision blurred, the world around him fading into a haze of shadows and flickering streetlights.

In the depths of his suffering, Seb began to hallucinate. The cold, grimy walls of the alley melted away, replaced by the familiar confines of a softly lit room from his childhood.

Suddenly, she was there. His mother. Her soft features, her long brown hair. Was it really her? Or just someone he had made up in his mind?

There were few pictures left of her. His father had made sure of that. He had hidden some of them in the drawer of his bedroom, until his father had found them and shredded them in a fit of rage.

She leaned over, her face a mixture of tenderness and sorrow. Her voice, soft and melodic, filled the room as she whispered sweet words to him. "Shh, my little one. Mommy's here. Everything's going to be alright." She caressed his cheek, her touch warm and comforting.

For a moment, the pain and desperation melted away, replaced by a fragile sense of peace. He looked up at her with wide, innocent eyes, reaching out.

But then, the scene shifted. The sweetness in her eyes turned to terror as a dark figure appeared behind her. Seb's heart raced as he watched, helpless.

A plastic bag was pulled over his mother's head, her hands clawing at it in a desperate struggle for air. The sweetness of her voice was replaced by muffled screams, her eyes wide with panic.

Seb's hands reached out, but he was powerless to stop what was happening. The room seemed to close in on him, the shadows growing darker and more oppressive. He watched, frozen in horror, as his mother disappeared into the darkness, leaving him alone once more.

The hallucination dissolved, and Seb was back in the alley, his body wracked with pain and his mind reeling from the vivid nightmare. Tears streamed down his face, mingling with the dirt and blood that clung to his skin.

He curled into himself, the agony of withdrawal and the ghosts of his past intertwining in a relentless torment. His breaths came in ragged gasps.

But there was no escape. Not in this alley, not in the drugs he craved, not in the fleeting memories of a mother who had never truly been there. Seb lay there, broken and lost, the darkness closing in around him as the hallucinations continued to torment his fragile mind.

※ ※ ※

Torre sat in the living room, flipping through the case file with a furrowed brow. The frustration was palpable in the set of his shoulders and the tense grip on the papers. They were no closer to catching the killer, and the weight of that failure gnawed at him.

"What's going on?"

He looked up as his father walked in, carrying the evening paper under his arm and glasses in hand, a nightly ritual. Ragnar seemed almost a relic in the digital age with his unwavering devotion to the physical newspaper, yet any hint of being outdated was instantly dismissed by his clear air of command. He was undeniably someone to be reckoned with.

Though in his mid-fifties, Ragnar possessed the athletic build and sharp looks of someone ten years younger, carrying a striking sex appeal that age had only enhanced. This formidable presence consistently left Torre feeling inadequate, almost diminished.

"What's going on?" Ragnar repeated as he placed the newspaper on the coffee table and settled into the armchair opposite Torre.

"Just going over some work, Dad. It's nothing," Torre replied.

Ragnar's eyes flickered with curiosity, a small smile playing at the corners of his mouth. "You seem quite troubled. Is it about the murders... the case you're working on?"

Torre sighed, rubbing his temples. "I can't discuss the details with you, Dad. You know that."

"Of course," Ragnar said. "But sometimes a fresh perspective can help. I might have some useful insights."

Torre hesitated, knowing how persistent his father could be. "It's just...frustrating. We have so many pieces, but nothing fits together."

"Frustration is the enemy of clarity. Sometimes, we need to step back and look at things from a different angle. Think about what the killer wants, what drives him."

Torre shook his head. "It's not that simple. There's too much at stake."

Ragnar leaned in. "Every mind has its breaking point, Torre. Find the weakness, and you'll find the man."

What is it they were missing?

Gustav Gyllenstierna and Marnix Castner.

"You have a theory," his father said. "What is it?"

"No, I don't... I..."

"Your gut feeling... what is it telling you?"

"Revenge. It's about revenge."

"Why?" his father asked.

"The women humiliated them... the husbands. The men feel disconnected, pushed out of their own home. Something similar happened to him."

"Or maybe he wants to teach the men a lesson," Ragnar said. "I don't know the details, but rumors go that he forced the men to watch while their families died, maybe they were even actively involved."

"How do you know all this?" Torre said and frowned.

"Dr. Gersson."

"He shouldn't have..."

"He didn't, but his entourage did."

Torre sighed and shook his head. "With what you've heard, how would your profile of the killer look like?"

Ragnar's gaze sharpened, his mind clearly already working through the possibilities. "Based on what we have so far, I'd say he's a man with deep-seated issues related to power and control. He likely experienced significant trauma or humiliation at the hands of a female figure in his life, which has translated into a hatred for women who he perceives as powerful or dominant. This hatred extends to the men who, in his mind, allowed themselves to be emasculated."

"So, he's trying to reclaim that power through these acts of violence."

"Likely," his father said and leaned back, a satisfied gleam in his eyes. "He forces the men to watch, to participate even, as a means of transferring his own feelings of helplessness and rage onto them. It's a twisted way of making them complicit in his pain. He's not just seeking revenge; he's trying to recreate his own trauma and force others to live through it."

Torre nodded slowly. "So, we need to look for someone with a history of familial abuse or neglect, someone who feels deeply wronged by women in positions of power."

"Yes," Ragnar agreed. "And he likely has a charismatic side, a way of manipulating those around him to achieve his goals. He might be hiding in plain sight, presenting himself as a victim or someone harmless."

"This is helpful... thanks," Torre said and closed the file. For the first time he noticed that his father looked tired. There were dark circles under Ragnar's eyes, and a weariness in his posture that Torre hadn't seen before.

"Are you okay, Dad?"

Ragnar waved a hand dismissively. "Just a bit worn out. Nothing to worry about."

"Mom was quiet at dinner. What happened? Something with Emil? Or Sam?"

"No, your brothers are fine," Ragnar said and looked down at his hands.

Torre noted the uncharacteristic hesitation. "It's more than just being tired, isn't it?"

Ragnar sighed, the confident façade slipping for a moment. "Your mother and I... we've been having some disagreements lately."

"Disagreements?" Torre echoed, though he had felt the strain between his parents for a while. The tension at home had been unmistakable.

It was a war fought in glances and cold silences.

"It's nothing for you to worry about," Ragnar said. "Marriages have their ups and downs."

"But it feels different this time," Torre pressed. "Like there's something you're not telling me."

Ragnar looked at his son. "Some things are private, Torre. Let us handle it."

"I don't want this to get out of hand," Torre said. "Not like the last time."

"It won't," Ragnar said.

"Dad... talk to me. What's wrong?"

Ragnar threw his head back and closed his eyes before letting out a sigh. "It's complicated. Your mother and I... we're going through a rough patch. It's nothing you need to worry about."

"But I do worry," Torre insisted. "I've seen the way you two look at each other. It's not just a rough patch. You don't talk."

Ragnar opened his eyes and met his son's gaze. "Your mother feels... neglected. She thinks I'm too absorbed in my work, that I'm not present enough for the family."

"And are you?" Torre asked.

Ragnar hesitated. "Maybe. Psychiatry isn't just a job; it's who I am. She doesn't see that I cannot just switch off. I take these things with me at home."

"Mom knows. She's a doctor herself."

"That's different. She gives lectures; she doesn't deal with the same level of personal trauma as I do. It's draining. I have to be there for my patients, to help them through their darkest times."

"I get that, Dad, but can't you also be there for her... for us?" Torre asked.

"Your mother doesn't understand the commitment it takes," Ragnar said. "I'm not just doing this for myself. I'm helping people, saving lives. She sees it as neglect, but it's dedication. Long days, endless nights—it's the price I pay to make a difference. She can sometimes be so... selfish."

He had never heard his dad talk about his mother like that.

"And...," Ragnar continued. "We did have a fight about Emil."

"What about him?"

"Your mother thinks I'm too hard on him," Ragnar said. "She thinks I expect too much, that I'm pushing him too far. But Emil needs structure and discipline. He needs to understand the world isn't going to hand him anything. The way he treated Delara is unacceptable. No sense of responsibility, no sense of decency. Your mother always had a soft spot for Emil. She cannot be objective when it comes to him."

Torre felt a pang of discomfort and disappointment at his father's words. "She's just worried about him, that's all."

Ragnar shook his head. "You don't see it, Torre. She coddles him, makes excuses for him. And it just makes him weaker. He needs to grow up."

"He needs guidance, not just discipline," Torre protested. "Maybe Mom has a point."

Ragnar's eyes flashed with irritation, but he said nothing.

"Maybe you should try to see it from her perspective," Torre said. "She's not against you; she just wants what's best for Emil."

Ragnar sighed and a rare moment of vulnerability crossed his features. "I just want him to be better than me. I want all of you to be better than me."

Torre nodded, the weight of his father's words sinking in. "I know, Dad."

"How's Delara? She must be devastated."

"She's okay."

"Maybe we should invite her and..."

Torre frowned. "Why?"

Ragnar's expression hardened. "She's part of our family too, Torre. She shouldn't be alone right now."

Torre shook his head, frustration creeping into his voice. "I appreciate that, Dad, but... that's weird. Inviting the ex-girlfriend of your son. Besides, she needs time to process everything that's happened. Emil wasn't exactly subtle."

Ragnar leaned back in his chair and studied his son for a moment. "You like her."

Torre almost jumped up. "Uh... no... what... how..."

Ragnar's lips curled into a knowing smile. "It's obvious. The way you talk about her, the concern in your voice. It's more than just feeling responsible for her because of Emil."

Torre felt a flush rise to his cheeks. "She's Emil's ex and we're colleagues. It would be... inappropriate."

"Inappropriate?" Ragnar echoed. "Sometimes, you need to go after the things you want. Life won't wait for you to decide when it's convenient."

"Dad, this isn't the time for this conversation."

Ragnar's gaze sharpened and he gave him a small smile. "Up to you."

Torre sighed. "I just don't want to make things more complicated than they already are."

Ragnar took the newspaper from the table, leaned backward, and started reading.

Torre studied his father in silence, the weight of his words settling deep inside him like a stone. As always, Ragnar had struck a nerve, leaving Torre tangled in the mess of his own emotions. If he was honest with himself, Delara had lived in his thoughts since the moment he first saw her—the day Emil brought her home.

Everything about her captivated him. Her kindness. That sharp, bright smile. The effortless way she commanded respect without demanding it. Even her stubbornness, which should have frustrated him, only drew him in deeper.

But it was her laugh that had ruined him. The way it had spilled out, warm and unguarded, at one of Emil's stupid jokes. That sound had burrowed under Torre's skin, a quiet revelation: *She was different. She was everything.*

And yet, she had been Emil's. So Torre had done what was right— kept his distance, buried the longing beneath his work, pretended it didn't gnaw at him in the quiet hours. But now, with everything unraveling, those old feelings surged back, relentless and inconvenient.

Colleagues. That's all they could ever be.

He shut his eyes, forcing the thoughts away. The case demanded focus; there was no space for distractions. But when he reopened the file, Delara's face flickered behind his eyelids, haunting him.

A ghost of what he wanted.

A reminder of what he couldn't have.

CHAPTER FOURTEEN

DELARA THREW BACK HER LONG BLACK HAIR and took the cup of tea Njord Dahlman handed her. She looked around. The house wasn't very special. Just a modest, two-story suburban home with plain white walls and minimalistic decor. The furniture was simple, functional, without any trace of personality or warmth.

But on the cupboard there were a bunch of family photos. Njord and a woman, likely his wife. She knew his wife had died five years ago. Then many pictures of children, young and old.

Delara quickly glanced through the window. Outside, it had started to snow again, the flakes falling gently and blanketing the ground in another pristine layer of white. She took a deep breath, letting the serene scene outside calm her nerves. It was rare to see the snow linger so long—these days, winters were more slush than silence, more gray than glittering. But today, the city held its breath under the frost, as if time had slipped backward.

Njord followed her gaze and smiled softly. "Beautiful, isn't it?

There's something peaceful about snowfall, a certain quiet that comes with it."

"Yes, it is," Delara agreed, turning back to him. "It's almost like a fresh start, everything covered in white."

Njord nodded. "A fresh start. We could all use one of those from time to time."

Delara took a sip of her tea, savoring the warmth. "Franck Juhlin mentioned you were one of the best detectives he's ever worked with. Do you miss it?"

Njord's eyes flickered with a mixture of emotions. "Sometimes. The thrill of solving a case, the satisfaction of bringing justice... it's hard to let go of that. But everything has its time."

"You must have some incredible stories," Delara prompted gently.

A small smile tugged at Njord's lips. "Oh, I do. Some incredible, some heartbreaking, some so devastating that it left its mark on all of us."

"The Svensson case," she said.

"Yeah," he said with a sigh, taking a sip of his tea. "I blamed myself... I still do. I should have seen it. How many times did Annika Svensson stand in the police station? How many desperate calls did we receive? She was afraid of him—afraid he would do something terrible. And he finally did."

"There's no doubt Harald Svensson killed his children?"

"None. He was at the scene when we arrived. He confessed almost immediately and has never changed his story."

"And the mother?"

"According to Harald, he waited for her that night—rifle in hand, children at his feet. Just sitting there on the couch. Calm. Like it was any other evening." Njord's voice dropped. "But when she walked in... he didn't move. Didn't even look at her. She was the one who called us. Frantic. In a panic. And when we got there?"

A pause.

"She wasn't screaming anymore. Wasn't crying. Just... empty. Staring at those little bodies like she'd already left hers behind. Took us hours to get a word out of her. After that?" He exhaled sharply. "Rotating between hospitals and halfway houses. She never really came back."

Delara felt a chill run down her spine. The image Njord painted was harrowing, and she could almost see it unfolding in her mind.

"So, she called the police?"

"Yes, but meanwhile also a neighbor did. He heard the gunshots." Njord's eyes darkened further as he recounted the events.

"And Harald? What happened to him?"

Njord's eyes darkened. "He was convicted and sent to prison. His lawyer argued insanity but the court didn't agree. He got life. But I always felt we missed something. I must say... that case regularly goes through my mind in the most unexpected moments. In my entire career, which spans more than forty years, I've never seen anything like it."

"It must have been devastating," Delara said.

"It was. Not just for the family, but for everyone involved—the officers, the investigators, the community. My partner at the time, Adam Wallin, resigned not long after. He never really recovered from what he saw that night. It broke him."

"What is he doing now?"

Njord sighed and took another sip of his tea. "He was a lot younger than I was... ten, fifteen years. We have no contact anymore. I think he went into private security... I think Nordisk Säkerhet. Last I heard, he was doing well, but that was a long time ago."

Delara took a sip of the tea. "Two of the children survived."

Njord nodded, looked at his hands for a moment and then said, "Yes. We thought they were all dead until the little boy, Stefan, opened his eyes." The memory was difficult. "I... have never seen so much confusion and fear in a child's eyes. It's a miracle he and his sister—I think it was Elena or something—survived. She was somewhat less lucky... paralyzed from the waist down. She will never walk again. Both were downstairs when it happened. According to what Elena told the child psychologist Stefan had woken up in the night, complaining of a dry throat. She took him downstairs to the kitchen. They heard the shots, but by the time she realized something was wrong, Harald had already found them. Elena tried to protect her brother. He shot her in the back. The bullet went right through her and hit Stefan. She took the full hit."

"Jesus...," Delara whispered, horrified by the vivid account.

"It was one of the worst scenes I've ever encountered. The resilience those children showed was extraordinary, but the scars—both physical and emotional—are something they'll carry for the rest of their lives."

Delara took a deep breath, trying to steady herself. "What happened to them after? Were they able to find some semblance of normalcy?"

But she knew all too well what had happened to them.

"They were taken in by their paternal grandparents," Njord said. "They took their grandmother's maiden name —the name Svensson was too loaded—and moved to a different city to start fresh. I kept in touch for a while, but eventually, I had to let go. I don't know what happened to the girl though... she was..."

"What?"

"I always wondered why she never officially identified her father as the shooter. I believe she was the only one who actually saw him."

"She didn't? Did you ever talk to her about it?"

Njord shook his head. "No, I didn't. By the time she was able to speak about it, she was already in the care of her grandparents, and they were very protective of her. They didn't want her to relive the trauma any more than necessary."

Delara frowned. "But if she saw him, wouldn't that be crucial evidence?"

"You would think so," Njord replied, a shadow crossing his face. "But trauma can do strange things to the mind. Maybe she couldn't bear to face the truth, or perhaps she blocked it out to protect herself. It's hard to say."

Delara sipped her tea, the warmth doing little to chase away the chill of the conversation. "It's heartbreaking to think she had to carry that burden alone."

"Yes," Njord agreed. "Sometimes the mind creates its own defense mechanisms to cope with such horrors. We may never fully understand why she made the choices she did, but we can only hope she found some peace in the end."

"Inspector Dahlman..."

"Njord, please. I haven't been inspector for a while now."

"Okay, Njord. I wonder... were there no other leads? What about other witnesses?"

Njord sighed and then looked her straight in the eye. "What is this about? Why are you here?"

"Benjamin Hartmann. Was that name ever mentioned?"

"Hartmann?"

Her eyes widened in surprise as she studied him. For a fleeting moment, she was certain he recognized the name—a flicker of acknowledgment passed across his features. But just as quickly, he masked it, his expression smoothing into practiced composure, leaving her to wonder if she had imagined it altogether.

"Do you know him?" she asked.

"No... no, I can't say I do."

"Are you sure? He's a painter, famous for his rather disturbing works." She pulled a paper from her purse and handed it to him.

The Children.

Njord took the paper, his brow furrowing as he studied the painting. It depicted a haunting scene of children with hollow eyes, their faces twisted in fear and despair, lying on the floor, hand in hand. The style was unmistakably dark, the emotions raw and unsettling.

"This is... disturbing," Njord said. "It's like..."

"The Svenssons... Benjamin Hartmann has been exhibiting a series of paintings that are eerily similar to several crime scenes. This one, titled 'The Children,' bears a striking resemblance to the Svensson case. The details are too close to be a coincidence."

Njord's eyes widened as he looked back at the painting. "You think this Hartmann knew something about the Svensson case?"

"I don't know," Delara admitted. "But we've been researching his work, and this isn't the only case. Someone is using his paintings as a blueprint for murder. The only difference is that 'The Children' was painted a year after the shooting, while the other crimes were done years after the paintings."

Njord leaned back in his chair, the gears in his mind visibly turning. "This is... intriguing. The Children. How does Hartmann know these details? Some of it was leaked in the press but not all of it, like the exact placement of the bodies, the chair on the floor, the pieces of glass next to the little boy on the very end. These were things only those on the scene would know."

"That's what makes this so concerning," Delara said. "We're dealing with someone who has either extraordinary access to confidential information or is somehow connected to the crimes in a way we don't yet understand."

"How does Hartmann explain it?'

"He says he got a letter about the Svensson case," Delara said.

"Really? Did you see that letter?"

"No. It's been more than twenty years. He claims he destroyed it."

Njord snorted softly. "That's convenient."

"But if it's true... someone on the inside knows a lot more and is involved in these crimes. Maybe Harald didn't kill his children."

"He confessed. Why would he do that if..." Njord's voice trailed off as he looked at the picture again, his brow furrowed in thought.

"What is it?" Delara prompted.

Njord shook his head slowly. "For a moment, I wondered if maybe we missed something crucial. Harald's confession seemed straightforward at the time, but what if there were external pressures or manipulations we didn't see? I remember there were witnesses and I guess you can find their statements in the file. I'm sure you have access to it, but..."

"What is bothering you?"

Njord sighed, running a hand through his thinning hair. "Nothing, but if he didn't do it and he confessed, he's protecting someone."

"Who? Hartmann? Harald's wife?"

"Annika? No, she loved those children. A mother would never do that." But he, just like Delara, knew all too well that there were plenty of examples where women, even mothers, had committed unimaginable acts of violence. "Though... there were rumors of an affair and like I said the number of household disturbances were numerous. There was always something going on in that house. It would have blown up at a certain moment. It was just a matter of time."

"What about the affair?"

"They were just rumors. Harald and Annika were in marriage counseling. I remember their counselor mentioned to the police that Harald was a very jealous man. He often suspected Annika of infidelity, but there was never any concrete proof."

Delara frowned. "Jealousy can be a powerful motivator. But was that enough to push Harald to such an extreme violence?"

Njord sighed. "It's hard to say. Maybe it was the culmination of years of distrust and resentment. We really didn't explore this any further. The focus was on the immediate evidence and Harald's confession."

"I know. Thank you anyway." Delara gave a small, appreciative smile.

Njord returned her smile. "I hope you find the answers you're looking for. Just be careful, Delara. The past has a way of reaching out to the present in unexpected ways."

"I will," Delara promised.

As she walked to the door, Njord's voice stopped her one last time. "If you need any more information, don't hesitate to reach out. I'll do what I can to help."

"Thank you, Njord. I appreciate it."

With that, Delara stepped out into the falling snow, the cold biting at her cheeks. The quiet of the snowfall seemed almost like a promise, a reminder that sometimes, beneath the surface, answers waited to be found.

But inside, Njord felt restless. There was something Delara had said which had triggered this feeling of foreboding. There was something he wasn't seeing, or he didn't want to see. Could it be?

And Hartmann.

After all those years.

Of course, he knew him.

How could he forget.

Maybe he should have told her.

He stared at the picture again, the unsettling details echoing through his mind. The children's eyes, their expressions—it was too lifelike, too accurate.

Njord's mind raced back to the days of the Svensson case, to the interviews, the statements, the hours of sifting through evidence. A memory surfaced: a piece of evidence dismissed too quickly, a name in a report that hadn't seemed important at the time. Could Benjamin Hartmann have been connected to someone within the investigation? Was there a mole, someone who had fed him details?

As much as he wanted Hartmann to be involved, there was no evidence that he had been connected to the case.

Njord grabbed his phone, his fingers trembling as he dialed the number. It was late, but this couldn't wait.

"Hello?" The voice on the other end was groggy, filled with the confusion of being woken up.

"It's Njord. I need to ask you something about the Svensson case."

There was a pause, then a sigh. "Njord? What's this about? It's been over twenty years. What's going on? I have a nightshift... I need my sleep."

"Do you remember any connections to an artist named Benjamin Hartmann?"

"Benjamin Hartmann? Why are you asking about him?"

"I've come across something disturbing. There might be a connection to new cases. A young inspector brought me information about Hartmann's paintings. They match crime scenes, including the Svensson case. He claims to have received a letter with details only we would know."

"Njord, that's... that's serious. But I don't recall any connection to Hartmann. We didn't focus much on anyone outside the immediate family and neighbors. And is this the Hartmann I think it is?"

"Yeah... it is," Njord said. "There's something here. Something we missed. I need to go back through the files."

"You are retired. Let it go. They have people looking at this. Don't get mixed up in this."

"But..."

"Njord, it was great hearing your voice, but I need to get some sleep. Okay?'

Njord hung up, feeling a mixture of dread and determination. He looked out the window, watching the snow continue to fall.

Beneath the surface, the past was stirring.

CHAPTER FIFTEEN

THE POLICE OFFICER WHO GREETED Stefan and Torre at the hospital looked like he'd lost a bet. Tall and lanky, he slouched beneath the weight of his own apathy. His uniform was wrinkled and ill-fitting, like it had been dug out of a laundry pile minutes before his shift. The tie dangled crooked and loose, the knot hovering halfway down his chest. A sheen of gel barely held back wisps of thinning hair, failing to conceal the bald patch that caught the overhead lights like a beacon.

His face was carved with scorn—deep lines etched into a permanent scowl—and his eyes were dull, lifeless, as if the job had drained the last of his curiosity years ago.

He barely acknowledged them, flipping through the clipboard in his hands with a look of mild irritation. When he did glance up, the expression was a cocktail of boredom and disdain.

"He's a mess," he muttered.

Stefan's jaw tightened. "Who found him?"

The officer shrugged. A lazy lift of the shoulders. "Some bystander."

The words came out clipped, careless, like even repeating them was beneath him.

He shifted his weight from one foot to the other, shoes squeaking against the linoleum in a quiet, impatient rhythm. His eyes drifted to his watch. Again. Then a sigh—loud, pointed, theatrical.

To him, this wasn't a victim. Just another box to tick.

But it was his voice when he mentioned Seb that cut deepest—flat, but tinged with contempt, as if Seb had brought this on himself. Not anger. Just a quiet, poisonous kind of judgment.

Stefan felt his teeth grind. Torre's fists clenched at his sides.

The officer didn't notice. Or didn't care.

"Save your sympathy," he said. "These types always end up back on the street—or in the morgue."

Stefan and Torre exchanged a glance. There was no point pressing the officer further. Whatever spark had once made him a good cop had long since burned out, leaving behind only habit and paperwork. He wasn't here to help. Just to endure his shift.

Without another word, they turned and headed down the corridor toward Seb's room.

Inside the room, Seb Hartmann looked every bit as wrecked as the officer had warned.

He lay propped up in the hospital bed, his face a mess of bruises and swelling. A thick bandage cut across the bridge of his nose, and dried blood crusted near his hairline. Each breath seemed to cost him, shallow and tight, his chest barely rising under the thin hospital blanket.

It was more than an assault. It looked personal.

Stefan stepped forward. "Sebastian Hartmann?"

Seb's eyes flickered open, and he groaned. "Who are you?"

"I'm Inspector Stefan Eklund, and this is Dr. Torre Nylander. We need to ask you some questions."

Seb tried to sit up but winced in pain. "About my attack?"

"Amongst others," Stefan replied. "What were you doing there?"

"What do you think?"

"We're not here to make assumptions," Torre said calmly, stepping closer. "We need your help to understand what happened."

Seb's eyes darted between the two men, assessing them. "I was... I was looking for a fix. I know it sounds bad, but that's the truth. I went to meet my dealer, but he never showed up. Next thing I know, I'm being jumped."

"Do you know who attacked you?" Stefan asked.

Seb shook his head. "It was dark, and they came out of nowhere. It happened so fast... I didn't see their faces."

"Did they say anything?" Torre probed. "Anything that might give us a clue about who they were or why they attacked you?"

Seb closed his eyes, trying to remember. "One of them... one of them mentioned something about 'paying the price.' I don't know what they meant."

Stefan exchanged a look with Torre, then leaned in closer to Seb. "We would like to talk to you about your father."

"My father? Yeah... that would be a great suspect."

Stefan frowned. "What do you mean?"

"You must know by now that my father hates me and likes to torture me."

"And why is that?"

"Because he blames me for my mother's leaving."

Stefan's frown deepened as he glanced at Torre, then back at Seb. "Your father blames you for your mother leaving? That's quite a burden to place on a child."

Seb laughed, his eyes hardening. "Yeah, well, my dad has a unique way of handling things. When my mom left, he needed someone to blame. I was the easiest target. It's been that way ever since."

"What do you mean by torture?" Torre asked.

Seb's expression grew darker. "He makes sure I never forget what he thinks of me. Verbal abuse, sometimes physical. And when I started using... it gave him even more ammunition. I think he enjoys watching me suffer."

Stefan leaned in. "Seb, do you think your father had anything to do with the attack on you?"

Seb hesitated, then shook his head. "I don't know. It wouldn't surprise me, but he's more about psychological torture. Hiring someone to jump me... that seems too direct for him. He prefers to make me self-destruct."

Torre took a step closer. "Seb, we're trying to piece together a larger puzzle here. We believe your father might be connected to some of the things we're investigating, indirectly or otherwise. Any detail, no matter how small, could help."

"What things?"

Stefan hesitated. "We can't give you the details."

Seb sighed, his eyes fluttering shut as if the weight of the moment was too much to hold. His skin had taken on a sickly pallor, more gray than pale, and a fine sheen of sweat clung to his brow despite the sterile chill of the hospital room. His hands trembled beneath the blanket, fingers twitching in erratic bursts like shorted wires. Every so often, a sudden jolt rippled through his body—a violent, involuntary shudder that made the bed creak faintly beneath him.

Stefan had seen withdrawal before. But this? This was different. Seb didn't just look sick. He looked like he was unraveling from the inside out.

"My father's been lying to me all my life," Seb muttered. "All my life..."

Stefan exchanged a glance with Torre.

"He's done so much damage," Seb continued. "Not just to me, but to everyone around him. You don't know what he's capable of."

Stefan leaned forward. "What did he do?"

Seb's gaze snapped to him, his eyes bloodshot and wild. For a moment, he looked like he might lash out, but then he slumped back against the pillows, his energy draining away as quickly as it had surged. "Forget it... he'll probably twist it in such a way that makes me look like the bad guy." His voice was bitter, tinged with a weariness that went beyond physical exhaustion. "He's always been good at that. Making me doubt my own reality, making everyone else believe his lies."

Stefan's expression hardened. "You seem eager to put all the blame for your problems on your father."

Seb's hands clenched into fists, the tremors momentarily stilled by the force of his anger. "He punishes me, he humiliates me, he... tortures me... how can I not?" His voice cracked, and for a moment, he looked like the child Stefan imagined he once was—scared, helpless, and desperate. "Every time I try to get clean, he finds a way to drag me back down. He manipulates everyone around him to believe he's this brilliant artist, but he's a monster."

Torre stepped closer, his voice softer but no less urgent. "Seb, we believe you..."

Stefan cut in abruptly, his tone almost businesslike. "Tell me about Castner."

Torre shot him a disapproving look, but Stefan ignored it. Seb blinked, visibly thrown by the sudden shift in questioning. "Castner? Who is that?"

"Marnix Castner. You had an altercation with him in the office of Dr. Elsa Larsson."

Seb's brow furrowed. "I... I can't remember," he stammered, his voice faltering for a moment. His hands began to shake again, and he wrapped his arms around himself as if trying to hold his body together.

"A month later, Mr. Castner and his entire family were murdered."

Seb's eyes widened, and for a moment, he looked genuinely horrified. "Wait... what... you think I did this?"

Torre stepped forward, placing a hand on Seb's arm. "Seb, no one is accusing you of that. We're just trying to understand what happened. Can you try to remember anything about that day in Dr. Larsson's office? I think... you do remember."

Seb's breathing quickened, his chest rising and falling rapidly. "I... I was in a bad place. My mind was all over the place. I just needed to talk to Elsa, but Castner wouldn't let me... he threatened me. I lashed out, but I didn't... I didn't kill anyone."

Torre stepped back. "Elsa? Why do you call her Elsa?"

Seb stared at him. For a moment, it seemed like he hadn't even heard the question. "Uh... she's my father's friend."

"Since when is she your father's... friend?"

"Since always... she was his shrink... since my mom left, at least that's what he told me."

Torre's gaze sharpened. "You don't believe him."

Seb shook his head, his movements jerky and uncoordinated. "Not really... she stayed with us for a while."

"She did? When? Why?"

"When I was a child. I have faint memories about her. She never liked me, even when I was her patient. She always took dad's side."

Stefan interjected. "So, your dad and Dr. Larsson had a romantic relationship?"

Seb let out a bitter laugh. "I wouldn't call it romantic. He fucks her. It was... I don't know what it was. They were close, but it always felt... transactional. Like she was getting something out of it, but it wasn't love. More like... control. I always felt like she was more involved in our lives than a normal therapist would be. She had this... hold over him. And over me, too."

His hands were trembling violently now, the withdrawal symptoms worsening by the minute. Cold sweat dripped down his temples, and his breathing was shallow and uneven. He looked like he was on the verge of collapse, his body betraying him in every possible way.

"I need help," he whispered. "I can't... I can't do this..."

Torre's tone was gentle but firm. "Seb, we understand this is hard. We're here to help you, but we need you to stay with us. Can you do that?"

Seb nodded, but his eyes were glassy, unfocused. The tears that welled up in them were as much from frustration as from pain. "I'll try... but please... I need something... anything..."

Stefan's voice cut through the room like a knife. "Elsa Larsson."

Seb flinched, his body jerking as if he'd been struck. "I don't know anything else about her," he yelled. The outburst drew a glance from several passing doctors, but no one stopped. "Look, talk to my father. He can probably tell you why and when and how. I had no choice."

"No choice about what?"

"Nothing...," Seb stammered, burying his face in his hands. His entire body shook with the effort to keep himself together.

Stefan pressed on. "Marnix Castner and Gustav Gyllenstierna, maybe?"

Seb looked up, his eyes wide and confused. "Who is Gyllenstierna?"

"Where were you last Tuesday, December 13, and Monday, December 5?"

Seb let out a strangled laugh, his voice rising in desperation. "Jesus... how would I know? Do you really think I keep track of dates? I was probably just trying to survive, find a fix... I don't know." His voice broke, and he looked at them with a mixture of anger and despair. "Why are you asking me all these questions? I've already told you: I didn't kill anyone!"

Stefan's expression didn't change. "Well, we found a mask worn by the killer in Gyllenstierna's house."

Seb froze, his breath catching in his throat. "And?"

"Gyllenstierna's DNA was found on it..."

"So, he's the killer," Seb said.

"And yours," Stefan added, his tone flat. "It was tiny, ever so small.

They almost overlooked it, but I guess you didn't clean it well enough."

Seb's face went pale, his eyes widening in horror. "What?! That can't be. What sort of mask is this? I don't understand. I don't know these people. How... I... I don't know what you're talking about. A mask? Are you saying I was wearing a mask?"

Stefan nodded, his gaze unwavering. "Yes. We found traces of your DNA on the inside of a mask left at one of the crime scenes. Lucky for us—unlucky for you—your DNA was in the system. You need to start being honest with us, Seb. This is serious."

Seb's eyes darted around the room, panic etched into every line of his face. "I swear, I don't remember anything about a mask." He closed his eyes. "No... it can't be me. I can't be that monster. No!"

Stefan's voice was cold and final. "Sebastian Hartmann, we are putting you under arrest for the murder of Marnix Castner, Vanja Castner..."

The rest of the words faded into a blur as Seb's world collapsed around him. His body went limp, his consciousness slipping away under the weight of his despair.

CHAPTER SIXTEEN

"WHAT WERE YOU THINKING?"

Torre could tell Stefan wasn't too happy. Although he didn't know him that well yet—only a few weeks, if he had to be honest—he had always thought of Stefan Eklund as someone who maintained a calm, almost unshakable demeanor. Stefan's laid-back attitude was something Torre had noticed from the start; it was as if nothing could disturb his peace of mind. It wasn't indifference, though—more like a protective mechanism, a way to keep his sanity.

Delara was different. Sharp and always ready for the kill.

"What's the problem?" Delara said, hardly looking up from the file in front of her.

"You harassed my sister," Stefan said. "Why?"

"Harassed? Really? I asked her a question."

"You're meddling in my private life. This has nothing to do with the case."

"It has everything to do with the case," Delara let out.

The Children. Torre had noticed it before. The subtle change in Stefan's demeanor. It was fleeting, almost imperceptible, but there, nonetheless.

And when he had confronted Stefan about it, he had waved it off.

Stefan's usually composed demeanor was slipping, revealing an edge that Torre hadn't seen before. Delara, on the other hand, seemed unfazed, her sharp eyes still focused on the file in front of her.

"The Children," Delara said, "that's what this is about, Stefan. Your family drama, this case—they're connected."

"Family drama?" Torre stammered. "What is she talking about?"

But both ignored him.

Stefan's jaw tightened. "You don't get to dig up my family's graves for your fucking hunch. My... situation has nothing to do with this investigation."

Delara finally looked up, her gaze piercing. "Everything is connected. The painting, your family, Seb—there's a thread here, and I'm not going to ignore it just because it makes you uncomfortable."

Stefan took a deep breath, forcing himself to regain control. "This isn't just about the case anymore. You need to back off. This macabre interest of yours..."

But Delara didn't flinch. "I'm not backing off until we get to the truth. And if that means stepping into uncomfortable territory, then so be it. Have you ever considered that your father might not have killed your sisters and brother? That he might be innocent."

"Don't go there," Stefan yelled.

Torre stood there, caught in the middle of the escalating tension between Stefan and Delara, his confusion quickly turning into frustration. He had always prided himself on being level-headed, able to mediate between different perspectives, but right now, he felt like an outsider in a conversation that seemed to run much deeper than just professional disagreements.

"Wait, hold on," Torre interrupted, his voice rising just enough to make them both pause and look at him. "What exactly is going on here? You're throwing cases and names around, digging into each other's personal lives—Stefan's father? What does any of this have to do with the case?"

Neither of them answered right away. Delara crossed her arms, while Stefan's expression was a mix of anger and something Torre couldn't quite pin down—fear, maybe? The kind of fear that comes when old wounds are torn open.

"This isn't just about the case, is it?" Torre continued, his irritation growing. "I've been working on this investigation with you two for weeks, and now I find out there's all this... this history? How am I supposed to do my job when I'm being kept in the dark?"

Stefan looked away, his jaw clenched tight, as if holding back words he didn't trust himself to speak.

Delara's eyes narrowed, sharp and calculating, flicking between him and Torre like a predator sizing up prey. The air grew dense, electric with the kind of tension that signals a storm—secrets wound tight, threatening to unravel.

Torre could feel it in his bones, taste it on his tongue—metallic, sharp, like blood. He wasn't sure he wanted to hear what was coming. But they were past the point of comfort. If they were going to move forward, the truth had to be dragged into the light—raw, ugly, and unflinching.

Delara broke the silence first, her voice firm but laced with a weariness that betrayed her usual composure. "You're right, Torre." She paused, her eyes locking onto Stefan, who still refused to meet her gaze. "You care to tell him, Stefan? Or should I?"

Torre stared at her, then at Stefan, who was now clenching his fists.

"Fine," Delara said when no reaction came from Stefan's side. "Torre, I advise you to look up the Svensson case, December 2000. "

"Svensson," Torre said. "Yes, I know the case."

The Children.

Of course.

How had he not seen it before?

Delara frowned. "How? That is so before your time."

"I... just know," Torre stammered and then turned to Stefan, but Stefan remained silent, his fists still clenched, his eyes fixed on a point somewhere far away.

"The Svensson case..." Torre started, trying to piece things together. "That was... your family, wasn't it? Your siblings? And you survived. You and your sister."

Stefan's jaw tightened, but he still didn't say anything.

"Dead children on the floor, holding hands... Hartmann's painting was a frightening depiction of the crime scene," Delara added. "Whomever sent that letter to Hartmann knew the details."

"If there was a letter," Torre said. "We've never seen it."

"I don't think Benjamin Hartmann did it."

"Of course not," Stefan let out. "We arrested Seb Hartmann."

Delara frowned. "Seb Hartmann? That makes no sense, Stefan. The person who killed Gustav Gyllenstierna's family and the Castners is meticulous, structured, well-organized, not a drug-addled mess like Seb Hartmann. Seb couldn't have pulled off something like this, not with his state of mind and his dependency. Whoever did this has a level of control and planning that Seb just doesn't possess. And you..." Now she pointed directly at Torre. As if he was to blame for the entire thing. "... you should have known. Why didn't you stop Stefan?"

"I tried but...," Torre stammered.

Stefan sighed and frowned. "Fact is we found Seb's DNA in both houses, on the mask, on the knife. And he gave no satisfactory explanation."

"He's an addict," Delara said. "What is the motive?"

"His father. Revenge for a lifetime of torment," Stefan said. His voice was cold and distant. "Maybe Seb snapped. Maybe the drugs made him finally act on all that hatred he's been bottling up."

Delara shook her head. "Revenge? Maybe. But revenge on the Castners and Gyllenstiernas? What did they have to do with his father? And what about 'The Children?' He can't have done it. He was... three or so."

"God, Delara. There is no link. Get over it."

"I think there is. Maybe not in the way we think, but..." She sighed and looked at the hands in her lap.

"Benjamin Hartmann is at the heart of all this," Torre said suddenly. "It's clear. The killer wanted us to make the link with the paintings. He set up everything. The killer wants revenge."

Delara looked him straight in the eye. "What is the profile?"

Torre tried to gather his thoughts. "The profile suggests someone highly intelligent, organized, and meticulous. This person is deeply methodical, planning each move with precision. The crimes are symbolic, almost ritualistic, which indicates a deep personal connection to the victims or the events surrounding them. The killer is likely someone who feels wronged, possibly by Benjamin Hartmann, and is seeking revenge by recreating or alluding to his paintings."

Delara nodded. "But that doesn't fit Seb. He's erratic, disorganized. There's no way he could pull off something this calculated, this precise."

"Exactly," Torre agreed. "Whoever did this is the complete opposite. But if we consider Benjamin Hartmann as the central figure, it changes the entire dynamic. The killer could be someone connected to him, someone who knows his work intimately and wants to expose or punish him for something. And then Seb still would fit. He hates his dad, blames him for pushing away his mother, blames him for..."

Bringing Elsa in their lives. Elsa.

Why didn't he see it before.

She played an important role.

"And?" Delara looked at him.

"Uh... nothing. Just saying that... it's unlikely and it's speculating, but Seb could be playing a role. The role of an addict."

Delara raised an eyebrow. "You're saying Seb could be faking it? That his addiction is an act?"

Torre shook his head. "Not exactly. I'm not saying he's faking the addiction itself, but maybe... using it as a cover. It's possible he's more aware than we think, playing into the perception that he's too disorganized and unstable to be the killer. It's a long shot, but if someone is manipulating him, or if he's somehow involved without fully realizing it, it could explain why his DNA was found at the scenes. And... I want to look into Dr. Larsson. She knows more than she's telling us."

Stefan threw himself in the chair opposite Delara. "Elsa was close to Benjamin, right? She's been in their lives for years, influencing both father and son. If there's anyone who could manipulate Seb—or even Benjamin—it might be her."

"But why?" Torre asked.

"That's for us to find out."

"I don't buy it. We can't dismiss the link to 'The Children'," Delara insisted. "Maybe it's not about Seb or Elsa, but about something deeper, something from Benjamin's past that's resurfacing. Whoever this killer is, they're playing a game, and we're missing the key pieces."

"We need to look at Benjamin Hartmann's life, his connections, his past," Torre said. "There's something there we're not seeing. The killer is driven by more than just a desire to kill. This is about sending a message, about making Benjamin face something he's been running from."

Stefan looked at Torre and Delara. "And you think this message is tied to what happened to my family?"

Delara met his gaze. "I do. How? I don't know."

"Maybe you need to talk to your father," Torre said.

"Never."

"The word came out like a gunshot, sharp and final. Stefan's face hardened as he stared at Torre, a storm brewing behind his usually calm demeanor. "That man is dead to me. There's nothing he can say that will change what happened, nothing he can offer that I want to hear."

Torre exchanged a glance with Delara.

"Stefan," Delara began. "We're not asking you to forgive him. We're asking you to consider the possibility that whatever is happening now might be connected to what happened back then. If there's even a chance that your father knows something, anything that could help us..."

Stefan turned away, his hands gripping the edge of the table so tightly his knuckles whitened. "You don't understand. You didn't live through it, Delara. You didn't see what I saw, felt what I felt."

"No, we didn't," Torre said quietly. "But we're here now, and we're trying to help you make sense of it. You don't have to like your father, Stefan. We just need to know what he knows."

For a moment, the room was silent. Stefan closed his eyes, taking a deep breath.

Finally, he spoke, his voice strained but steady. "I'll think about it. But I'm not making any promises."

"That's all we ask," Delara said. "We'll keep digging on our end. Elsa Larsson and Benjamin Hartmann."

Elsa Larsson and Benjamin Hartmann.

What if...

The sound of a cell phone interrupted the heavy silence, its shrill ring cutting through the tension like a knife. Delara glanced down at the screen, her brow furrowing as she saw the caller ID. She hesitated, her thumb hovering over the decline button.

Torre, noticing the shift in her demeanor, raised an eyebrow. "Everything okay?"

Delara pressed her lips together, then shook her head. "It's just someone I don't want to talk to right now. He's been calling me all day."

Torre's curiosity was piqued, but he kept his voice neutral. "Someone important?"

She didn't answer right away, her eyes fixed on the phone as it continued to ring. Finally, she let out a small sigh and silenced the call. "It's... complicated. I'll deal with it later."

Torre nodded, but a thought nagged at the back of his mind. Could it be Emil? He knew Delara had ended things with his brother weeks ago, but persistent calls weren't Emil's style—he was usually the type to move on to the next girl before the last one had even left his bed.

Delara tucked her phone back into her pocket and straightened up. "Elsa Larsson and Benjamin Hartmann," she repeated, bringing the focus back to the investigation. "Let's figure out what they're hiding."

CHAPTER SEVENTEEN

THE SNOW CRUNCHED softly beneath Njord Dahlman's boots as he walked the forest path with Loki, his loyal Labrador, trotting beside him. The world lay hushed beneath a pristine white blanket, pine branches bowing under the weight of fresh snow, their frosted needles glittering in the pale light. This was why he'd chosen to leave Stockholm—this crisp, clean air that filled his lungs like redemption, this silence broken only by the rhythmic panting of his dog and the occasional creak of burdened trees. Up here in the north, he could almost believe the past stayed buried.

At the hill's crest, he paused, gloved hands resting on his hips as he surveyed the valley below. Quaint houses with snow—capped roofs dotted the landscape, smoke curling from their chimneys in lazy spirals. Children's laughter carried on the wind, the sound so innocent it made his chest ache. For a moment, peace settled over him—the kind of deep calm he'd spent a lifetime chasing in the city but only found here, where the horizon stretched uninterrupted, and the air didn't smell of exhaust and regret.

Loki's sudden growl shattered the silence. The dog stood rigid, ears pricked forward, staring intently at the shadowed tree line to their left. Njord's breath stilled. That familiar unease—the one that had dogged him since Delara's visit—coiled tight in his gut. His hand automatically went to his hip, where his service weapon used to rest, finding only the coarse wool of his parka.

Old habits. Older fears.

The forest offered no answers. Only the wind sighing through the pines and the distant cry of a raven. But as Njord squinted into the gathering dusk, he couldn't shake the feeling that something—or someone—was watching them from the silent woods.

"Easy, boy," he murmured, placing a calming hand on Loki's head. But the dog remained rigid, his instincts on high alert.

He was being watched. He could feel it. It had started subtly—a fleeting shadow, the sensation of eyes boring into his back—but now it was pervasive. Every rustle of leaves, every distant snap of a twig set his nerves on edge.

Deciding it was best to head back, Njord gave a gentle tug on Loki's leash. "Come on, let's go home."

Darkness fell swiftly this far north, even though it was only mid-afternoon.

They retraced their steps, the descent quicker than their ascent. But with every step, the feeling intensified. The hairs on the back of Njord's neck stood on end, and he found himself glancing over his shoulder more than once, each time met with the same haunting stillness.

Halfway down, he heard it—a faint crunching of snow, distinct and deliberate. He stopped abruptly, his heart pounding in his chest. Loki growled again, turning to face the direction of the sound.

"Who's there?" Njord called out, his voice echoing amidst the trees.

Silence answered.

A surge of adrenaline coursed through him. Gripping Loki's leash tightly, he quickened his pace, nearly breaking into a run.

Finally, the familiar sight of his house came into view. Njord breathed a sigh of relief, but the unease lingered. As he approached the front door, he cast one last glance toward the forest's edge. For a fleeting second, he thought he saw movement—a dark figure slipping behind a tree—but when he blinked, it was gone.

He ushered Loki inside, locking the door behind them. Leaning against the wooden frame, he tried to steady his breathing, the pounding of his heart echoing in his ears. Loki sat by his side, eyes still fixed on the window, ears alert.

Njord moved to draw the curtains, his hands trembling. Before pulling them shut, he peered out into the inky darkness, searching for any sign of the elusive presence. But the only thing he could see was the snow-covered landscape.

Njord knew better. The feeling was too strong to dismiss as mere paranoia. Someone—or something—had been out there, watching, following.

And deep down, he feared the shadows he thought he'd escaped were finally catching up to him.

It had all begun with the woman's visit a few days ago. Since then, a quiet dread had taken hold of him, growing heavier with each passing hour. Her questions—sharp, deliberate—had reached into places he'd long sealed off, unearthing something dark and dangerous he'd spent years trying to bury.

She had been relentless. The Svensson case, Benjamin Hartmann, and the truths he'd prayed the world had forgotten. But it was the knowing glint in her eyes that truly unsettled him—the way she looked at him, like she already knew.

He spun around, breath catching in his throat. The sound was no longer just a rustle in the distance—it was inside the cabin now. Close.

Too close.

"Who's there?" Njord's voice trembled.

Silence followed. Thick, suffocating. As if the very walls were holding their breath.

Loki, usually alert and quick to respond, stood frozen at his side. Ears flattened. A low, uneasy whine curling from his throat. The dog sensed something—something Njord couldn't see, something wrong.

Njord's heartbeat pounded against his ribs, loud in his ears. The shadows clinging to the corners of the room shifted, deepening, as if the light itself was retreating from whatever had entered.

Every instinct screamed at him to get out, to run.

But he couldn't move. His legs refused to obey. He stood rooted, eyes fixed on the darkened doorway to the next room. The noise had come from there—a faint shuffle, barely more than a whisper—but it was enough to send a jolt of pure terror through him.

Loki let out another whimper and stepped back, eyes locked on the same doorway. Njord forced himself to move. One step. Then another. His hand reached for the light switch, fingers skimming the wall.

A click—and nothing.

Darkness held.

The lights didn't come on.

A cold draft slithered through the room. Loki growled, low and guttural, fur bristling along his spine.

The sound came again—closer now. Measured. Patient. As if whatever was inside was watching, waiting.

"Who's there?" he repeated.

No answer.

Just get out.

Now!

Only his ragged breathing and the faint thud of movement just out of sight.

And then the dark closed in. A blinding impact exploded at the base of his skull—cold, solid, shattering.

Pain flared.

The world spun violently, floorboards rushing up to meet him. He hit hard, the air driven from his lungs. A heavy weight crushed his chest, pinning him. The rough texture of wool pressed against his cheek, smelling of pine needles and cold sweat.

Loki's barking was a frantic, distant storm muffled by the roaring pressure in his head. Pinpricks of light danced in the thickening shadows before winking out.

His fingers clawed at the rough wood, finding no grip. The darkness wasn't just visual; it pressed in, heavy and absolute, stealing breath, stealing consciousness.

Loki's frantic defense faded, replaced by a final, choked-off yelp.

Then the roaring subsided, leaving only... silence.

Utter. Black. Silence.

CHAPTER EIGHTEEN

TORRE CLOSED THE FILE. Reading Gustav Gyllenstierna's statement hadn't helped his growing unease.

While the third hypnosis session had reconstructed the night's events in gruesome detail, it provided no new leads. The killer remained as elusive as ever.

They had to let Seb go. The evidence simply hadn't been that strong, and his father's expensive lawyer had torn through the prosecution's argument like it was paper.

It had earned them a summons to Franck Juhlin's office, where he had unleashed ten minutes of thinly veiled disappointment—lecturing them on elite standards, investigative gaps, and the mounting political pressure. At one point, Juhlin was threatening to give the case to Quinten Arning.

And, frankly, Torre had to admit he was right. Stefan had been too impulsive in arresting Seb.

This killer was shrewd. His cruelty was methodical. He hadn't just murdered Gustav's family—he'd forced Gustav to participate, making him choose who would die first and who might live a few agonizing minutes longer. The psychological torture had shattered what remained of Gustav's mind. Yet for all its horrifying clarity, the hypnosis revealed nothing concrete about the killer's identity—only the brutal precision of his game.

Torre leaned back, kneading his temples as if he could push out the dread settling in his bones. This wasn't just murder—it was a calculated performance of power, one where the police were perpetually two moves behind.

Only one detail emerged consistently from Gustav's fractured memories: the voice. Cold. Commanding. Completely unremarkable—no accent, no discernible quirks, nothing to trace. Worse still were Gustav's terrified insistences that he wasn't the killer's first "player"... nor would he be the last. These phantom victims haunted Torre's investigation, taunting him with connections he couldn't prove.

His thoughts turned to Benjamin Hartmann. Something had always felt off about that case. In focusing on Benjamin and Seb, they'd overlooked the missing piece—the wife who vanished when Seb was just a toddler.

Benjamin's official statements painted her as unstable—a woman who had simply walked away. But the timing was too neat, the disappearance too clean. No struggle. No paper trail. Just a mother erased from her child's life.

Torre reached for another file. Anna Grinberg-Hartmann. Missing twenty-four years. The photo showed a woman frozen in time: blonde, delicate features, an ethereal quality that seemed ill-suited to harsh reality. As Torre studied her face, recognition prickled at him—the slope of her nose, the particular curve of her lips. Seb had his father's intensity, but in unguarded moments, his mother's ghost surfaced in his expressions.

That resemblance unsettled Torre more than he cared to admit. Because if Anna hadn't simply left... what had happened to her?

A profound sadness washed over Torre as he considered Seb's fractured childhood—raised on half-remembered whispers of a mother and whatever distorted fragments Benjamin had fed him. He snapped the file shut, his mind swirling with unanswered questions.

Then he felt it—that dangerous pull he recognized immediately. Like standing at the edge of a cliff, toes curling over the void of obsession that had nearly consumed him before.

His mother's warning surfaced with startling clarity, her voice echoing across the years: "Torre," she'd said, her knowing eyes searching his, "you see into people's souls better than anyone. But don't let their darkness swallow yours. Some cases will eat you alive if you let them."

At the time, he'd dismissed it as maternal worry, though she understood his work better than anyone. Now, he recognized the painful truth—he had a tendency to disappear into the cases he investigated, until the boundaries between his life and his subjects blurred beyond recognition.

The warning signs were all there again. This was treacherous ground, and Torre knew it.

Pushing back from his desk, he paced the small office like a caged animal, trying to steady himself. He needed clarity. Discipline. Most of all, he needed to speak with Anna's mother—the woman who'd filed complaint after complaint against her son-in-law for years. Her deep-seated hatred of Benjamin wasn't just grief; it was suspicion given form.

And Torre intended to find out why.

***

Time and grief had sculpted Mrs. Grinberg into a woman of hardened edges. Torre saw it in the canyons carved into her face, in eyes that might once have sparkled but now reflected only loss. As she sat stiffly on her floral-print sofa, fingers knotting together in her lap, he felt her decades-long vigil pressing against his ribs.

The cramped living room was a museum of interrupted happiness—faded birthday photos, Anna's childhood portraits yellowing at the edges, ceramic knickknacks frozen in happier moments. Even the dust motes swirling in the afternoon light seemed to move slower here, as if burdened by memory.

"Thank you for seeing me," Torre began, measuring each word.

This wasn't just an interview; it was an excavation of a mother's open wound.

Her gaze never left the mantelpiece photograph. "You're here about Anna." The name left her lips like a confession.

Torre leaned forward. "I think there's more to her disappearance than the official records show."

Her eyes snapped to his—suddenly, startlingly alive. "They called her troubled. Said she abandoned her child." A vein pulsed at her temple. "My Anna would've died before leaving Seb."

"I've read your complaints against Benjamin Hartmann." Torre kept his voice neutral. "What made you suspect him?"

A lifetime of bitterness condensed into one exhale. "I warned her about him. Charming? Yes. But like a spider spinning its web." Her knuckles whitened. "He was controlling, possessive. He didn't like anyone getting too close to Anna, not even me. After Seb was born, it got worse. He was obsessed with the boy, in a way that wasn't right. And Anna... she was afraid. She never said it outright, but a mother knows."

"What do you mean by obsessed?"

"He was... I don't know how to put it," she said, frowning as she searched for the right words.

"He was overprotective, almost paranoid. He wouldn't let her take Seb anywhere without him, wouldn't let her make any decisions about the boy on her own. It was like he wanted to keep them both under his control, to keep them isolated from the rest of the world."

"Did she ever try to leave?"

"Twice." The word came out sharp. "First time, she stayed here three days before his promises reeled her back in. Second time... she just vanished."

Torre watched grief fracture across her face like ice giving way. "You think Benjamin—"

"I've always believed that," Mrs. Grinberg replied. "He was too calm, too composed when she disappeared. And when I tried to talk to him about it, he just shut me out, said I was imagining things, that Anna had left because she was unhappy. But I knew better. Anna wasn't the type to just walk away from her son. She loved Seb more than anything." She sighed and let her glance go over the pictures of her daughter and grandson. "I miss her... I miss them."

"Them? Seb?"

Her hand trembled as she reached for the framed photograph resting on the side table. The glass caught the light as she lifted it, her fingers tracing the picture frame—Anna holding her son Seb at some long-ago beach. "Benjamin erased me from Seb's life. He made sure I never got to see my grandson. I missed most of his life... until one day, he was standing on my doorstep. He was in a pretty bad shape, and I must admit I thought he wanted money, but..."

"But?"

"He wanted to talk about his mom. He had the same suspicion as I had, that something must have happened to her. There was this dream and memory he had about his mom suffocating. Ridiculous, right? He was barely three. He couldn't have remembered."

"Flashbulb memory," Torre said.

"What is that?"

"Most people cannot recall events from before the age of about 3-4 years old because the brain structures necessary for forming and storing long-term memories, such as the hippocampus and prefrontal cortex, are still developing during this period. But some individuals may have what are called 'flashbulb memories,' which are vivid, detailed memories of a specific event, particularly if it was traumatic, emotionally charged, or involved strong sensory experiences. These memories can sometimes be retained from a very young age, even 2-3 years old. So he might be right. But likely this memory will be tainted with his emotions and the stories he heard later in life. Memories from such a young age can be fragmented, and it's possible that what he remembers is a combination of actual events and things he was told or imagined as he grew older."

Mrs. Grinberg nodded, her eyes distant as she processed this information. "So you think... there's some truth in what he remembers?"

"It's possible," Torre said. "But memories from that time are often unreliable. It could be a genuine recollection, or a reconstructed memory influenced by later experiences. The important thing is that it troubled him enough to seek answers. We need to take it seriously."

"Then she's dead." The tears welled up in Mrs. Grinberg's eyes, her voice breaking as she spoke. "I've always feared the worst, but hearing it like this..."

"We don't know that for sure. But we do need to prepare for every possibility. Whatever the truth is, it's important that we uncover it, for both your sake and Seb's."

Mrs. Grinberg wiped away a tear that had escaped. "I've lived with this uncertainty for so long, Dr. Nylander. Not knowing what happened to her, if she's suffering somewhere or if she's... gone. It's like a wound that never heals."

"I need your help, Mrs. Grinberg."

She nodded. "I'll try to help you as best as I can."

"Elsa Larsson. How does she fit in this story?"

When he mentioned Elsa's name, the old woman's mouth twisted. "That witch? She was Benjamin's fiancée before Anna. Called off the wedding so abruptly people thought she'd been threatened." Her smile held no warmth. "Six months later she married someone else. Benjamin never recovered."

"But Elsa lived with them when Seb was younger."

"Elsa moved in with them right after Anna vanished," Mrs. Grinberg said. "Her own marriage had collapsed—no surprise, given how she'd kept Benjamin warming her bed the whole time." A mirthless laugh escaped her. "When Anna finally discovered the affair... that was the last straw. Benjamin had already hollowed her out with his control. This? This broke what was left."

Torre's pen hovered over his notebook. "How did Anna react?"

The old woman's knuckles whitened around the photograph frame. "She confronted him. Called me after—her voice was so shattered I barely recognized it. He didn't deny it. Just told her if she ever left, she'd never lay eyes on Seb again."

Torre's jaw tightened. "And that's when she disappeared."

Mrs. Grinberg nodded, the tears now spilling down her cheeks. "And I think Elsa played a part in whatever happened to my daughter. After Anna was gone, Elsa moved in with Benjamin and Seb. She took over Anna's role like she had been waiting for that moment, like it was all part of some sick plan. I could never prove it, but in my heart, I've always believed she knew something. Maybe even that she helped him cover it up."

"Yet Benjamin and Elsa didn't last."

"Oil and fire never do." She dabbed her eyes with a crumpled tissue. "The fights started within months—screams that rattled windows, squad cars lighting up the street at 3 a.m. They were poison to each other, but too addicted to the burn to walk away."

Torre leaned forward. "Then why stay?"

"Power," Mrs. Grinberg said. "Elsa craved control, and Benjamin offered her a way to get it. She never got over losing him to Anna in the first place. She thought he'd come after her, beg her to choose him, and save her from her marriage. I think moving in after Anna's disappearance was her way of reclaiming what she thought was hers, but it backfired. Their toxicity only fed off each other, turning the relationship into a battlefield."

Torre nodded. "But it couldn't last. Relationships like that never do."

"No, it didn't," Mrs. Grinberg agreed. "Eventually, their relationship fell apart too. She left him again, but this time it was different. It wasn't just a separation—it was like she wanted to disappear, to erase herself from everything connected to Benjamin. She went back to her husband."

"Her husband must be a very patient and forgiving man."

Mrs. Grinberg let out a dry, humorless laugh. "Patient, perhaps. Forgiving? I'm not so sure. I don't know him, but what Seb told me is that he is a complicated man—cold, calculating, and far from the forgiving type. He was more concerned with appearances than emotions. When Elsa left him the first time, it wasn't out of love or desire for Benjamin. It was out of defiance, a way to assert control over her own life. But her husband wasn't the kind of man to take that lightly."

Torre frowned. "Why would she go back to him, then?"

"Desperation, I suppose. By the time her relationship with Benjamin imploded, Elsa had burned almost every bridge. He offered her a way out, a chance to escape the mess she'd created. But it wasn't out of the goodness of his heart. Her husband had his reasons for taking her back, though I can only speculate what they were."

"What do you think his motivations were?" Torre asked.

Mrs. Grinberg hesitated, choosing her words carefully. "By taking her back, he reasserted his dominance, not just over her, but over everyone who had witnessed her affair with Benjamin. It was his way of showing that no one leaves him, and no one defies him without consequence. Of course, that is just speculation. I never met the man, don't even know his name."

"Do you think Elsa is still involved with Benjamin?"

Mrs. Grinberg sighed. "I don't know. But if she is, it's only because they're tied together by whatever they did to Anna. If there's one thing I know about Elsa, it's that she'll do whatever it takes to protect herself. If that means keeping ties with Benjamin, she will. But I wouldn't be surprised if she's just as desperate to break free from him as he is from her."

"Mrs. Grinberg, what do you think happened to Anna?"

Mrs. Grinberg looked down. Her voice was barely audible when she finally spoke. "I've asked myself that question every day since she disappeared. At first, I hoped she had just run away, that maybe she had found a way to escape from Benjamin and start a new life. But deep down, I knew that wasn't true. Anna would never have left Seb behind."

She paused, her eyes distant as if she were reliving the memories. "The more I think about it, the more I believe that something terrible happened to her. Whether it was Benjamin, Elsa, or both of them together, I'm convinced they had something to do with it. Anna wasn't just unhappy—she was terrified. I could hear it in her voice the last time we spoke. She said she was trapped, that there was no way out."

Torre leaned in closer. "Do you think they killed her?"

A tear slipped down Mrs. Grinberg's cheek as she nodded slowly. "I don't want to believe it, but it's the only thing that makes sense. If Anna had simply run away, she would have found a way to contact me, to let me know she was safe. But there has been nothing—no word, no trace. It's as if she just vanished."

She looked up at Torre. "I think they made her disappear, Dr. Nylander. I think they took her life and then covered it up, made it look like she left on her own."

"I'm going to find out the truth," Torre said. "Whatever happened to Anna, I won't stop until we uncover it. You have my word."

Mrs. Grinberg nodded. "Thank you, Dr. Nylander. That's all I've ever wanted—to know the truth, no matter how painful it is. But if I were you,

I'd look a bit into Benjamin's past."

"Oh, why?"

"There were never official charges, but when he was a teenager, he and his friends were involved in the death of a young woman. Her death was ruled a suicide, but there were rumors."

"Rumors? What kind of rumors?"

Mrs. Grinberg's gaze grew distant, as though she was recalling some long-forgotten details. "It was a long time ago, but I remember hearing about it from a friend who lived near the Hartmanns back then. The girl's name was Lena... I don't know her last name anymore. She was just seventeen, a quiet, unassuming girl from a modest family. She ran with a different crowd—Benjamin and his friends were wealthy, privileged. But somehow, she got mixed up with them."

"What happened to her?"

"She was found dead in the woods near their school. The official report said she'd taken her own life—overdose, I believe. But there were whispers that she didn't go there alone. Some said Benjamin and his friends were with her that night, that they had been playing some sort of cruel game."

Torre's frown deepened. "A game?"

Mrs. Grinberg nodded slowly. "There were stories about how Benjamin and his friends liked to push people to their limits, to see how far they could go before they broke. Some said they manipulated Lena, pushed her too far. But there was never any proof, and the Hartmann family was very influential. The whole thing was hushed up quickly."

"Do you think Benjamin was responsible for her death?"

"I can't say for sure," Mrs. Grinberg replied. "But I believe that whatever happened to Lena, it wasn't as simple as the authorities made it out to be. Benjamin was involved, one way or another. And if he was capable of something like that back then... who's to say he wouldn't do it again? When Anna told me Benjamin was her new boyfriend, I knew from the start that it was asking for problems. He is evil."

"I'll look into it. Thank you for telling me, Mrs. Grinberg. This could be crucial."

She nodded, her expression one of weary relief. "I hope it helps, Dr. Nylander. I've carried this fear for so long… the thought that Benjamin might have done to my Anna what he did to that poor girl all those years ago. Please, find out the truth. For her sake, and for Seb's."

CHAPTER NINETEEN

THE NIGHT THROBBED WITH TENSION, the air thick with the ozone sting of an approaching storm. The stalker crouched deeper in the shadows, his binoculars pressing cold against his eye sockets as he watched through the uncurtained window. The house offered no mercy—no drapes to obscure the raw, unfiltered view of the rot festering between Benjamin Hartmann and Elsa Larsson.

They stood frozen in the lamplight's flickering glow, their argument humming through the glass. Even at this distance, the stalker could taste the venom in their silence—years of shared guilt and mutual loathing crystallizing in the space between them.

This was no lovers' quarrel. It was a reckoning.

Benjamin struck first. His palm cracked across Elsa's cheek with a sound the stalker imagined he could hear. A strand of blonde hair caught on her split lip, glued there by a bead of blood that shimmered in the unstable light. She didn't cry out. Just stood there, breathing shallowly through her nose before turning back to him with deliberate slowness. Her tongue darted out, collecting the blood at the corner of her mouth. When she smiled, it cut like a razor.

The stalker's pulse hammered in his throat as Benjamin's fists trembled at his sides. But Elsa moved first—not to strike, but to seize. Her fingers clawed into his hair, yanking his face down to hers. Their lips collided in a savage, teeth-first kiss that drew fresh blood. Benjamin's hands tore at her blouse until the fabric split with a sound like a stifled scream.

The stalker's grip on the binoculars tightened. They weren't lovers—they were animals, feeding on each other's poison. Benjamin's mouth trailed down Elsa's throat, biting hard enough to bruise, and she threw her head back with a gasp that twisted into laughter—harsh, unhinged, euphoric. The lamp shuddered as he slammed her against the wall, their shadows merging into a single monstrous shape that convulsed across the ceiling.

This was the truth the world never saw. Not passion. Not love. Just two parasites devouring each other alive.

The stalker's breath came in ragged bursts now, his body taut with a perverse thrill he refused to name. He could almost taste the copper tang of blood through the glass.

Then—Elsa went perfectly still.

Her gaze snapped to the window, eyes wide and unblinking, pupils dilated like a shark's in hunting mode. The stalker froze, his lungs burning as he held his breath.

She saw him. She knew.

But Benjamin gripped her chin, wrenching her face back to his. Elsa's lips curled even as she kissed him again, her hand sliding behind her back—slow, deliberate.

She knew.

Yes, she knew.

The first icy raindrops needled the stalker's skin as he retreated into the blackness. Lightning flashed—not the summer's jagged forks, but a diffuse blue glow that lit the snowfield like an X-ray. The thunder came seconds later, a dull growl as if the storm itself was frozen.

The game had begun.

***

Delara looked down at the file. *The Svensson case.* Stefan and Elena Svensson—the only survivors. She flipped through the pages, pausing at a crime scene photograph. Though the image was black and white, the horror needed no color. The bodies of the Svensson children lay on the floor, their hands clasped together in a final, desperate act of unity.

She turned to the next page—interview transcripts from Annika Svensson's psychiatrist, statements from neighbors, Annika's own fractured account.

The phone on her desk buzzed again.

Ten calls in half an hour.

She should probably answer it. He clearly wasn't giving up. Irritation prickled at her—this was the worst possible distraction. Yet the insistent vibrations demanded acknowledgment.

With a sigh, she glanced at the screen. The number was familiar, though not one she'd expected to see so persistently today. Her finger hovered over the answer button. She knew what this was about. Or rather, *who* it was about.

She had a good guess, but that didn't make her any more eager to pick up.

Still... ten calls? That suggested urgency.

Her gaze drifted back to the file.

Maybe she should answer.

* * *

Katherine stood, her fingers resting on Stefan's shoulder as if to steady herself—or him. Another bolt of lightning split the sky, drawing her gaze to the window. Then she said, "Maybe it's time you talked to Elena."

Stefan didn't respond immediately, his eyes fixed on some invisible point on the floor. Two hours had passed since Katherine had appeared unannounced at his door, suitcase in hand—her silent declaration that she'd left Xander for good.

"I don't know," he finally murmured. The weight of decades pressed down on him—the unspeakable past, the unbearable present. "Elena's already spoken to Dad. She'll be thrilled about this. For years she has tried convincing me to do the same. She's always doubted... always believed he didn't kill them."

Katherine studied him carefully. "Maybe that's exactly why you should talk to her. Different perspectives don't mean wrong ones." Her voice gentled. "You've both carried this alone too long."

Stefan finally met her gaze. Her sudden return had shocked him yet somehow anchored him too. But the thought of peeling back those carefully scarred-over wounds terrified him.

"She wants to believe in his innocence," Stefan said. "But what if she's wrong? Or worse—what if she's right?"

Katherine knelt before him, hands settling on his knees. "From everything you've told me, this case was never black and white." Her thumbs made small circles. "You owe them all the truth—your siblings, your mother... even your father."

The lump in his throat threatened to choke him. "And if she is right? If he's innocent?"

"Then you face that truth together," Katherine said. "But at least you'll know." Her eyes searched for his. "You're so good at hiding it, but this has defined your entire life. Part of you wants what Elena wants—to believe he didn't do this."

"I've tried so hard to hate him," Stefan whispered. "It's easier that way. But if he didn't—"

Katherine caught the tear tracking down his cheek. "Then you learn to see him differently. It will hurt, Stefan. But you deserve the truth."

Stefan closed his eyes, letting her words settle in the spaces between his ribs. The fear was paralyzing, but deeper still—that fragile, forbidden hope.

"I'm scared of what this might do to me," he admitted.

Katherine cradled his face, tilting his chin up. "You're not alone anymore," she promised. "I'm here now." Her hand drifted to her stomach. "We both are. The baby..."

The word *baby* struck Stefan like a physical blow. His breath hitched, and suddenly the fear he'd carried for years paled against this new, overwhelming terror.

A child—*his* child—changed everything.

What if the darkness ran deeper than his choices? What if one day, despite all his vows, he became the monster whose shadow had shaped him? The image flashed unbidden: his father's bloodstained hands, the hollow eyes of a man who'd slaughtered his own family. Stefan had built walls for this exact reason—to protect others from the poison in his blood.

Katherine had scaled those walls. But this? Fatherhood required a faith in himself he didn't possess.

His trembling hands closed over hers, his voice breaking. "I can't— What if I'm like him? What if I—"

"You're *not* him." Katherine cut through the spiral, her palms firm against his cheeks. "You've spent your life running from that fear instead of toward it. That's how I know you're different."

Her certainty should have soothed him. Instead, it laid bare the chasm between the man she believed in and the broken boy he still felt like inside. The ghosts weren't so easily banished.

Stefan crushed her against his chest, his grip bordering on pain. She anchored him—this woman who'd chosen him despite knowing his demons.

For now, her faith would have to be enough for both of them.

CHAPTER TWENTY

TORRE FOUND HIMSELF WALKING DOWN a familiar hallway, the wooden floors creaking beneath his feet. The house was his parents' home, yet something felt wrong—off. The walls seemed to pulse, the shadows too thick, too dark, as if the house itself was alive, breathing in the gloom that surrounded him.

"Mom?" he called out. His voice echoed through the empty corridors. But no answer came, only the eerie silence that wrapped around him like a shroud.

He moved from room to room, each more distorted than the last. The furniture was familiar yet wrong, twisted and warped in ways that made his skin crawl. Photos on the walls melted into shadows, the faces of his family members blurred, indistinguishable.

His mother's absence clawed at him, each passing moment winding the tension in his chest tighter.

"Mom!" he called again, louder this time.

Still, there was no response.

He reached the stairs, the ascent slow and torturous. Each step groaned underfoot, the sound reverberating through the house. The upstairs hallway stretched before him, impossibly long. He knew where he was going, where he had to be, but his body resisted, every fiber of his being screaming for him to turn back.

But he couldn't.

Something was drawing him forward, a force he couldn't resist.

The door at the end of the hallway was ajar, a thin line of light spilling out from the crack.

He approached it slowly, dread curling in the pit of his stomach.

He pushed the door open.

The room was bathed in a sickly yellow light, casting long, distorted shadows on the walls. And there, in the center of the room, was his father, Ragnar, his back turned to Torre.

His father's movements were slow, deliberate, the glint of a knife catching the light as it rose and fell, over and over again.

Torre's heart pounded in his chest. He took a step closer, and the scene before him came into horrifying focus.

His mother lay on the bed, her eyes wide with terror, her mouth open in a silent scream. Blood pooled around her, seeping into the sheets, dripping onto the floor. Next to her, on the floor, were his two brothers, their lifeless bodies twisted in unnatural angles, their eyes staring blankly at nothing.

"Dad... no," Torre whispered, his voice trembling as his mind struggled to process the horror before him.

Ragnar turned slowly, his eyes cold and devoid of emotion, his face a mask of calm as if he were performing some mundane task.

There was no remorse, no recognition, only a chilling detachment.

He tilted his head, studying Torre with an unsettling calm.

Then, without warning, Ragnar lunged at him, the knife gleaming as it arced through the air.

Torre tried to move, tried to scream, but his body was frozen, paralyzed by terror. The blade descended, and in that split second before it struck, everything went black.

A scream tore from his throat as he lurched upright—
—and then choked off, strangled by the dark.

The room pressed in around him, air thick with the stench of sweat and something sharper, metallic. His pulse roared in his ears, so loud he barely heard his own ragged gasps. The sheets clung to him, damp and cold, but the dream's heat still licked at his skin: the knife's arc, his father's hollow eyes, the click of the bedroom door as it swung shut—

Had that been real?

His hands fisted in the blankets. No. Just a dream.

But something was wrong, terribly wrong, but he couldn't pinpoint what.

Unconsciously, he had always felt it, a darkness that he could never quite understand.

A darkness in his family.

Who? What?

He didn't know.

But now, after the dream, that feeling was no longer just a vague unease. It was a cold, hard knot of fear in the pit of his stomach, a gnawing certainty that something was very, very wrong.

He shifted under the covers.

And then he saw it—a shadow, darker than the rest, sitting in the corner of his room.

It wasn't just a trick of the light; it was too defined, too solid. The figure was hunched, staring at him. Torre's breath caught in his throat, his body freezing in terror.

The shadow didn't move, didn't make a sound, but he could feel its eyes on him, boring into him, filling him with a dread that made his skin crawl.

His heart raced, every instinct screaming at him to move, to run, but he couldn't.

Then, as suddenly as it had appeared, the shadow was gone. The corner was empty, the darkness once again just darkness. But the fear remained, coursing through his veins, urging him to get up, to do something.

Torre threw off the covers and swung his legs over the side of the bed. His feet hit the cold floor, and he stood, unsteady, his heart still pounding.

The room was silent, but it wasn't a comforting silence.

He needed to see them, needed to make sure they were okay. The dream had left him with a deep, irrational fear that something had happened.

His parents' room was just down the hall, a few short steps away, but it felt like a mile.

He forced himself to move, his legs trembling as he walked to the door. The hallway was dark, the only light coming from the faint glow of the moon filtering through the windows, the snow outside amplifying the light and casting an eerie, pale glow over everything.

He hesitated for a moment, his hand hovering over the doorknob.

Finally, he pushed the door open.

The room was dark, but he could make out the shapes of his parents, lying peacefully in their bed, their breathing slow and steady.

They were fine.

They were just sleeping.

He stood there for a long moment, watching them, as if expecting something to happen, something to confirm the fear that had taken root in his mind.

But nothing did.

They continued to sleep peacefully, oblivious to the turmoil raging inside him.

Torre quietly closed the door and backed away, his mind still racing. The fear hadn't left him. If anything, it had only grown stronger, feeding off the darkness that seemed to lurk in every corner of the house.

He returned to his room, but sleep didn't come easily. The shadow, the dream, his father—everything felt wrong, twisted in a way he couldn't fully grasp.

Something terrible was just out of reach, something that was waiting, watching, hidden in the shadows of his family.

✳ ✳ ✳

Torre sat at his desk in the police station, the remnants of his unsettling dream still clinging to him like a heavy fog. He rubbed his eyes, trying to shake off the lingering anxiety, but the uneasy feeling refused to leave. The cold knot of fear that had lodged itself in his stomach during the night was still there.

He turned his attention to the file on his computer screen.

Lena Vinter. Seventeen years old, found dead in the forest under circumstances that were both mysterious and brutal.

He clicked on the file and began to read.

Lena Vinter had been found in a remote area, her body discovered by a hiker early one morning. The official report listed Lena's cause of death as a drug overdose—suicide. But as he delved deeper into the file, Torre found the details that didn't quite add up. There were the bruises on her arms and legs, the signs of a struggle, the odd, almost ritualistic way her body had been positioned—all of it pointed to something far worse than a simple case of overdose or suicide.

But it was the names mentioned in the file that truly made his blood run cold.

Lena had last been seen with four boys on the night of her death—

Benjamin Hartmann, then nineteen, and three minors. They had all been interrogated, but nothing had come of it. The case had been ruled a suicide, despite the unsettling inconsistencies.

Torre's eyes lingered on the names of the three minors, his breath catching as he realized who two of them were.

Gustav Gyllenstierna.

Marnix Castner.

The connection was undeniable now, and Torre felt a cold dread wash over him as the pieces began to fall into place.

Benjamin Hartmann's involvement in Lena's death, the brutal fashion in which their families had been killed—it was all connected. But how? And why had these connections been buried for so long, left to fester until they exploded in such horrific violence?

Torre leaned back in his chair. He needed to talk to Delara and Stefan.

This case was the key to everything.

He looked up from the computer, his eyes scanning the people around him. So much activity, a constant hum of voices, ringing phones, and the clatter of keyboards. Officers moved briskly through the corridors, some with files tucked under their arms, others deep in conversation.

But the absence of Stefan and Delara was real, a strange void in the midst of all the chaos. They were usually at the center of things.

He never was.

Nobody ever noticed him.

His eyes wandered over the scene, taking in the faces of his colleagues, some familiar, others not.

A laugh erupted from a cluster of officers nearby. Torre didn't turn. Their camaraderie was a language he'd never learned—words like trust and belonging twisting into static when he got too close.

He had never felt so disconnected as at that moment.

What was he doing here?

"What's going on?"

Torre nearly jumped out of his seat at the sound of Delara's voice. She was standing right behind him. Her sudden appearance broke through the fog of his thoughts, grounding him in the moment.

"What's going on?" she repeated. She had a way of cutting through the noise, of seeing things others missed—like how out of place he felt right now.

"Lena Vinter. She is the link between Hartmann, Castner, and Gyllenstierna."

Delara frowned. She put her bag on the table and sat next to him. "How?"

"I think they all had something to do with her death and now someone is making them pay."

"Are you sure? Why didn't Hartmann mention he knew them."

"He's hiding the truth about her death," Torre said.

Delara leaned in, her sleeve brushing his wrist. The sweet scent of jasmine. His breath hitched.

Focus, idiot.

A girl was dead. Families were slaughtered. But his traitorous mind whispered: She's close enough to kiss.

He had tried to keep his feelings at bay, to remain professional, but moments like this made it difficult.

He had hidden his feelings when she was still with his brother Emil. He had hidden his feelings when she became his colleague, but they were still there, clearer than ever. More painful than ever.

"Torre," Delara said, bringing his attention back to the screen. "If you're right, this changes everything. We need to find out what really happened to Lena, and fast. Before anyone else gets hurt."

He nodded, forcing himself to focus on the conversation. This case wasn't the only thing he was losing control over. His emotions for Delara were becoming harder to ignore, and as much as he tried to push them aside, they lingered—like the scent of her perfume, sweet and impossible to forget.

"You said there were four boys. Who is the fourth one?"

"Uh...," he scrolled through the file. "Let me see... uh. Here it is. The fourth one is... Axel Bergström."

Delara nodded, but then her gaze shifted back to Torre, her eyes narrowing as she studied him with an intensity that made him uncomfortable. It was as if she could see right through him.

"You look tired," she said. "Is everything okay?"

Torre forced a smile. "Yeah, I'm fine. Just... this case, you know? It's been keeping me up at night."

She leaned in closer, her eyes searching his face as if trying to read the truth in his expression. "Is everything okay with your parents? With Emil?"

He hadn't been expecting her to bring up Emil, and it caught him off guard. "Why do you ask?"

Delara shrugged, her eyes never leaving his. "I don't know, Torre. You just seem... different. Distant. Like there's something on your mind that you're not talking about."

"Why would you care about my parents and... Emil? You broke up."

"It might surprise you, but I truly enjoyed being part of your family. I'm sorry that things didn't work out between Emil and I, but that doesn't mean I don't care. I really like your parents."

"Really? Mom?"

She smiled. "Even your mother. I know she doesn't like me, but that's the prerogative of any mother-in-law."

"I guess you're right about that."

"She's protective of you and your brothers, and I understand that. It's just... I never meant to hurt anyone. I care about your family, about you too. That hasn't changed." She looked down at her hands for a moment. "But Emil needs to grow up. He craves attention. That's not healthy."

"I don't think he craves the attention. He *gets* the attention."

"He's handsome and charming... I give you that, but he only exists in the spotlight. He needs that constant validation, and it's exhausting to keep up with. I didn't realize how much it drained me until it was too late."

"He's always been that way," Torre admitted. "Even when we were kids. Everyone loved Emil, and he knew how to work it. But... I don't think he has ever really understood what it means to be in a relationship."

Delara looked at him, her eyes softening. "You're different. You don't need the attention, and that's what makes you stronger in a way he can't be. You see people for who they really are, not just how they make you feel. That's rare."

He felt his cheeks warm at her words. "I don't know about that. I just... I try to be there for people. That's all."

"And you are," Delara said gently. "You've always been there for your family, for Emil. But don't forget to take care of yourself too."

"Uh... thanks. I'll keep that in mind."

He had never expected her to be that open. She usually had her defenses up. She could be direct and harsh, to the point of bullying, but this was a different side of her he had rarely seen.

"Axel Bergström... he could be in danger." Her words cut through his train of thought.

Torre blinked. The warmth from Delara's unexpected openness had momentarily distracted him, but her shift in tone brought him back to the harsh reality of their work.

"He was the fourth boy in Lena Vinter's file," she said. "If something's happening to those involved in her death, then he could be next."

Torre nodded. "We need to find him, warn him. If someone is targeting them, he might not have much time."

"We need Stefan," Torre said.

"I'll call him," Delara said and took her cell phone from the bag. "We need to find Axel Bergström."

"We also need to talk to the family of Lena Vinter. The killer likely wants to take revenge for what happened to her. You can do that."

Delara nodded, her fingers already dialing Stefan's number. "I'll let Stefan know we're splitting up—he can help track down Bergström while you visit Lena's family. We need to cover all our bases."

"Let's hope we're not too late."

Delara glanced at him. "We won't be. We're going to stop this before anyone else gets hurt."

CHAPTER TWENTY-ONE

THE CAR SWALLOWED THE ROAD WHOLE, headlights drowning in the black. Trees clawed at the windows. Somewhere ahead, a light flickered—weak, like a dying pulse. The world beyond the windshield felt claustrophobic, as if the night itself was closing in on them.

Stefan quickly looked at Delara, sitting next to him and then gripped the steering wheel tightly. The rhythmic thrum of the tires on the gravel road was the only sound, a monotonous, almost hypnotic buzz.

"Are we even on the right road?" Delara's voice broke the silence.

Stefan glanced at the GPS. "We should be close, but everything looks the same out here."

Delara stared out the window, her eyes straining to make sense of the shifting shadows that flickered past them. They hadn't seen another sign of life for what felt like hours. The countryside was a vast, empty void, devoid of the comforting markers of civilization. No streetlights, no distant glow from a neighboring house—just an unbroken sea of darkness that seemed to stretch on forever.

As they rounded a bend, the car's headlights swept across something in the distance—a faint glimmer of light, barely visible through the dense undergrowth. The first flicker of life emerged from the silence, but it didn't soothe Delara—it unsettled her, a cold shiver prickling her skin.

"There," Stefan muttered. "That has to be it."

The light grew closer.

The gravel driveway they turned onto was uneven, the car bumping and jolting as they made their way deeper into the unknown. A dilapidated sign came into view, the name "Bergström" barely legible in the light, its wooden surface weathered and cracked.

Then the house itself emerged from the darkness. It was old, far older than they had expected, with sagging walls and a roof that seemed to dip in the middle.

Stefan killed the engine, and they sat in silence for a moment, neither eager to step out into the night, and the cold air hit them like a slap when they finally opened the doors.

Delara wrapped her coat tighter around herself, the hairs on the back of her neck prickling as they approached the house. "I don't like this," she whispered.

"Me neither."

The light from the bulb barely reached beyond the porch, casting long, distorted shadows that made the place feel even more ominous.

Stefan hesitated at the bottom of the porch steps, his fingers brushing against the rough, weathered wood of the railing. "Ready?"

Delara nodded. "Let's get this over with. The faster we can get out of here, the better. This place gives me the creeps."

Stefan reached for the door, ready to ring the bell, but it creaked open with a sound that made Delara flinch.

"What the...," Stefan let out.

"The door is open. That's not good."

Stefan pulled his gun. Delara's breath hitched as she mirrored

Stefan's movements, her own gun drawn and held firmly in her hands. "Stay sharp," she whispered, more to herself than to Stefan, though he nodded in acknowledgment.

"Mr. Bergström?" Delara called out. "Police."

Inside, the house was eerily silent. The faint light from the bulb outside barely reached beyond the threshold.

As they stepped inside, the stench coiled around them—wet iron, spoiled meat, and beneath it, something sweet. It was a smell that didn't belong in a house meant for the living.

"What the hell is that?" Delara muttered.

Stefan didn't answer, but the tension in his posture was enough. He took a cautious step forward, the floorboards creaking under his weight.

"Something is wrong," Delara whispered.

Stefan nodded, his eyes still fixed on the dark hallway ahead. "We must find Axel. If he's here..."

"This doesn't look good." The walls wept red. Not smears—spatter. High-velocity arcs, like someone had swung a bucket of paint in a frenzy.

But it wasn't paint.

It was blood.

And the blood was everywhere.

Stefan took another step forward, his flashlight illuminating the trail of blood that led deeper into the house, vanishing into the dark maw of the hallway.

Delara's fingers tightened around the grip of her gun.

The hallway seemed to stretch on forever, each step taking them further into the unknown.

They reached a doorway at the end of the hall, the wood splintered and stained. Stefan hesitated for a moment, then slowly pushed the door open with his foot, his flashlight cutting through the thick darkness that filled the room beyond.

"What do you see?" Delara asked.

Stefan's breath caught in his throat as the light fell on the scene before them. The room was in shambles—furniture overturned, shards of glass littering the floor, and in the center of it all, a large pool of blood, still fresh, glistening under the harsh light of the flashlight.

"This is bad. Really bad."

Delara stepped closer, her own flashlight sweeping the room. "Where is Bergström?"

Stefan's hand trembled as he reached for his cell phone.

He dialed Torre's number.

Torre picked up on the third ring, his voice sounding distant, distracted. "Stefan? What's going on?"

"Listen," Stefan began. "We're at Axel Bergström's place. It's bad. There's blood everywhere, and we can't find him. I need you to do something for me."

"Go ahead."

"I need you to look up what other paintings there are in the 'Darkness and Light' series. Axel is alone—no wife, no children."

There was a brief pause on the other end, then Torre's voice came back, more focused. "I'll look into it right away. But Stefan, I was planning to meet with Lena Vinter's family. I think they might have some crucial information about her connection to Hartmann and the others."

"Delay it if you can," Stefan said. "Axel might be in serious danger. We need to know what painting the killer is going to use as example for his murder."

"I'll call you as soon as I find anything."

Torre hung up, his heart pounding as he rushed to his computer. The screen flickered to life as he quickly navigated through his files.

∗ ∗ ∗

Torre navigated the digital gallery with methodical keystrokes, pulling up

Benjamin Hartmann's 'Darkness and Light' series. His pulse hammered against his ribs, each thumbnail loading slower than the last—as if the screen itself resisted showing him what came next.

Then he paused.

The painting filled his screen. Leaning closer, Torre studied the details: a man hung by a rope coiled taut around his neck, the fibers biting into his skin. Streaks of blood darkened the collar of his torn shirt. The figure's posture was unnervingly still, head tilted at an angle that strained the tendons of his neck, yet his expression held an eerie resignation. The smile was all wrong—lips parted like a lover's, but the eyes were glazed, dead. As if the man had welcomed the rope's embrace.

Shadows pooled around the man like smoke, dense and restless, but a stark beam of light cut through the gloom. It sharpened every detail—the gaunt hollows of the man's cheeks, the glisten of blood on his hands, the rope vanishing into the darkness. The longer Torre stared at it, the more the scene blurred the line between art and reality.

This wasn't a painting. It was a blueprint.

He called Stefan. Once. Twice. Three times. No answer. His thumb hovered over Delara's contact next, but her phone rang to silence too.

If Hartmann's work mirrored reality, Axel Bergström's fate—or Stefan's, or Delara's—might already be sealed.

Torre stumbled back. The chair shrieked against the tile, tipping over like a fallen body. He grabbed his jacket just as the crash still echoed.

But too late.

The painting's rope was already around someone's neck—he felt it tighten in his own throat.

※ ※ ※

A creak—soft, deliberate—cut through the silence. Stefan's finger twitched against his trigger.

Delara's breath stopped mid-inhale.

Someone was here.

They weren't alone.

As they moved through the narrow hallway, the sound came again, a soft, almost rhythmic creak that echoed through the stillness. It led them to the back door, where a cold draft slipped through the gaps in the old, weathered wood.

Stefan nudged the door open with his shoulder, and they stepped out into the night. The biting chill of the air immediately hit them, but it was the sight before them that made them both pause.

There, a short distance from the house, stood the barn. It was large, its silhouette stark against the sky, and though the structure was ancient, its presence was unsettling. The wooden planks were dark with age, many of them warped and splintered, giving the building a crooked appearance, as though it were bowing under some great, unseen weight.

The roof was steep, with shingles missing in patches, revealing the skeletal framework beneath. The dim light from the house's back porch flickered across the barn's surface, casting jagged patterns of light and shadow that made the barn appear almost alive.

At one end of the barn, a large set of double doors hung slightly ajar, swaying ever so gently with the wind. Above the doors, a small, broken window gaped like a dark, empty eye, its glass long shattered, leaving behind jagged shards that glinted dangerously in the faint light.

Stefan's gaze traveled over the barn. The place looked abandoned, forgotten, yet something about it drew his attention, a pull he couldn't quite explain.

Delara's breath clouded in the air as she stood beside him, her eyes narrowed as she studied the barn. "This doesn't feel right."

Stefan nodded, his grip tightening on his gun. "We need to check it out. Whatever made that noise—it's in there."

They moved as one, crossing the short distance with cautious steps.

As they approached the barn, the sense of foreboding grew stronger, the air around them thickening with an almost tangible tension.

Stefan reached the doors first, pausing just outside the threshold. He glanced back at Delara, who gave a brief, tight nod. With a deep breath, Stefan pushed one of the doors open, its hinges protesting loudly in the otherwise still night.

Inside, the barn was eerily illuminated by a single, flickering bulb hanging from the rafters. The weak light did little to pierce the darkness that clung to the corners of the barn, where the beams of their flashlights cut through the blackness, revealing the interior bit by bit. A dirt floor littered with debris, old hay bales stacked haphazardly against one wall, and more tools scattered around—rusted scythes, pitchforks, and other implements whose metal edges caught the light in brief, ominous flashes.

But in the center of the barn hung a large, heavy object, draped with a torn and dirty tarp. It was impossible to tell what was beneath it, but the shape of it was vaguely human, and that alone was enough to give them the shivers.

Stefan took a step forward, his flashlight trained on the tarp. "Let's see what we're dealing with," he whispered, more to steady his nerves than anything else. Delara followed closely behind, her own light sweeping the barn's shadowed corners, searching for any sign of movement.

Stefan's fingers trembled as he reached for the edge of the tarp.

The tarp slid away.

Axel hung like a marionette, his neck bent at a butcher's angle.

Blood crusted the rope where it sawed into the skin.

His eyes—God, his eyes.

Still wet.

Still aware.

As if he'd watched his own death unfold.

Blood stained the front of his shirt, a dark rivulet running down from the wound where the rope had bitten into his skin.

The faint, unsettling smile on Axel's face was the final, chilling touch.

Delara swallowed hard, her heart pounding in her chest as she tried to process the sight before her. The stench of death was overwhelming, a sickly sweet odor that made her stomach churn. She forced herself to look away, her flashlight sweeping the barn once more, desperate to find something—anything—that could explain this nightmare.

Then they heard it—a noise, faint but unmistakable, coming from the back of the barn. Stefan and Delara both froze, their guns drawn, the beams of their flashlights converging to the source of the sound.

It was a soft, pitiful whimpering, like the cry of a wounded animal.

Stefan moved first, taking slow, cautious steps toward the sound, his gun raised. Delara followed, her own weapon steady in her hands, her senses on high alert. The noise grew louder as they approached the dark corner of the barn, hidden behind a stack of old, moldy hay bales.

They rounded the corner, and there, huddled in the shadows, was a boy. He couldn't have been more than ten or eleven years old, his small frame shaking with sobs. His clothes were dirty and torn, and his face was streaked with tears.

Stefan immediately holstered his gun, his instincts kicking in as he crouched down to the boy's level. "Hey, hey, it's okay. We're here to help."

The boy's whimpers died in his throat.

His hands clutched something—a small, blood-caked knife.

Not a weapon. A tool.

The kind you'd use to cut a rope.

Delara knelt beside Stefan.

"What's your name?" Delara asked gently.

The boy didn't respond, his sobs growing quieter but still shaking his small frame. He looked up at them with eyes filled with a deep fear, his gaze darting back and forth between Stefan and Delara as if unsure whether to trust them.

Delara reached out. "You're safe now. We won't let anything happen to you."

For a moment, the boy seemed to relax, his sobs subsiding into quiet sniffles.

Then the boy's eyes locked onto something behind them.

A shadow peeled away from the barn wall.

And the rope began to swing.

CHAPTER TWENTY-TWO

TORRE'S FINGERS TWITCHED TOWARD the crime-scene photos—Axel's corpse, the rope, the boy's tear-streaked face.

The killer needed a witness.

A child.

Innocence, corrupted.

Across the table, Benjamin Hartmann sat like a king dethroned, his tailored suit rumpled, his eyes sharp as scalpels.

Torre knew this power—the kind that didn't need to raise a voice to make a room suffocate.

When Hartmann's gaze settled on Torre, he felt insignificant. Torre knew this feeling all too well. His father had wielded a similar power—the ability to fill a room, to command attention without effort. It was a kind of dominance Torre had never understood, let alone mastered. Yet here it was again, embodied in Hartmann, who seemed to bend the air itself to his will.

The door opened, and Stefan entered, shifting the atmosphere. Torre glanced at Hartmann and caught a flicker of unease in his eyes. It was subtle, fleeting, but undeniable—a crack in the man's otherwise impenetrable armor.

"So, Mr. Hartmann," Stefan began as he sat beside Torre, his voice calm but laced with authority. "Here we are again. You know Dr. Nylander. He'll be assisting me today."

"What is this about?" Hartmann's tone was sharp, condescending, and it grated on Torre's nerves.

"Why didn't you tell us you know Gustav Gyllenstierna and Marnix Castner?"

"I didn't think it was relevant," Hartmann replied.

"I showed you Gustav's picture. I explicitly asked if you knew him, and yet... you said no. You lied."

"I haven't spoken to them in over thirty years."

"That isn't quite the truth, is it?" Stefan countered.

Hartmann blinked, caught off guard.

"You recommended Dr. Elsa Larsson to Gyllenstierna two years ago. He told us everything. What he didn't tell us is why he contacted you in the first place. Care to elaborate?"

"Not really," Hartmann said, folding his hands.

"And Marnix Castner?" Stefan pressed. "If we dig deeper, maybe speak with Dr. Larsson, will we find a similar story?"

Hartmann sighed. "Fine. I admit I reconnected with Gustav and Marnix a few years ago. It was like a reunion—old friends catching up. They were both struggling in their marriages, and I merely suggested Elsa as someone who might help."

"Was Axel Bergström there?"

Hartmann frowned. "Axel? No, he wasn't."

"Isn't it time you told us about Lena Vinter?" Stefan asked.

Hartmann's composure faltered, just for a moment. "Lena Vinter?

What does she have to do with this?"

"You, Gyllenstierna, Castner, and now Bergström," Stefan said. "That's a lot of coincidences."

Hartmann leaned forward. "What happened to Axel?"

"He was found dead," Stefan replied. "Beaten, stabbed, dragged, and hanged in his barn. His ten-year-old nephew witnessed the entire thing."

Torre slid a set of photographs across the table. Hartmann's face drained of color as he stared at the gruesome images.

"Silent Ascension," Hartmann whispered, his eyes wide with shock. "Why? How?"

"Correct," Stefan said. "I'm trying to understand your 'Darkness and Light' series. It's all so..."

Hartmann swallowed. "That series... it was born out of despair. After Anna left me, I..." He trailed off, shaking his head. "In 'Darkness and Light,' there is no light."

Stefan's eyes narrowed. "Let's talk about Anna, then. Your marriage wasn't a happy one, was it? There were three people in that marriage—you, Anna, and Elsa Larsson, your mistress."

Hartmann's face darkened. "There's nothing to talk about. Anna and I grew apart, that's all. And Elsa... she was just someone who understood me when no one else did."

"Understood you? Or enabled you?" Stefan asked. "You paint a picture of a man consumed by darkness. Did Elsa feed that darkness, or was she the light you lost?"

Hartmann's composure cracked further. "Elsa was... everything I couldn't have. She was the passion, the fire, the life that Anna never was. But it was all wrong. I knew it was wrong, and I couldn't stop myself. In fact... Anna was the light, but she drifted away from me. And when it ended, when I lost her... that's when the darkness came. That's when I started the series."

"Anna was the light? Then... where is your light right now?"

"I don't know," Benjamin hissed.

"A woman just doesn't disappear from the face of the earth," Stefan said.

Benjamin's eyes narrowed as he stared at Stefan. He looked like a man on the edge. His hands clenched into fists, his knuckles turning white as he tried to maintain control.

"She didn't disappear," Benjamin finally said. "She left. She walked out, just like that. And Elsa... Elsa was supposed to fill that void, but she couldn't. She wasn't Anna. No one could ever be Anna."

"You're flipping the coin," Torre said. "Anna had to make space for Elsa and that's why she left or rather... is no longer there."

"No," Benjamin shook his head.

Stefan leaned in, his voice a blade. "Where. Is. She."

Benjamin's mask slipped—just a crack. A vein pulsed in his temple. "I told you. She left."

"And yet," Stefan tapped the file, "no bank withdrawals. No calls. No sign of life."

"I don't know!" Benjamin's voice rose, his composure slipping further.

Stefan leaned in. "You don't know, or you don't want to know? Benjamin, people don't just vanish without a trace. If you want to help yourself, now's the time to come clean. Where is Anna?"

"I told you! I don't know!" Benjamin snapped, but there was a crack in his voice now, a thread of desperation woven through his anger. "Are you accusing me of her disappearance? You think I did something to her? First you go after my son for these disgusting murders, and now you're pointing the finger at me."

Stefan didn't respond immediately. Instead, he let the silence stretch. When he finally spoke, his tone was measured but firm. "Mr. Hartmann, whatever happened, we need to know. If you're hiding something, it will eventually come out. You don't want to be on the wrong side of this."

Benjamin held Stefan's gaze, his own eyes a storm of emotions—anger, fear, and something deeper, harder to name. Regret, maybe.

At last, his shoulders sagged, the fight seeping out of him. He lowered his gaze. "I hired a private investigator when she left. I needed to know where she went, what happened to her. For years, I tried. But they never found her. Not a single trace."

"And that didn't strike you as odd?" Stefan asked.

"Of course, it struck me as odd!" Benjamin exclaimed. "It has haunted me every single day—how someone could just vanish without a trace. No credit card activity, no phone calls, nothing. It was as if she'd been wiped off the face of the earth."

Stefan said nothing, his gaze steady as he watched Benjamin, searching for cracks in his armor. "And you didn't find that suspicious? Didn't it cross your mind that... something else might have happened?"

Benjamin's eyes snapped back to Stefan. "You think I didn't consider that? That I didn't play out every possible scenario in my head? But there was nothing—no leads, no evidence, not a single clue to where she might have gone. It was like she just disappeared into thin air. And the longer I searched, the more I realized..." His voice faltered, dropping to a whisper. "I didn't want to find out."

"You were the last person to see her," Torre interjected.

Benjamin stiffened, his head snapping toward Torre. "What do you mean by that?"

"That you killed her," Stefan said. He didn't even look at Benjamin as he delivered the accusation. "You killed her because Anna wasn't your light... Elsa was."

The words hung in the air like a thunderclap.

Benjamin froze.

"Elsa," Stefan continued, "was the woman you truly loved. Your equal in every way that mattered—passion, creativity, intellect. But Anna? She was an obstacle. One you couldn't get rid of... until she left. But when she didn't just leave, when she disappeared without a trace..." He turned to face Benjamin. "You knew. Deep down, you knew she wasn't coming back."

Benjamin's face drained of color as he shook his head repeatedly. "No, that's not true. I didn't kill her! I would never—"

"Then where is she?" Stefan's voice was sharp, slicing through Benjamin's denial like a blade. "If you didn't kill her, then where is she? Because right now, all the evidence points to you. You had motive, you had opportunity, and now we're uncovering just how deep your obsession with Elsa Larsson ran. Anna found out about it. Maybe she threatened to expose you, to ruin you—and that's when you decided she had to go."

Benjamin's jaw tightened as he stared at Stefan, his hands trembling at his sides. "Then prove it."

Stefan leaned back. A slow, calculating smile spread across his face. "Maybe we should talk to Dr. Larsson again."

A flicker of panic crossed Benjamin's eyes before he could hide it. "She has nothing to do with this," he said quickly, the words spilling out too fast.

"Well, I think she does," Stefan countered. "The same month Anna disappeared, Elsa moved in. Funny, isn't it? You'd think the police would have looked into that more seriously."

Benjamin's face darkened. "Elsa moved in because I needed help with Sebastian. There was a toddler—a toddler I didn't know how to take care of!"

Stefan's eyebrows lifted, a mockery of sympathy in his expression. "So, she was the nanny?"

"No, of course not! She's a friend. She took care of us."

"And what did her husband think about that?"

"Her husband?" Benjamin scoffed. "That douchebag? He's an idiot... but a dangerous and violent one."

"Oh? Why?" Stefan pressed.

Benjamin's expression darkened. "He hits her. Threatens her."

"Domestic violence," Stefan said, leaning back. "Did she ever report it?"

A bitter, sarcastic smile twisted Benjamin's lips. "You really don't know."

Stefan's gaze flicked to Torre, a silent exchange passing between them, before he refocused on Benjamin. "What don't I know?"

Benjamin let out a dry, humorless laugh. "He's a cop. Or was. I'm not exactly sure what he's doing now, but trust me, he's still the same violent, manipulative bastard he's always been."

Stefan's jaw tightened, and he leaned forward. "Did Elsa ever talk to you about leaving him? Did she ask for your help?"

Benjamin hesitated for a moment but finally nodded. "A few times. She'd get close to making a decision, but then... he'd find a way to drag her back. He knows how to get under her skin, make her feel like she can't live without him. And when that didn't work, he'd use his fists."

"You took her in," Torre said. "You offered her a way out."

Benjamin's eyes moved toward Torre. There was something unreadable in his gaze. "I tried. But it's not that simple when someone like him is involved."

Stefan studied Benjamin's face. "How did Elsa feel about Anna? You had a relationship with Elsa before, then suddenly chose Anna. That must have been painful."

"I didn't choose Anna over her. Elsa chose her husband over me. It was painful for me."

Stefan's gaze sharpened. "So, Elsa left you for her husband, and you settled for Anna. Is that it?"

Benjamin sneered. "Settled? No, Anna was... different. Stable, secure. The kind of woman who could keep everything in order. Predictable. But Elsa... she was fire, passion. She made me feel alive in a way Anna never could."

"So why marry Anna? Why not wait for Elsa to leave her husband?"

Benjamin's irritation flared. "You don't understand, do you? Like I said... Anna was safe. She gave me a respectable life."

"Safe," Stefan echoed. "Yet you think she just walked out on you? That doesn't sound like a 'safe' person. That sounds like someone pushed to the brink."

Benjamin's expression darkened. "Anna was weak. She couldn't handle the pressures, the expectations. I gave her everything, and she just... couldn't deal with it."

"Or maybe she found out you were still seeing Elsa," Torre said. "Maybe she knew you'd never really let Elsa go. And that drove her away."

Benjamin's eyes snapped to Torre. "You don't know what you're talking about. Anna knew what our marriage was. She knew her place."

"Her place?" Stefan raised an eyebrow. "And where exactly was her place? As the wife you paraded around in public while Elsa was the one you really cared about? When Anna disappeared, it was convenient, wasn't it? No more wife to pretend to care about—just you and Elsa, playing house with Sebastian."

Benjamin's face twisted in frustration. "You think you've got me all figured out, don't you? Like I'm some kind of monster. But you're wrong. I loved Anna, and I love Elsa. I just..."

Stefan leaned back. "And now you have neither. Anna's gone, and Elsa lives in fear of her husband. You say you didn't kill Anna, but everything points to a man desperate to get what he wants, no matter the cost."

"I'm not a killer," Benjamin said. "You can't prove anything. You have nothing on me."

"The fact is, one woman disappeared, and another is dead."

Benjamin frowned. "Who?"

"Lena Vinter," Stefan said.

Benjamin's expression shifted. "Oh, my God. That's ages ago. Lena killed herself."

"But there were doubts," Torre added.

"Never proven."

"What happened that night?"

"Lena went to the woods, took an overdose, and died," Benjamin said.

Stefan nodded, his eyes locked on Benjamin. "That's the official story, isn't it? Lena Vinter took an overdose and wandered into the woods to die. But I've spoken to people, Mr. Hartmann. People who knew her. People who knew you. They all say the same thing: Lena wasn't the type to give up. She was full of life, passionate, and strong-willed. Does that sound like someone who would just go into the woods and kill herself?"

Benjamin's face remained impassive, but his eyes told another story—fear, annoyance. "Lena had her demons, like everyone else."

"That's not what her family told the police more than thirty years ago."

"Her family?" Benjamin shook his head. "I blame them. They put so much pressure on her that—"

"Well, they had another story," Stefan interrupted. "They said Lena was happy, with plans and dreams for the future. But the relationship with her boyfriend? That was another matter. It was strained. Toxic. He put unreasonable demands on her. And she was planning to leave him."

Stefan glanced at the picture in the folder before him. Lena Vinter lay sprawled on the forest floor, surrounded by a thick carpet of pine needles and fallen leaves. Her body was partially obscured by the underbrush, limbs splayed out unnaturally, as if she had fallen or been carelessly placed there.

Her face was pale and still, framed by dark hair fanned out around her head like a halo. Her eyes were closed, lips slightly parted—as if she had been about to speak or take a breath that never came.

Stefan frowned. He still couldn't understand why the police hadn't investigated her death more thoroughly. Suicide? This wasn't a scene of suicide.

"Your relationship. You were her boyfriend."

"I loved her," Benjamin replied.

"A twisted version of love. What happened that night? You were there—Gustav, Marnix, Axel, and you."

"I had nothing to do with Lena's or Anna's death."

"Anna's dead?" Stefan pressed, eyes locked on Benjamin.

Benjamin's face froze in shock. "No... I didn't say that. Maybe. I don't know. You're twisting my words—just like you did with Seb."

He stood abruptly, his chair scraping loudly against the floor. "This conversation has taken long enough. I assume I'm free to go."

"We still have more questions," Stefan said.

Benjamin's voice turned cold. "Then you can take that up with my lawyer."

CHAPTER TWENTY-THREE

THE DOORBELL'S ECHO FADED INTO SILENCE.

Again.

Njord's car sat in the driveway, dusted with snow.

He was there.

But the curtains were drawn.

And the house?

Too quiet.

Should she go in?

No, she couldn't. She had no warrant.

But what if something had happened to him?

She had to talk to him. The last conversation with Benjamin Hartmann at the police station had triggered something. And she just had to know.

"Are you looking for Njord?"

Delara jumped up and turned around. An older woman, dressed in a striking colorful ensemble, met her gaze. She appeared to be in her sixties, perhaps nearing seventy. The woman's purple coat and turquoise scarf clashed violently with the winter gloom—a deliberate act of defiance, Delara guessed.

She quickly composed herself and forced a polite smile as she faced the woman. "Yes, I am. Do you know where he is?"

The woman shook her head, her eyes narrowing as she studied Delara. "I'm Inga, Njord's neighbor," she said, glancing at the house. "His curtains are drawn. That's unusual for this time of day. He's usually up and running early, even in this weather." She gestured toward the snow gently falling around them. "But I haven't seen him for a few days. Last time was when he was walking his dog, late in the afternoon. Haven't seen him since."

Inga's brow furrowed as she looked back at Delara.

"You're concerned?" Delara asked.

Inga nodded. "I haven't heard his dog either these past days. He did have a visitor, though."

"Oh? Who?"

"It must have been the day before I saw him last."

"I was here four days ago," Delara said.

Inga raised an eyebrow, her expression skeptical. "I know," she replied slowly. "It wasn't you. It was a man—much younger than Njord, but older than you. They were arguing. I could hear them from my window." Inga's gaze sharpened as she studied Delara more closely. "And who exactly are you?"

Delara showed her badge and said, "Inspector Delara Holm."

The woman studied the badge for a moment and then nodded. "Is Njord in some sort of trouble?"

Delara hesitated. "I'm just trying to find him, make sure he's safe. You mentioned a man. Can you describe him?"

"I only saw him very briefly. He was middle-aged, had grey hair, but he was tall and athletic... I could tell he worked out."

"Did you hear what they were saying?"

The woman pursed her lips. "Not really. Like I said, I could only make out bits and pieces. The man was speaking loudly, almost shouting at times. It sounded like he was accusing Njord of something, but I couldn't catch the words. There was a lot of anger in his voice, and I heard something about keeping quiet and minding his own business."

Delara frowned. "Did Njord respond? Did he seem afraid?"

Inga thought for a moment, then shook her head again. "Not really. Njord is a stubborn old man. He stood his ground, but he didn't raise his voice. It was more like he was trying to reason with the man, calm him down. But then the man just stormed off. I saw him get into a black car and drive away."

"A black car?"

"A BMW. I couldn't see the license plate," Inga said apologetically. "But it looked fancy, like one of those expensive models."

"And you saw Njord the day after walking his dog?"

"Yes, that was the last time. I..." Inga quickly looked at the house. "Do you think something happened to him?"

Delara ignored the question. "Did you see the black BMW again?"

Inga shook her head. "But then again, I wasn't paying attention."

Delara didn't believe that for a second. Inga was the type of woman who noticed everything happening in her neighborhood. Delara could tell just by the way she had described Njord's routines and the visitor with such precision. Inga was one of those watchful neighbors who kept tabs on everything, even if she tried to act otherwise.

"Okay," Delara said softly, "if you see anything unusual or remember more details, will you let me know? It's important."

She reached for her pocket and took out a business card which she handed to Inga.

The woman nodded, her eyes still lingering on Njord's house. "Of course. I'll let you know if I see anything. I hope he's all right. He's a good man, you know. Always keeps to himself, but kind."

Inga gave her another glance and then slowly continued her way down the snowy sidewalk, her colorful ensemble standing out against the white landscape.

Delara watched her go.

Then she turned to Njord's house, a deep frown settling on her face. She had to find a way in. An unease clawed at her chest—something about this whole setup felt off. The drawn curtains, the silence behind the door, the vague account of an unknown visitor—it all sharpened into an urgency she couldn't ignore.

She decided she couldn't just walk away. She had to check the property, look for any signs that could give her a clue. If nothing else, she might find a reason to justify coming back with a warrant.

Njord had kept something from her and if she turned back to their conversation in her mind, she knew she should have pressed on.

But about what?

Benjamin Hartmann? He knew Hartmann and he hadn't told her. Why?

The Svensson case?

She made her way around the side of the house. She peered into the windows, but the curtains were tightly drawn, giving her no view inside. The unease she felt grew with each step.

She reached the back of the house and saw a small patio. There was an old, weathered chair and a small table covered in snow. Njord's dog bowl was there, but it was empty and clean, as if it hadn't been used in days.

Where was the dog?

During her visit, Njord had put the dog in the back room, and she hadn't seen him.

She hesitated for a moment, then tried the back door. It was locked and she bit her lip in frustration. She could call for backup, but without a clear sign of foul play, she knew no one would authorize a forced entry.

Taking a deep breath, she decided to try one last thing. She pulled out her phone and dialed Njord's number. She listened as it rang and rang, the sound echoing in the still, snowy air. Then, after what felt like an eternity, it went to voicemail. She hung up and stared at the house, her mind racing.

Maybe she was overreacting. Maybe Njord had simply gone away for a few days. Maybe he was celebrating Christmas and New Year with his family. Or maybe he was just sick and didn't want to see anyone.

But then why hadn't he answered the door?

The fear was mounting.

She needed to do something.

Delara circled to the other side of the house.

Another window, but this time the gap in the curtains revealed part of the interior, and it wasn't good. The dog lay motionless on the floor—not sleeping.

Dead.

Her heart skipped a beat.

Without another thought, Delara made her decision. She needed to get inside, and she needed to do it now. She quickly looked around for anything that could help her force the door open.

Her eyes landed on a small garden tool, half-buried in the snow near the patio. It wasn't much, but it was sturdy enough.

She took it and the next moment, the garden tool bit into the wood.

One heave. Two.

The jamb splintered with a sound like a gunshot in the silent air. The door only creaked open, just enough for her to slip inside.

The house was dark and cold. Delara's breath caught in her throat as she stepped inside, gun drawn, her senses on high alert.

She carefully moved through the kitchen. Somewhere deeper inside the house, on her right hand side was the room where she had seen the dog. The narrow hallway led to a closed door at the end.

Delara's pulse quickened as she approached, every instinct screaming at her to be ready for anything.

She reached out, slowly turned the handle, and pushed the door open.

The scene that greeted her chilled her to the bone.

Njord lay sprawled on the floor beside the dog's lifeless body. For a horrifying instant, she thought he was gone too.

A gaping wound marred his head.

But then, her fingers found a faint pulse, a fragile flutter beneath her touch.

His breathing was barely there.

She needed an ambulance.

Quick.

* * *

Stefan's voice was a blade. "Dahlman. Really?"

Delara's pulse spiked. She'd seen that look before—icy, controlled, the kind of anger that didn't shout.

The kind that burned.

"I was going to tell you," she said.

"When? After you dug up my siblings' graves too?"

"Stefan..."

"You know everything. Why did you need to talk to Dahlman? I told you I would talk to my father, but you just couldn't let it go."

They were standing in the corridor of the hospital, and passersby gave them a strange look.

Delara took a deep breath, struggling to keep her composure amidst Stefan's escalating frustration. "This isn't just about your family, Stefan. Dahlman had information crucial to the case, and time was running out."

Stefan's jaw tightened, his eyes flashing with a mix of anger and hurt. "You should have trusted me enough to handle it. Going behind my back like this makes me question where your loyalties truly lie."

"Loyalties? Jesus, this is my job, and you are making it personal. I think Dahlman knows more. The link to Benjamin Hartmann triggered a reaction. He must have his suspicions."

"Do you have proof?"

"Njord was attacked. Isn't that proof enough?"

Stefan exhaled sharply, his frustration palpable. "It's circumstantial. We can't base everything on gut feelings and coincidences. This can be just an ordinary home jacking."

Delara stepped closer. "Stefan, you really believe that? Besides his phone, nothing was stolen. You know there's more to this. Njord was silenced because he was onto something. Do you know Njord was the investigating officer in the Lena Vinter case?"

Stefan frowned. "I... no."

"He had a visitor a few days ago. They were arguing. A man in a black BMW. We need to find him. He might know more."

"That's not very specific."

"And we need to check Njord's phone records. He likely called the man. There is a reason why his phone is missing. It was still active when I tried to reach him. Now, it's dead."

Stefan sighed and then looked at the doctor who was walking toward them.

"Are you the police officers... for Njord Dahlman?" the doctor asked.

Delara and Stefan turned to face the doctor.

"How is he doing?" Stefan asked.

The doctor's pen tapped the clipboard. "His brain activity is... minimal. Borderline... brain dead. Even if he wakes up, which I doubt, he might not be able to tell us anything. His brain sustained serious damage."

Stefan clenched his jaw. "Did he say anything?"

The doctor shook his head. "No. He never regained consciousness. I'm sorry."

"Thank you, doctor," Stefan said. "Please let us know when there is a change in his condition."

"Okay. Given the circumstances, we've also informed hospital security to keep a close watch on him." The doctor then gave a curt nod and continued down the corridor, leaving Delara and Stefan standing in uneasy silence.

Stefan finally broke it. "He was nice."

Delara frowned. "Who?"

"Njord Dahlman. I remember him. He came to see us... Elena and I... in the hospital. He was nice. He was so... kind to us, especially to Elena. He brought candy and toys. I never forgot that." Stefan's voice softened, the anger from earlier replaced by a quiet sadness.

Delara walked up to him. "And that's why we need to find whoever did this to him. All these cases are connected."

"But who?"

"Dahlman made me believe he didn't know Hartmann, but he did. Why didn't he tell me? He was the one who voiced concerns about the Lena Vinter case. We need to find out what happened to her. The answer is there. We just can't see it yet."

"Gustav Gyllenstierna. He was there. He knows."

"What about the little boy at the Axel Bergström's farm?" Delara asked.

Stefan let out a deep sigh. "He isn't talking... too traumatized. He's the son of Bergström's sister. He was visiting his uncle. God... he must have seen everything."

"That was the killer's intention. To inflict trauma, to cause emotional pain. Just like in the painting. The killer is targeting the group, but specifically Hartmann, directly or indirectly through his son."

Stefan nodded. "You're right. And Lena Vinter is the key."

"Let's talk to Gyllenstierna," Delara said.

"No, we'll have *Torre* talk to him. Gustav is still in the psychiatric ward. This needs a professional. The man just realized he was an active participant in his family's killing. I can't say his state of mind is good."

※ ※ ※

Gustav sat in his small room at the psychiatric hospital, staring blankly at the walls. The sterile white paint made everything feel hollow, like the echoes of his thoughts were the only sounds left in the world. His hands trembled in his lap, though he barely noticed it anymore. The medication dulled his senses, but it couldn't stop the memories from creeping in.

He closed his eyes, hoping for a moment of peace, but instead, the vivid images of that night rushed back. The terror. The voices. The blood. He could hear his children's cries, the killer's cold commands, and the horrible choices he'd been forced to make. The guilt crept in, tightening around his chest like a noose.

There was a soft knock on the door, but Gustav didn't respond. A moment later, the door creaked open, and Torre stepped inside.

Gustav finally looked up, meeting Torre's eyes. "He'll never stop, will he?" he whispered. His voice was raw and fragile.

Torre moved closer. "That's why I'm here, Gustav. We're going to stop him. But I need your help."

"I told you everything I know. I... cannot go through that again."

"I understand," Torre said and sat down next to him. Gustav gave him a quick look and then turned his gaze to the barred window. There wasn't much to see. Just the blackness of the winter night, occasionally interrupted by the flicker of a distant streetlamp. He could barely make out the silhouettes of the leafless trees, their bare branches like skeletal fingers reaching toward the sky.

"You were right," Torre continued. "This isn't just about revenge. It's about sending a message. There's a pattern to his actions, a logic that we're still trying to understand. You're one of the few who knows him, truly understands what he's capable of. We need your insight."

Gustav's hands gripped the sides of his chair, knuckles turning white. "You don't understand. He gets into your head. Makes you believe things... do things. Even when you think you're in control, he's the one pulling the strings. I tried to resist, but he's always there, always watching."

Torre leaned in, his voice lowering. "Who, Gustav? Who are we talking about? Is it someone from your past? Someone connected to your family or to Lena Vinter?"

"Lena Vinter?" Gustav stared at him.

"Marnix Castner, Axel Bergström and Benjamin Hartmann. Do you see the pattern?"

When Gustav finally spoke, his voice was barely audible. "Lena was sensitive... such a beautiful soul, but so fragile. Benjamin and she... they weren't a good match. She idealized him for a while, until she saw what he really was."

"And that is?"

"A bully, a manipulative monster," Gustav continued. "Benjamin has this way of charming people, making them think he is someone they can trust. But behind closed doors, he is cruel, always looking for control. He twisted Lena's mind, made her doubt herself, doubt everyone around her." He shook his head. "And we went along with it. Jesus, it was like we were a cult or something."

"Still, you sought his advice when your marriage was falling apart," Torre remarked.

For a moment, a glint of anger crossed Gustav's face, and Torre knew he was going to downplay his part in the entire Lena Vinter story.

"It was just a reunion, and we got to talk about our lives. Marnix was there too."

"What about Axel?"

The expression on Gustav's face suddenly changed. It became

gloomier and sadder. "No, not Axel. And I can understand him."

"Why?"

Gustav sighed and shrugged.

"Come on, Gustav. You haven't told me much. Was there a fall-out between you, Benjamin, Marnix and Axel? Has this to do with Lena?"

"It was a stupid game. That evening we got together... like we always did in the forest. It was quiet, secluded. We used to go there to drink, party..."

"Drugs?"

Gustav nodded. "Benjamin always had these... weird games to push you to the limits. This time he was stressed out, angry, even more than usual. Everything Lena said was annoying him and he lashed out at her a lot. He told me before he thought she had someone else and that she was going to break it off."

"And was she?"

Gustav looked down. "We didn't mean for it to happen. It just... did. Lena and I, we had this connection, something real. I didn't want to hurt Benjamin, but the more I was with Lena, the more I realized how toxic he was. She needed to get away from him."

"Did Benjamin know about you and Lena?"

"I think he suspected it. That night in the forest, he was on edge, watching us all the time. I tried to keep my distance from Lena, but he wasn't stupid. Benjamin could read people, and he could tell something had changed. When he cornered me later, he asked if I knew anything. I denied it, of course, but I don't think he believed me."

"And then what happened?"

"We were drinking... a lot. Axel had nicked his father's entire liquor cabinet. Whisky, tequila, vodka. We were already wasted when he started this stupid game. The pills came out."

"What was it?"

Gustav swallowed a few times. "Russian roulette, but with drugs.

Benjamin called it 'Chasing the Edge.' You mix a handful of different pills, take one without knowing what it is, and see what happens. It could be something harmless, or it could be something that puts you on your knees. Benjamin liked to watch us squirm, liked to see who could handle the risk and who couldn't. He said it was a way to prove you could handle anything life threw at you."

Torre's face hardened. "And Lena? Did she play?"

Gustav's expression grew even more serious. "She didn't want to. I could see it in her eyes; she was scared, but Benjamin kept pushing her. He taunted her, called her weak, said she didn't belong with us if she couldn't handle a little fun. The others joined in, laughing, egging her on. I... I tried to tell them to stop, to leave her alone, but Benjamin... he wouldn't let it go. He put the pills in her hand and dared her to be one of us."

Gustav's hands were shaking now. "Lena looked at me, her eyes pleading. I should have stopped it, should have taken her away from there. But I didn't. I just stood there like a coward, watching her take the pill, watching her face as she swallowed it. And then... and then everything went to hell."

Torre's eyes bore into Gustav's. "What happened after she took the pill?"

Gustav's breath came in shallow gasps, the memory clawing at him. "She... she started to convulse, her body shaking violently. Her eyes rolled back, and she collapsed. I tried to go to her, but Benjamin held me back, said she was just faking it, that she wanted attention. But she wasn't faking. Her lips turned blue, and... and she stopped breathing. We all just stood there, too shocked to move. Benjamin... he just watched, a sick smile on his face. Like he enjoyed it."

Gustav's hands clawed at his thighs, nails biting through the fabric. His voice shattered: "I watched. I let it happen. And when she hit the ground, Benjamin laughed."

Torre leaned back in his chair, eyes still fixed on Gustav. "The autopsy report showed a mix of drugs in Lena's blood. There were traces of alcohol, a mild sedative—something like Valium. But there was also a more potent substance."

Gustav's eyes widened, confusion and fear flashing across his face. "What do you mean, a more potent substance? What are you saying?"

"Barbiturates," Torre replied. "Someone spiked her drink. The whisky bottle next to her contained traces of it. Combined with the sedative and the alcohol, it created a deadly cocktail. It slowed her heart and breathing until she couldn't recover."

Gustav's mouth opened as if to protest, but no words came. Finally, he whispered, "No, that can't be right. Benjamin only gave her one pill. I saw it. I..." His voice faltered, his eyes widening in realization. "Unless... unless he already put something in her drink before that."

Torre kept his gaze steady, watching Gustav as the truth sank in.

Gustav's face went pale as the realization began to take shape in his mind. His voice was trembling as he spoke, barely able to get the words out. "Maybe... maybe someone else put something in the bottle. Benjamin was always paranoid, always thinking someone was out to get him. He made me watch Marnix pour the drinks. Axel was distracted, and Marnix... he poured from a different bottle for himself. At the time, I thought it was just Marnix being picky about his drink. But what if..."

He trailed off.

"What if what, Gustav? What are you thinking?"

"What if Lena wasn't the target, but Benjamin. Marnix wasn't trying to kill Lena? What if he was after Benjamin?"

Torre paused. "Go on."

"Marnix... he hated Benjamin, more than anyone. He always acted like he was Benjamin's lapdog, but there was resentment. He never liked being treated like he was second best. He wanted to be the one in control, the one who called the shots. He wanted to get rid of Benjamin."

"So, you think Marnix spiked the drink and his target was Benjamin.

What went wrong?"

"Benjamin wasn't in the mood to drink, and he gave the liquor to Lena. I remember Marnix trying to intervene, but it was already too late."

"Interesting theory," Torre said.

"It must have been Marnix," Gustav said.

Torre stayed quiet for a moment, leaning back in his chair as he processed everything Gustav had revealed. His eyes drifted to the barred window, where the skeletal branches of the leafless trees swayed slightly in the winter wind, casting flickering shadows against the cold, dark sky.

Then he glanced at Gustav, who was staring blankly ahead, the lines of anguish etched deeply into his face. The silence stretched between them.

Torre's phone buzzed on the table, jolting him from his thoughts. He glanced at the screen—Stefan's name flashed up.

He ignored it. He needed to order his thoughts.

The threads were finally coming together, but the tapestry they wove was twisted and dark, filled with secrets and lies that had been buried for too long. And still the main actors in the story were holding back so many secrets.

He sighed, rubbing his temples as if trying to ease the ache that had settled there. "Gustav... I don't think that was what happened that night. If I had to guess, I'd say you were the one gaining most from Benjamin's death. The way you talked about him, you were scared of him, and you were scared of what he would do when he found out about you and Lena. You killed Lena and for years, you tried to blame Benjamin. You spiked the drink, thinking Benjamin would take it. But he gave it to Lena."

Gustav's expression hardened as he clenched his fists. "You're wrong! I didn't kill Lena, I swear it! You're twisting everything—Benjamin is the one responsible! Or maybe... Marnix."

Torre sighed, standing up and glancing once more at the barred window before meeting Gustav's gaze. "Maybe I can't prove it yet, but I'll do everything I can to reopen the case. And when I do, the truth will come out—every bit of it."

CHAPTER TWENTY-FOUR

STEFAN AND DELARA STEPPED INTO the Vinter family restaurant. The warmth of the small space was a sharp contrast to the biting cold outside. The air smelled of hearty Swedish food, but the atmosphere quickly shifted when Karl and Björn Vinter noticed them. Karl, still wearing his apron, looked up from behind the counter, while his son Björn busied himself stacking plates, his movements becoming more rigid the moment he saw them.

Karl's hands stilled over the counter. The rag in his grip was stained—grease, or something darker.

"A table for two?" Karl asked. "The kitchen's slow this early, but I could—"

Stefan's badge glinted in the lamplight. Delara mirrored him.

"Police?" He barked a laugh. "Here to tell me you've finally pinned my daughter's death on someone? Or just to reopen old wounds?"

Delara held his gaze. "We need to talk. About Gustav Gyllenstierna. Marnix Castner. Axel Bergström. Benjamin Hartmann."

The names landed like blows. Karl's knuckles whitened around the rag. "Those bastards? Why drag them up now?"

Björn slammed a plate down. "Thirty years too late. We're done talking."

Stefan took a step closer. "There's been a series of attacks—Axel is dead and so is Marnix and his family... and Gustav's family."

Karl gave them a sarcastic grin. "Good. Whoever did this, I give them a round of applause. Those bastards killed my daughter."

"And where were you the night of 5 December, 13 December and 20 December?" Stefan said.

Karl looked him straight in the eye, a smirk playing on his lips. "Listen, kid. I know you think you've got it all figured out with your shiny badge and your textbook questions, but you don't have a clue what you're dealing with."

Stefan's jaw tightened, but he held his ground, his eyes fixed on Karl's. "Just answer the question, Mr. Vinter."

Karl chuckled, shaking his head. "How old are you anyway? Twenty-five? Thirty? You think you can waltz in here and understand what my family's been through. You weren't even around when Lena died. You don't know anything."

Björn watched them in silence, his jaw clenched, while Delara stepped forward. "We're trying to stop this from happening to anyone else, Mr. Vinter. Your cooperation could make a difference."

But Karl just scoffed, crossing his arms. "Save your breath. We've been dealing with this pain for longer than you've been alive. Now get out of our restaurant and let us grieve in peace."

"We can't do that," Delara said.

Karl's eyes flashed with defiance as he sneered at her. "You think we care about your case? We've spent thirty years with no answers, no justice for Lena. And now you show up, hoping we'll play nice? You're wasting your time."

"We can either talk here or at the station. Your choice." Delara's eyes were locked on Karl's.

"Okay... what do you want to know?"

"Dad," Björn tried to interject but his father raised a hand to calm him down.

"As you've noticed, we're not exactly fan of that particular quartet. They took advantage of a vulnerable young woman. Even if they didn't give her the pills, although I think Hartmann did, I hold them responsible. They were bullies. They took pleasure in manipulating her, in making her feel small and scared. They twisted everything around her until she didn't know who she could trust. That's what those bastards did, and I'll never forgive them for it."

Karl's voice shook with the weight of his anger, his hands clenched into fists at his sides.

Björn shifted uncomfortably, his eyes darting to his father. "We all know what they did to Lena, but that doesn't mean we—"

"Björn, enough," Karl snapped, though his gaze softened when he turned to his son. He took a deep breath, then faced Delara and Stefan again, his expression hardening once more. "Ask your questions. But know this—I'm done covering for anyone. We lost Lena, all because of the poison those men spread. So if there's justice coming for them now, I won't shed a tear. I admit I've threatened Hartmann in the past—"

"Dad, stop! We've already lost enough."

"I've had enough of this shit. I don't care what happens to me as long as it is fair. I admit to harassing him, only him. He's the mastermind. The others are followers. But I didn't kill anyone. I would never hurt innocent people. Their families had nothing to do with this."

"You threatened him," Stefan said. "What did you do?"

Karl smiled and then said, "Phone calls, letters, unexpected visits to his house."

"Letters? What kind of letters?"

Karl shrugged and let out a deep sigh. "Stupid letters... in hindsight, childish letters threatening to do to his son what he did to my daughter."

"That's not so childish. You threatened his son, an innocent boy."

"Mmm... innocent? I'm not so sure. He liked his addictions from a very young age. A long, painful journey to death. It's unavoidable." Karl's face showed a sarcastic grin.

And suddenly Stefan froze. Karl and Björn weren't just holding onto their anger; they were actively fueling a vendetta that went beyond harassment.

"You're his suppliers," Stefan said. "You've been feeding Seb drugs, keeping him hooked to get back at Benjamin."

Björn's eyes widened, darting to his father, but Karl didn't flinch, his expression cold and unrepentant. "Benjamin ruined my family. It's only fair that he watches his own family fall apart, piece by piece."

"Did you attack Seb?" Delara asked.

Karl just stared at her and then a sarcastic grin played on his lips. "No comment."

"And you also tried with the paintings," Stefan said.

"Paintings? I don't know what you're talking about."

Delara injected, "Gruesome scenes where people die... you've been feeding Hartmann those ideas. You've been stalking him."

Karl leaned forward, "Stalking... yes, I did, for many years. He, his wife, his mistress, but then came Seb. I thought he was a better target than Hartmann."

It was clear Björn didn't agree with his father's confession. The entire time he was fidgeting, his eyes darting between his father and the officers, his jaw clenched tight as if he were biting back words. Finally, he couldn't hold it in any longer. "Dad, you've said enough! This isn't going to fix anything—can't you see that?"

Karl shot Björn a warning glance, but the younger man's expression was a mix of anger and desperation. "Stop talking... please. You are all I have left."

Karl's expression briefly turned soft. "And I am an old man. I should be enjoying life while I still can, but I can't. The last thirty, forty years have been hell." He turned to Stefan and Delara. "Luckily, my wife and I stayed together, but it was hard. We were always at a different pace in dealing with our grief. I was stuck in anger and resentment and she... she could forgive. She thought everything had a purpose. She believed that the universe had a plan, that somehow all of this pain was leading somewhere better. But me? I never found that peace. I couldn't let go of what they did to Lena. I saw Hartmann live his life, and it just ate away at me, day after day. I wouldn't have stopped. Seb Hartmann is a lost cause anyway."

"And do you know what happened to Anna?" Delara asked.

Karl shook his head. "No... but I can't blame her that she ran away. Though, she might have gotten a few spicy pictures about her husband and his mistress."

"Elsa Larsson," Stefan said.

"Yeah... that woman is a freak," Karl hissed.

"Why do you say that?"

"I was stalking Hartmann, but she was stalking his wife."

Stefan and Delara exchanged a look of disbelief. The web of deceit and obsession was unraveling before them, but the revelation about Elsa Larsson added a chilling new dimension.

"She was stalking Anna?" Delara repeated.

Karl nodded. "She was always there. At first, I thought she was just another one of Hartmann's flings, but it became clear that she was obsessed. She would follow Anna everywhere, take pictures."

"Did she do anything?"

"No... but Anna disappeared. You might wonder..."

"... if Elsa had something to do with it," Delara finished.

"And Elsa had a stalker of her own," Karl said and smiled while he wiped the last breadcrumbs from the table.

"Wait," Stefan let out. "The stalker had a stalker."

"Oh... maybe it wasn't a stalker, but there was always a guy following her. I saw him many times. I've seen him recently peeping through Hartmann's windows. Hartmann and Larsson were going at it. Luckily, he didn't see me. Hartmann really has some problems."

Stefan frowned. "Can you describe this man?'

"Fifties, maybe sixties now but he was a real looker when he was young... athletic, tall... blond, grayish hair. Though he always seemed angry. There was a cold intensity in his eyes, like he was always on edge, ready to explode. Oh, and he drives a black BMW now."

"A black BMW?" Delara said and quickly looked at Stefan.

"You don't have the license plate by any chance?" Stefan asked.

"No, not really. I couldn't care less about the guy."

"Mr. Vinter, you do realize that I need to arrest you and your son for contributing to the delinquency of a minor, assault, and possession of drugs." Stefan stared at Karl.

Karl's eyes narrowed. "Is that all?"

Stefan leaned in slightly. "For now, but that's more than enough to start with."

Delara chimed in. "Inspector Eklund, I still think we should consider looking at their whereabouts when the Castner family, Gustav Gyllenstierna's family and Axel Bergström died."

"We had nothing to do with that," Björn yelled.

Karl shot his son with a warning glance, his jaw tightening. "Quiet, Björn," he hissed, then turned back to Stefan and Delara. "You've got what you came for. Now do your worst."

✳ ✳ ✳

Delara put the phone down and stared at the screen in front of her. Somehow it felt it was her fault. If she hadn't gone to Njord Dahlman, he wouldn't have been attacked in his own home and he wouldn't have been dead now. She'd led the killer to him. And now his blood was on her hands.

Stefan, at the desk next to her, was also staring in front of him. She knew he had overheard the conversation, and at the moment it had become clear that Njord hadn't survived, his expression had become wary.

Another conversation with Stefan's sister Elena had made it clear that Stefan hadn't met their father. Elena had even considered asking Katherine to persuade him, even though she wasn't a great fan of her so-called sister-in-law.

The trauma ran deep and Delara knew it. But the more she thought about it, the more she was convinced the shooting of the Svensson kids was key to solving the murders. Karl and Björn Vinter were a distraction and so was Seb Hartmann.

Who was the man in the black BMW?

Back to square one. But they didn't have much time.

She pulled the file toward her. For days now, a little voice in her head was saying she needed to look at Elsa Larsson again. Lena Vinter had been a convergence point, but according to her a dead end. Karl and Björn Vinter had been charged with drug possession, but there was nothing that could link them to the Castner and Gyllenstierna murders, and the death of Axel Bergström.

Axel's nephew was still not talking. A trauma he would carry for the rest of his life.

How can people be that cruel to each other?

Elsa Larsson. Delara had asked one of the juniors—although in many ways she was a junior herself—to put a file together on her.

Fifty years old. Psychiatrist. Began her career at Karolinska University Hospital in Stockholm, working in the psychiatric unit for nearly a decade. She had been well-regarded there, known for her work with patients suffering from severe depression and trauma. But something had changed about ten years ago. She left the hospital suddenly, transitioning into private practice.

"Is that Larsson's file?" Stefan asked.

"Yeah. Seems Dr. Larsson specializes in marital issues, emotional manipulation, and psychological abuse in relationships. She even published papers on the subject. A lot of people see her as an expert in the field. She's been consulted in high-profile divorce cases."

"And she's in the perfect position to manipulate men in distress like Marnix Castner and Gustav Gyllenstierna," he said.

"But did she? And why?"

"Hartmann leads them to Larsson, and she finishes the job," Stefan said and turned his glance to the screen of his laptop.

Delara sighed. "It's not that straightforward." She shook her head and continued reading the file.

There was something they hadn't looked into. Lack of time and still, in the back of her mind, it was important.

There it was.

The husband.

Adam Wallin.

She had seen that name before.

Where?

And then she knew.

She quickly opened the file on her computer.

They should have known.

Damn. Axel Bergström might still be alive.

"Stefan," she said. "We need to talk to Larsson's husband."

"Why?"

She turned the screen of the computer toward him. "You know him."

Stefan's eyes widened as he saw the name on the screen. "Adam Wallin? The name sounds familiar."

"Njord Dahlman's partner. He was there where they found you. He was a cop, and he owns a private security company now. We need to check if he set up the security in the Castner and Gyllenstierna homes. If so, it must have been easy for him to get in. He knew exactly where everything was, the routines of the families. Everything." She got up and took her coat. "And now, he's going after Hartmann. We need to find him."

CHAPTER TWENTY-FIVE

OUTSIDE THE SNOW WAS FALLING STEADILY. Things had never been so clear in his head than at that moment.

Enough playing.

It was time for the real work.

But somehow, there was still some lingering doubt in his mind. Hartmann had to die, but what if the deed itself wouldn't give him the satisfaction he craved for. Years, decades even, he had festered maybe even nurtured this anger, the resentment. At times it almost felt like he had become addicted to the rage itself. The bitterness, the hatred—it had been his constant companion for so long, a dark force that fueled him through the years.

But what if, once it was gone, he felt empty? What if Hartmann's death didn't fill the void, but only deepened it?

And it was largely her fault. The woman who had triggered both their obsessions.

Elsa.

She played them so well, like puppets on strings, pulling at their darkest desires and feeding their insecurities. She had known exactly how to manipulate them both, weaving herself into their lives, twisting their minds until they could no longer see straight.

Hartmann and he had never met. But it was like an invisible force had put their lives in an entanglement of fate, bound together by the twisted machinations of Elsa Larsson. Hartmann had no idea how deeply their paths had been intertwined, nor how much damage had been caused by her delicate manipulations.

It was almost poetic, the way she had orchestrated their mutual destruction, using one against the other without either of them ever realizing it. Hartmann's life had crumbled, piece by piece, and now, so had his.

But there was still one final act left in the tragedy Elsa had set in motion. He wasn't sure if it would bring him peace or just more torment, but it didn't matter anymore.

It had to end, one way or another.

And he knew exactly where and how it would happen.

Elsa had left him twice. Maybe a hundred more times in her head, but once she had moved out of the house and a second time, she had told him she would leave him.

In 2003 she had left him a first time, though it didn't really come as a surprise.

But when he had learned about the affair, something twisted had stirred deep within him. A sick plan had begun to form in his mind, dark and insidious. Instead of confronting Elsa or Hartmann, instead of demanding answers or seeking the truth, he had decided to let his darker urges take over. This was his chance—an excuse to release the pent-up fury that had been festering inside him for years.

He had studied Hartmann, almost obsessively. At first, it had been about learning the details of the affair—when and where they met, the way they looked at each other—but then it became something else. He couldn't stop watching, analyzing, dissecting every part of Hartmann's life. There was something about him, something that fed his need for control, for destruction. It wasn't just about revenge anymore—it was about power.

The obsession deepened, growing more intense. And in a moment of pure madness, he had written a letter to Hartmann about the Svensson case. He knew Hartmann wouldn't be able to let it go. He was as sick as him.

He walked up to the house. The snow was falling gently, blanketing the world in white. The dark night seemed to deepen the silence, muting every sound.

His footsteps barely made a sound on the snow-covered ground. It was the kind of quiet that felt oppressive, where every movement felt wrong, intrusive.

It was eerie, almost surreal, as though time itself had slowed down. The world was a void, and in that silence, his thoughts echoed loudly in his head.

The house itself was dark, but he knew Hartmann was home. He had made sure. This time of the day and this moment of the year, he usually retreated to his studio, turning all his darkest thoughts into obscure art.

He had seen it before. Every time Hartmann faced personal problems, he would lose himself in his work, pouring every twisted emotion onto the canvas. The more chaotic his life became, the more disturbing the art. It was as if Hartmann needed that darkness to create, to make sense of his own torment.

And he had watched it all—every breakdown, every brushstroke—fueling his own sick satisfaction. His son's addiction, Elsa's fickleness, Anna's disappearance.

A cruel smile appeared on Adam's face as he took the leather gloves from his pocket.

He had studied this moment for months, knowing the layout of Hartmann's security system better than Hartmann himself. Years of experience with home security systems had given Adam an edge most intruders could only dream of.

Hartmann's house was equipped with a high-end system—motion detectors, glass-break sensors, and reinforced locks. But Adam knew how to bypass them all. He crouched near the side of the house, where Hartmann's system had a minor flaw—a blind spot in the camera coverage that Hartmann had probably never noticed. Adam had chosen this entrance for exactly that reason.

Using a slim, customized bypass device, Adam connected to the external security panel, tapping into the main feed. He didn't disable the cameras outright—that would have been too obvious. Instead, he looped a few minutes of old footage back into the system, creating the illusion that everything was fine while he moved undetected.

Next was the door. The reinforced lock on the back entrance was no challenge. With a set of professional lock-picking tools and knowledge of the model's weaknesses, Adam had the lock disengaged in less than a minute. He slipped inside with practiced silence, closing the door softly behind him.

He didn't hear a sound.

Everything was so quiet.

He had seen Hartmann enter the house.

Maybe he was wrong?

***

"Where is your husband?"

Elsa ran her hands through her hair, eyes narrowing as she gave Delara a hard, tired look. "I don't know. I haven't seen Adam in days."

Delara studied her, trying to gauge whether Elsa was telling the truth, but all she saw was exhaustion.

"You don't think it's strange that he's disappeared?" Delara asked. "Given everything that's been going on?"

Elsa scoffed. "Strange? Adam's always been like this. Disappearing when it suits him. If you're asking whether I think he's involved in all this madness, I don't know."

"Where does he go when he vanishes?" Delara pressed. "Does he have places? Contacts?"

"What about Benjamin Hartmann?" Torre said.

Elsa's gaze iced over. "What about him?"

"Everything he's done is because of Hartmann and your relationship with him. He's going after him." Torre took a seat next to Elsa.

He quickly looked around. He didn't feel comfortable. It was too sleek and minimalistic for him, but the sharp lines and a cold elegance did match Elsa's controlled demeanor.

Expensive leather furniture and modern art pieces adorned the walls, while large windows framed the snowy landscape outside.

He turned to her and looked her straight in the eye. "You know. You've known all this time. You've played both men."

Elsa took a deep breath. "I never believed it would get this far."

"When did you suspect Adam?" Delara asked.

"When I noticed he had been going through my patient files," she said. "Marnix Castner and Gustav Gyllenstierna."

"Why didn't you tell us?" Delara hissed. "Axel Bergström could have been saved."

Elsa looked down at her hands and shook her head.

"I'll call Stefan. I think he was right. Adam is going after Hartmann. I just hope he'll be in time."

* * *

Adam continued on. Through the windows, he saw the snow falling in thick, silent flakes. It was almost peaceful. The untouched snow mirrored the stillness inside the house, where everything was in its place.

Or maybe not?

And then he felt the cold steel against the back of his neck. He knew immediately what it was.

"Drop it."

He was surprised. The voice was a lot younger than he had expected. This wasn't Benjamin Hartmann.

"I won't tell you a second time."

Adam dropped the bag. Then he felt the hand push him forward, pinning him against the wall. The man began searching him. His hand moved with precision, patting down his coat, his sides, and then his legs. The cold steel of a gun was pulled from his waistband, followed by a smaller one strapped to his ankle.

"Thought you might be carrying," the voice said. "An old cop always does."

The man yanked Adam by the neck, shoving him through the doorway into a brightly lit room. The sudden brightness momentarily blinded him, but as his eyes adjusted, he saw Hartmann.

Hartmann was slumped in a chair, his face bruised and swollen, wrists cuffed tightly to the armrests. Blood had dried on the corner of his mouth, and his shirt was torn, exposing more bruises. His head was tilted forward, but as Adam stumbled into the room, their eyes met.

"Surprise, surprise," the man said.

And only then he knew who was standing behind him.

A twisted, unsettling laugh escaped the man's lips. "Look at him... my dear father! He's just like any other man. Weak."

"Seb," Benjamin whispered. "Don't..."

"Don't what?!"

Adam felt another sharp push against his back, and he stumbled forward toward Benjamin, barely keeping his balance. Seb was still right behind him, so close that Adam could feel his breath, hot and steady, against his neck. The cold pressure of the gun dug deeper into his spine, forcing him toward the empty chair beside Hartmann.

"Sit," Seb hissed.

Adam hesitated for a moment, glancing at Hartmann's bruised face. There was no way out. Reluctantly, he lowered himself into the chair, the metal of the gun never leaving his back.

"See I did some of the groundwork for you, Adam," Seb said. "He's there. All ready for you."

Benjamin's swollen eyes flicked up to Adam, pleading, but the defeat was unmistakable. "Seb... this... isn't you."

But Seb laughed. "Oh, but it is, Dad. More than you know. Can't you see it?"

"What?" Benjamin said. He was struggling to keep conscious.

"The monster you made is just in front of you. All those years of humiliation, of anger, of fear. But you underestimated me. You thought I was an addict... weak, submissive, miserable."

"I didn't...," Benjamin tried.

"You did. For years, I knew what you were doing. Elsa Larsson." Then Seb moved closer to Adam, his gun still pointed at him. Adam could finally see him. Seb looked tired and hollow, as if the weight of everything had drained the life from him. His eyes were bloodshot, filled with a dangerous mix of rage and satisfaction. "And you killed Mom."

Benjamin's breathing was labored, his bruised chest rising and falling heavily. "No, Seb, you've got it wrong. I didn't kill Anna. She left me."

Seb's eyes darkened, cutting him off with a bitter laugh. "I remember. You killed her."

"You can't remember. You were too young."

Seb's hand trembled as he kept the gun trained on Adam. "She would never have left me. My life would have been so much different with her in it."

Adam, sensing Seb's unraveling control, spoke up. "You're right. He killed her."

Seb looked at him and then his eyes narrowed. "You think you can manipulate me? Are you trying to set me up against my father?"

Of course he did. He was annoyed that he wasn't in control of the situation, but if he played it well, he could still turn it around. Seb's intention was clear enough. Benjamin had to die, and Adam was going to be the culprit. Seb would likely tell the police he managed to kill his father's murderer, and no one would ever know. A classic tale. But something was off.

The phone in Seb's pocket buzzed. He took it and quickly looked at the message on the screen. "The police are on their way. We'll have to hurry up."

"How... who...?" But then he knew who. "You concocted this together with Elsa? She's manipulating you. You know that, right?"

"She helped me," Seb said. "That's more than good old dad here can say. You had her in your bed, but I had her in my mind. All these years you thought you were in control, but she was."

He turned to Benjamin. "You made a big mistake, Dad. You should have called the police when you realized I killed that girl in high school... the one they never dug up. She wasn't the only one. You see... I wanted to be like you. You killed a girl in high school and I did too. But it wasn't enough, was it? You still didn't see me. And then I realized that the way to understand you is to look at your paintings. And I realized what you couldn't. You are weak. You didn't manage to put your sick fantasies into reality."

A glance at Adam, then back.

"You thought you could fix me. Elsa knew better. She saw me. Listened. Didn't even blink." His laugh was a dry crack. "Monsters recognize their own."

Benjamin's mouth moved, but the sounds were barely audible. "Seb... you don't know what you're saying."

"I know exactly what I'm saying." Seb took a step forward, his voice low, measured—almost tender. "You lied for me. Covered for me. Maybe I could've been... normal... if you hadn't."

A cold laugh.

"But you were weak. Just like the police—too blind to see what was right in front of them. They were on the right track. And Bergström?" His smile didn't reach his eyes. "He'd still be breathing if you hadn't called your lawyer to keep me out of prison."

A pause.

"Too late now. The only one who ever looked at me and saw me? The only person who has really been honest with me is Elsa."

"Honest?" Adam let out. "You must be joking. You want to know who killed your mother?"

Both Seb and Benjamin looked at him, surprised by the sudden statement.

"Elsa did," Adam said. "She pointed you to Gyllenstierna, Castner and Bergström, didn't she?" Then he turned to Benjamin. "She wants to get rid of us, and she used your son to do it."

"And what exactly did you come to do here?" Seb yelled. "I don't believe a word you said."

"I came to confront your father," Adam said.

"And what does that mean? Confront? Kill? What?!"

"I admit I was jealous and frustrated. Then Elsa was with me, then she left me. It drove me crazy. And for whom? That piece of crap." He pointed to Benjamin. "What did he have that I don't?"

"Money?" Seb said with a sarcastic grin on his face. "Anyway, enough with the talking. I've waited long enough. Gyllenstierna, Castner, Bergström... it was all much fun... liberating even, but it didn't exactly turn out the way I had hoped."

"And that is?" Adam asked.

Seb turned to Benjamin and fired the gun.

The shot rang out. Benjamin's body jerked in the chair as the bullet tore through his chest. Blood sprayed from the wound, and for a moment, his eyes went wide with shock, before they glazed over. His head slumped forward, the life drained from him in an instant.

Adam froze, his breath catching in his throat. The room felt colder, the silence deafening after the gunshot. He hadn't expected Seb to actually pull the trigger, and now the situation had spiraled out of control.

Seb lowered the gun, staring at his father's lifeless body. For a brief second, he looked lost, as if the reality of what he had done hadn't fully sunk in. His hand trembled again, but then his expression hardened. "It's done. It's finally over."

Adam kept his eyes on Seb. What was he really feeling right now? And then his own mind started working overtime. He was angry because Benjamin's demise had been his prerogative, and at the same time he knew what was going to come and he didn't want to die. "You think Elsa cares about you? She used you to do this—she'll discard you the moment you're no longer useful."

Seb's face twitched, his grip tightening on the gun. "Shut up. This is nothing. I'm lost anyway. When I killed Gyllenstierna's wife and children, Castner and his family and Axel Bergström, I pretty much knew there was no turning back. She might have manipulated me, but I wanted it." He turned to Adam while retrieving a second gun from his pocket. "This is yours by the way. The gun that killed my father. It will end up in your hands after your death."

"She killed your mother," Adam said. "You can still save yourself."

"Stop."

"Your mother was alone at home with you. Elsa rang the bell with the excuse to talk about your father."

"Stop."

"When your mother went to check up on you in the bedroom, Elsa followed her and put a bag over her head and suffocated her. That's what happened."

"How would you know?" Seb cried.

"Because... I saw it... through the window."

"You were following her?" Seb said. He could barely contain the tears.

Adam nodded. And that knowledge had served him well. At least that's what he had thought.

"What did she do with the body?" Seb asked.

"Your father helped her. He came home that evening and saw her sitting next to the body. They put her in the car later that night. I don't know what happened after that."

"All of you knew?" The tears were now running over Seb's cheeks. He took the gun and aimed it at Adam. He couldn't keep the sobbing under control. "They screamed... they pleaded for their lives... I can still hear their voices. And for what?"

"Don't do this," Adam said, his voice low but firm, trying to reason with Seb, who was barely holding it together.

Then, in the next instant, both men jumped at the sudden faint noise coming from the hallway. Seb's eyes darted to the door, wide with panic. Adam saw them—police officers. A dozen of them, scattered through the hallway, moving silently like shadows. Some were positioned at the windows, their guns raised, others inching closer toward the room.

Seb's breathing quickened as he realized what was happening. His grip on the gun tightened, but his face was a mess of confusion and fear.

"Seb, it's over," Adam said. He could see the desperation in Seb's eyes, the war raging in his mind. "There's no way out of this. Don't make it worse."

He wanted to live. He didn't want to die. Not for this.

Seb glanced back at his father's lifeless body, the reality of what he'd done sinking in. The police were closer now, their voices low but commanding as they took up positions at every possible exit.

One of the officers shouted, "Drop the weapon! Now!"

Seb froze, his gun still pointed at Adam, but his hands trembling violently. Tears streamed down his face as he looked back at his father. Lost.

Then, without warning, Seb let out a guttural cry and aimed the gun at his father's lifeless body. The shots rang out in rapid succession, echoing through the room as each bullet tore into Benjamin's already still form. It was a final act of rage, a twisted need to destroy what had already been taken from him.

The police surged forward, their shouts drowned out by the gunfire. Adam could only watch in horror as Seb's body jerked back, the bullet from the police gun tearing through his chest. Seb collapsed to the floor, his eyes wide in shock, staring at the ceiling as blood pooled around him.

Suddenly, the room fell eerily silent. Adam could hear his own ragged breathing, the metallic scent of blood filling the air. The police officers rushed in, but it was too late. Seb lay still, his chest no longer rising, his hands limp at his sides.

From the shadows of the hall, a young blond police officer emerged. There was something about him that tugged at Adam's memory, something in his eyes. The officer's gaze lingered on Seb's lifeless body before he shifted his focus to Adam.

Their eyes locked in a peculiar gaze.

"You," Adam whispered. He knew this boy—or rather, the man he had become. It was the same boy Adam had once seen lying on the floor of his family home, bloodied and barely clinging to life. The boy's father had gone on a murderous rampage, shooting his children, leaving only two survivors—this boy, and his sister. A circle of seven children dying on the floor of their home.

Adam had never forgotten that day. It was the case that had planted the twisted seed in his mind, the one that would lead him down a dark path—a path that eventually drove him to write those letters to Benjamin Hartmann, to feed Hartmann's twisted art with macabre inspiration, all in a jealous rage over Elsa.

And now, here he was, face-to-face with the very boy whose life had been destroyed, whose gaze seemed to bore into Adam's soul. The weight of everything—the deaths, the manipulation, the lies—pressed down on Adam as the young officer stepped closer.

"I remember you," Stefan said.

Adam could only nod.

There were no words to say anymore.

CHAPTER TWENTY-SIX

STEFAN PUT HIMSELF IN THE CHAIR at the desk. He needed a moment for himself. His father's case, his sister's constant nagging to reach out to him, and the baby—all of it swirled in his mind, relentless. He loved Katherine deeply, but sometimes she could be too much. The way she pressed him, especially with the baby on the way, weighed on him. He wanted to be a good partner, a good father, but the pressure of it all was suffocating.

He stared blankly at the stack of files on his desk, trying to push aside the whirlwind of thoughts. When he turned to face Delara on the other side of the room, he realized his attempt at finding peace, even for a few moments, would have to wait. She was standing by the window, her eyes watching him intently.

"You okay?" she asked.

Stefan rubbed his temples, tension building behind his eyes. "I'm fine. It was a complicated case."

"To say the least," she replied, settling into the chair beside him. "The report's longer than a novel, and it still feels like we're missing pieces. It's tragic though. Seb Hartmann. A monster shaped by abuse. I checked the archives. A girl vanished when he was seventeen. Viktoria Dahl. She was never found and now there is no hope anymore to ever find her." She sighed. "Adam Wallin and Elsa Larsson are in custody, but neither of them is talking. He insists she killed Anna, and that Hartmann helped dispose of the body. Personally, I doubt it. I think he helped her after witnessing the murder—Hartmann genuinely believed his wife left him. Those 'Darkness and Light' paintings say more than he ever did."

She paused, glancing at Stefan.

"Wallin also claims she manipulated Seb Hartmann into killing the families, Axel Bergström, and his own father. He downplays his own role, of course. Says all he did was stalk Hartmann and send the letters."

"What about Njord Dahlman?"

"We all know Adam Wallin is responsible for his death. Wallin admitted arguing with Dahlman on the phone, but he refuses to admit he dropped by. The phone records show that Dahlman called Wallin after I met him. I assume Dahlman remembered Wallin's fascination with paintings and with Hartmann in particular. If I read the report of your family's case again, Stefan, there are a few hints to his partner's unusual behavior."

Stefan sighed. "But killing Dahlman? That looks like a bridge too far. Are we sure about Wallin?"

"Who else could have done it?" Delara asked and then looked out the window again.

It was a bright day, the sun gleaming off the snow-covered streets. The storm had passed, but the world outside still looked cold and unforgiving. Frost clung to the edges of the glass, a reminder that even in daylight, the chill lingered.

"It has stopped snowing," she said softly, "but it's still freezing out there." She turned back to Stefan. "Just like everything in this case. On the surface, it looks calm, but underneath, it's still ice cold."

"You're getting poetic," Stefan said and a faint smile appeared on his face.

Delara shrugged, her smile lingering for just a moment before fading. "Maybe. This whole thing gets to you after a while."

Stefan nodded. "It doesn't sit right with me. Wallin is a manipulator, sure, but murder? That's another level."

"Maybe he panicked."

Stefan sighed, rubbing his hands together as if trying to chase away the cold that had settled into his bones. "Anyway, there's nothing we can do at this moment." He got up and took his coat. "I need to take Katherine to the doctor."

"Everything okay?"

"Yeah. Just a regular checkup."

There was a distant look in his eyes as he put on his coat.

"Why didn't you go and visit your father?" Delara suddenly asked.

"That is private," he said.

"I understand this is still a trauma for you and your sister. But it is intriguing how you both look at this in different ways."

"She has her opinion. I have mine. It's nothing new. We have disagreed on this for years."

"She was older than you when it happened," Delara said. "Have you ever considered that she might know more than she's saying. Maybe that's why she's so hesitant to condemn your father."

Stefan contemplated for a moment. He hadn't given it much thought before, at least not seriously. "But... no... why can't she tell me?"

"Maybe you should ask her," Delara said. "And maybe you should ask yourself what your mother's role is in this."

Stefan looked up from buttoning his coat. "You've been reading my file... our file."

"I had to," Delara said. "Your case was so intertwined with Hartmann's."

"And in a way it has... but now you can leave it to rest," he said and walked to the door.

"But Stefan..."

He had already disappeared.

Delara glanced around the nearly empty police station, her sense of disappointment growing. The holidays had come and gone without much fanfare, and it hit her that she hadn't even noticed. Christmas and New Year had passed in a blur of long hours and mounting stress from the case.

It stung a little.

She loved Christmas. People might be surprised to hear that—after all, she was Iranian, though adopted as a baby. But Christmas, with all its warmth and lights, had always been special to her. Her adoptive parents had made sure of that, creating magical holiday memories every year. For her, Christmas wasn't just about religion or tradition; it was about family, about love and belonging.

But this year had been different. The case had consumed her, leaving little room for anything else. She realized with a dull ache that she hadn't even decorated her apartment, something she usually looked forward to.

She sat down and opened the file of the Svensson case.

She could just leave it, or... Delara hesitated, fingers brushing the edges of the file.

The Svensson case had been a complex web of emotions, deception, and family secrets. It felt wrong to walk away now, knowing there were still threads left to unravel. She knew Stefan wanted to let it go, to bury it with everything else he'd been trying to escape. But there was something in his story, something in the file, that still bothered her.

Delara leaned back in her chair, staring at the pages in front of her. Stefan had made it clear he wasn't ready to dig any deeper. Would pushing further only make things worse for him?

But she couldn't let it go.

And then the phone on the table started buzzing. She looked at the screen, hesitated for a moment, but then took the call.

"Hello," she said. "Sorry for not calling back. It was pretty busy."

"I understand," the man on the other side of the line said. "I'm not sure if you... I mean..."

She straightened in her chair, sensing the hesitation in his voice. "I'm listening."

"Sorry for being so persistent, but I need to know if you are okay... and maybe we can meet, but only if you want to."

Delara exhaled, caught off guard by the gentle insistence. She had to think for a moment. What would she say now?

"Sorry, I just... haven't had much time to think about anything outside of work." She knew it wasn't the full truth, but it was close enough.

There was a pause, the silence between them stretching out. Then the man spoke again, more softly this time. "I just want to make sure you're not carrying all of this alone. If you need anything... even if it's just to talk. I know it might be strange, but I am worried about you."

"I appreciate it, and yes... maybe we should meet. What about tomorrow?"

"That sounds good. Take care of yourself, okay?"

"I will."

When the call ended, Delara placed the phone back on the table and looked back at the file.

And one name in particular.

She wasn't ready to let it go.

By far not.

* * *

Torre put the steamy pot on the table and then sat down next to his mother.

"Where's Dad?"

"He'll be here," his mother said and gave him a reassuring smile, though her eyes darted toward the clock on the wall.

Torre noticed the small, anxious gesture but said nothing. His father had been coming home later and later these days, and while his mother always had a calm explanation, Torre could sense the tension beneath her words.

The smell of the stew filled the kitchen, warm and comforting, but the silence between them felt heavier than usual. His mother busied herself, placing bowls and utensils on the table, her movements a little too precise, a little too hurried.

"Did he say why he'd be late?" Torre asked.

"He's just finishing up at work," she replied. "You know how it is."

"Are you guys okay?"

Torre watched her carefully, her response accompanied by the same overcompensating smile she always used when deflecting.

Deflection.

A classic avoidance strategy, especially when the emotional truth was too uncomfortable to face. And he had to admit his mother's gestures were too deliberate, too controlled, as though she were desperately trying to maintain an appearance of normalcy.

"Yes... sure... why do you ask?" she said.

Torre mentally cataloged her behavior: forced cheerfulness, subtle signs of hypervigilance, like the way her gaze darted toward the door every few minutes. She was likely experiencing anticipatory anxiety, a hallmark of someone trying to manage an escalating situation. His mother was clearly worried about his father's increasing absences but wasn't ready to confront it, either with Torre or herself.

"Just seems like something's been... off lately," he said, keeping his tone as neutral as possible, like a therapist broaching a sensitive topic in a session. He didn't want to push too hard, but he also wasn't going to let it go unnoticed.

"We're fine," she said. "Your father's just been busy at work. It happens, you know. By the way, how was your first big case?"

Torre reached for the ladle, the warmth from the pot rising up to meet his face as he carefully scooped a portion of the stew. The thick, hearty broth sloshed gently, chunks of meat and vegetables nestled in it. With deliberate motions, he poured it onto his mother's plate first, watching the steam curl upward before setting the ladle back into the pot.

He paused for a moment, staring down at the food, and then said, "Interesting, complicated... but not finished."

"Oh... I thought you found the killer?"

"We did, but somehow I feel the case is not over."

And that feeling was growing stronger by the minute. And it all converged with Stefan and what had happened with his family.

The Svensson case.

Somehow, Torre couldn't shake the sense that he'd been drawn into it long before he realized—maybe even by design.

Like someone was whispering in his ear.

Little, subtle manipulations.

At that moment, his father came in the room. His coat wet from the snow, his face lined with fatigue, and a tension in his jaw that hadn't been there before. He put his phone and the key of his BMW on the table, and his briefcase on a chair in the corner of the room. Then he hung his coat on the nearest hook without a word and moved toward the table.

Torre glanced at his mother, who flashed a tight smile, one that didn't reach her eyes.

"Long day?" she asked.

"Yes... many patients," he said, gave her a quick smile and then filled his plate with stew.

It was a play. It wasn't real.

What was going on?

Torre's unease deepened with every glance exchanged between his parents. His father's distant expression, his mother's darting eyes—something was wrong, deeply wrong. He had felt it for weeks now, the lingering sense that the case involving Stefan wasn't truly over, that something unresolved still hovered in the shadows.

But tonight, it hit him like a punch to the gut.

Whatever was lurking wasn't tied to Stefan. It wasn't out there, in some distant place he could analyze and investigate.

It was here.

In this house.

He looked at his father, and then at his mother. He could feel it, but he couldn't point it out.

It was something evil. And it was already here, lurking in the shadows of their lives, watching, waiting.

Torre's pulse quickened, a sense of dread tightening in his chest. Whatever it was, it was coming for them.

And it wasn't going to wait much longer.

THE END

ABOUT THE AUTHOR

Venezia Miller is a bestselling author known for her gripping Nordic noir thrillers, blending psychological depth with chilling suspense. Before turning to fiction, she built a distinguished career as an engineer and researcher in nanoelectronics, publishing extensively and editing technical books under a different name. Yet storytelling was always her true passion, and in 2020, she took the leap, releasing her debut novel, *The Find*.

Since then, Miller has captivated readers with her dark, atmospheric crime novels set in Sweden's High North, including *Evil Beneath the Skin*, *Retribution*, *The Storm*, *The Vanishing*, and *Darkened Heart*. Her stories are praised for their intricate plots, richly drawn characters, and haunting sense of place.

Now, with *Painter*, Venezia Miller launches a brand-new series, *The Stockholm Killings*, diving deeper into the shadows of Sweden's capital. With her signature blend of taut suspense, emotional complexity, and forensic precision, Miller invites readers into a world where secrets run deep and the hunt for the truth can be as dangerous as the killer themselves.

Printed in Great Britain
by Amazon